DEATH
OVER
NEWARK

DEATH
OVER
NEWARK

Alexander Williams

COACHWHIP PUBLICATIONS
Greenville, Ohio

To
Jean Wick Abdullah,
wise counsellor and a staunch friend.

Death over Newark, by Alexander Williams
© 2017 Coachwhip Publications

Title published 1933
No claims made on public domain material.
Front cover images: © Vanalem; Ioan Masay

CoachwhipBooks.com

ISBN 1-61646-413-5
ISBN-13 978-1-61646-413-4

1

DAWN RACING IN over Sandy Hook hurdled Brooklyn and New York Bay then, holding its nose with rosy fingers, crept over the effluvious marshes of the Hackensack and Passaic Rivers to Market Street, Newark. The chill breeze swirled about Stanislas Pazco, embodying the Merchants' Patrol and Night Watch Service, Inc., who pulled the collar of his coat a hitch higher on his neck and was glad. In two hours now he could go home to breakfast and bed. He rattled the front door of the Bon Ton Store, peered through the glass from behind the cupped palm of his hand and felt rather than heard the heavy rolling vibration of a high-powered motor swell above him. Together with the dawn haze he was saturated with sound.

"Tchk! Tchk!" he clicked his tongue. "Them aviators! It's a wonder the police wouldn't enforce the ordinance against low flying. If I was the chief, I betcha I'd raise some stink out at the airport—"

Muttering to himself, he stepped from under the shelter of the Bon Ton marquee and peered upward. The plane was unusually low unless the early hush accentuated its clamor. Trying to see through the ground haze, Stanislas squinted his eyes, his nose wrinkling, his upper lip lifted in the effort of concentration.

Nearer and nearer, the rapid, whirling crescendo of sound swooped and stopped abruptly. Instinctively Stanislas sprang back into the frail shelter of the corrugated glass awning. In silence more startling than the blast of full motor a huge bird-shape loomed, so close the watcher could hear the shriek of the air plucking at taut guy-wires. It swept downward until Pazco thought the undercarriage brushed the cornices of the roof; in a great explosive burst the

5

motor thundered into new life and as sharply as it had dived the plane zoomed upward out of sight.

The watchman had a distinct impression of a helmeted figure leaning over the side, of black letters and numerals on under wing surfaces, of a scarlet splotch on the fuselage; all of this at the instant of lowest descent. In that same instant a sprawling, awkward object catapulted downward, gangling, dissymmetrical, tumbling over and over as it fell, assuming gigantic proportions. It struck with a terrific crash, smashed through the iron and glass of the Bon Ton's marquee as if it were so much matchwood and paper.

The watchman's leap to the recessed entrance of the store was one reflex; the motion of hand and arm that yanked at the alarm placed there in the doorway for the protection of the Bon Ton's merchandise against riot and burglary was another. From above Pazco's head a klaxon grated, and in the headquarters of the Merchants' Patrol and Night Watch Service, Inc., the emergency squad was prodded into instant action by the rattle of an electric gong. The Bon Ton's protective apparatus was in good working order.

Nearly three blocks away the policeman on the beat started out of his early morning calm at the sound of the airplane swinging downward. He ran three steps forward, swerved out into the middle of the street and peered upward, his general behavior that of a hen when a chicken hawk appears. With the crash of glass and the blare of the alarm all hesitation vanished. He ran in the direction of the sound, his shoulders hunched in momentary expectation of another crash.

Safe in the entrance, crouched, white and shaking, Pazco gaped terror-stricken at the thing that had hurtled from the air and now lay inert.

"What is it? A bomb?" the policeman shouted.

Pazco tried to shriek but couldn't. He clutched at his parched throat, his tongue stuck to the roof of his dry mouth.

"My God! No!" he croaked. "It's a man!"

SHORTLY BEFORE SEVEN O'CLOCK the telephone interrupted Detective Sergeant Tonelli's second cup of coffee. He forestalled Mrs. Tonelli who, due to a figure as wide as her smile, moved slowly, and answered it himself. Tonelli's bulk did not interfere with speedy and decisive action.

"Detective Sergeant Tonelli speaking."

"Captain Henessy calling you, Sergeant." The operator at headquarters switched the call through.

"Hello, Pete?"

"Mornin', Captain."

"Pete, you better hop over to the tube and take a trip across to Newark."

"O.K. Chief. How come?"

"Seems like they've started taking 'em to ride in airplanes. Dr. John R. Holstead, who lives or did live up in Gramercy Park West, either jumped or was thrown from a plane about dawn this morning and landed in the middle of Market Street. Get on over to headquarters there and check up. I'll take care of the routine on this end."

"Murder, Chief?"

"Be yourself, Pete. No man who lived in Gramercy would jump out of a plane in Newark. Not of his own free will. But go easy on the wisecracks. Be official as hell. This is inter-city courtesy. Chief Hobson of Newark, when he rang up to give me the lowdown, laid that co-operation stuff on thick, so play up to him."

"Right. I getcha, I won't steal none of Hobson's thunder."

"I've got an idea Hobson called the papers before he called us—"

"Yeah?"

"Yeah. Watch your step. We don't want any part of this. No more than we have to take. It happened in Jersey, let them sob."

"O.K., Chief."

Tonelli was on the platform of the Hudson Tube Station at Christopher Street four minutes after his telephone had rung. It was characteristic of him that although he barely missed a train and had to wait a long two minutes for another, he neither paced the platform nor fidgeted. His theory, or rather one of his theories regarding his job as a professional policeman, was that it was the principal business of a detective to wait, wait until an opportunity for action presented itself and then act with the celerity of a high-explosive shell. He sat quietly in the train, his mind easy. He might have plenty to worry about later, but now there was nothing to do. The time to think would come—when he had something to think about.

There was a milling mob in the outer room of the Chief of Police at Newark Headquarters. The newspapers had certainly been notified. The sergeant had to shoulder his way through a mass of reporters and cameramen to reach the door, but he was admitted immediately to the presence of Chief Hobson. The chief was perspiring at his desk, the center of a whirlwind of activity.

"Detective Sergeant Tonelli, Homicide Squad, New York City Police Department." Calm in the midst of the hurly-burly, Tonelli introduced himself formally.

"Glad to see you, Sergeant," Hobson barked. "Where's Captain Henessy?"

"The captain is sorta tied up this morning—" Tonelli began.

"Tied up? Tied up? Too busy to attend to murder?"

'Why no sir, he's never too busy to attend to his business, but you see we didn't know it was murder, and besides we haven't any jurisdiction. Captain Henessy didn't wanna butt in on your territory—"

"Izzat so?" Hobson was flustered. He took it out on Tonelli, whose shoulders looked broad and capable enough to stand the burden. "Izzat so? Well, he can't pass the buck to me. This ain't my case, it's yours. All we got here is a cadaver, that's all. This man was murdered in New York. If you fellows over there can't bury your own dead, seems to me the least you can do is to make a stab at doin' your own police work. You tell Henessy if his department ain't capable of handlin' this, the Newark police will come over and show him how."

Hobson was talking for the benefit of the three or four reporters standing inside the door who with open eyes, ears and mouths drank in every word. Tonelli noted that all of the reporters in the room were representatives of local papers. The New York newspapermen were outside. The detective grinned to himself. This was Hobson's big moment, let him have it.

"Thanks, Chief," he said smoothly, "I'll report to Captain Henessy you offered the full co-operation of the Newark police. Is there anything I can do now? Could one of your men give me the lowdown up to date?"

"I'll give you all the facts there is," Hobson boasted. His bluster waned. Tonelli's imperturbability rather took the wind out of his sails.

"The body has been identified?" Tonelli, notebook in hand, had the situation under control. He never used a notebook when he really wanted information. Notebooks brought wariness with them, made people less loquacious. In this instance he knew it would calm Hobson down. It worked. The routine, official manner was almost instantly effective. The chief settled back in his chair.

"Certainly we've identified the body. It's Dr. John R. Holstead of New York City."

"How did you verify that, Chief?"

"I didn't haveta. Look! He had this in his pocket."

Hobson tossed a fat billfold across the desk. It contained a number of identifying papers. A membership card for the Chemists' Club. An automobile operator's license, with an owner's certificate and an identification card issued by an insurance company. There was a home address in Gramercy Park and a business address in Pearl Street. Also there was a pocket-size, indexed notebook with many neat entries.

Tonelli whistled as he shuffled over the cards and riffled through the notebook.

"Jeest! This is a pretty big shot, Chief."

"Yeah?"

"Yeah. If he's the guy I think he is, he's the head of that big wholesale drug house, Holstead & Co., Inc."

"Pretty smart, you New York fellas. Put somethin' under your noses an' you can smell it right away."

Tonelli nodded. It was no part of his business, as Henessy had warned him, to antagonize the New Jersey official.

"Did you say he was murdered in New York?" he enquired casually.

Hobson waved a triumphant paw.

"You tell him, Doc," he said magnanimously, willing to share his glory. "Sergeant, meet Dr. Loomis, our Chief Medical Examiner."

Tonelli turned to the professional-seeming man seated beside the chief's desk.

"It's murder all right, Sergeant," Loomis spoke quietly and competently, "the man was dead when he was thrown from the plane. The body was considerably mangled and the autopsy wasn't easy, but I would be glad to have any of your professional men check up on my findings."

"That won't be necessary I guess, Doctor. We'll take your say-so."

"I should think you would," Hobson blared, "Doc Loomis is an A Number One man—"

"Would you care to look at the body?" the medical examiner cut into any eulogies Hobson may have had in mind.

"Maybe I'd better, just for the record," Tonelli admitted. Still maintaining his meticulous attitude of respect he added, "If that's agreeable to you, Chief?"

"Why not? We ain't obstructin' the wheels of justice over here in Newark. Anything the Newark police has got is at your disposal. We're wide open to help all we can. You won't find no petty jealousy in this department, Sergeant, and you won't find none of our responsible officials too busy to do his duty either, and you can tell *that* to Captain Henessy with my compliments."

No doubt about it, Tonelli thought, it would be some time before Hobson got over the affront to his dignity that had resulted from the detailing of a mere detective sergeant from New York to the chief's prize news story. It wasn't often that murdered men dropped from airplanes in Newark's main street, and the chief resented any diminution of his place in the sun. Too bad, in a way, Captain Henessy hadn't come over.

"That's fine," Tonelli said aloud. "You won't mind giving me a look at the record then, will you, Chief?"

"Mind?" Hobson snorted. "I'll let you talk with the men who know. I got 'em here for you in person! Hey! Bring in Patrolman Brown an' that watchman—what's his name—Stanislas Pazco."

"Would it be possible for you to look over the body first, Sergeant? I'd rather like to get away as soon as possible—" Dr. Loomis spoke from Tonelli's elbow.

"O.K. by me," Tonelli agreed. "Can these officers wait a minute, Chief?"

"Why not? Holstead ain't ever goin' to be any deader than he is now." Chief Hobson, with some of his spleen vented on the New York officer, felt better. Perhaps, too, he was a trifle relieved at the thought that this case was being passed over the Hudson to the men of Centre Street.

"The chief's a little excited this morning, but he's a good capable officer," Dr. Loomis said as he and Tonelli elbowed their way through the group outside Hobson's door and moved off down a corridor.

"You bet he is. We know all about him in New York," Tonelli assured him.

"I guess you're used to this sort of thing, Sergeant?"

"Yeah, I been in a few."

"The sight of this body won't upset you, then?"

"I've seen 'em pretty bad in my day, Doctor."

They turned the corner of the corridor.

"What d'ya figure is the cause of death, Doctor?"

"Stabbing. Unless I am very much mistaken Dr. Holstead was stabbed in the back with a knife."

"Any idea what time?"

"I should say between two and three o'clock this morning. Furthermore, from the position of the wound and the direction of the thrust as well as what can be deduced from the internal evidence I should say the murdered man was seated, leaning forward, when he was stabbed. Probably leaning over a desk or a table."

The doctor turned near the end of the long corridor and opened a door, motioning the sergeant to precede him inside.

In spite of his boast that he was used to all of the horror of murder, Tonelli braced himself as he entered the room that had been pressed into service as a morgue. The body lay on a table covered over with a sheet, and Dr. Loomis moved forward to turn it back.

Tonelli was surprised. He had not known exactly what to expect but he was astonished to see the body so little mutilated.

"Say Doc," he exclaimed, "he ain't bad. I thought he'd be all cut up. Didn't he bounce through a plate glass what-do-you-call-it?"

Dr. Loomis smiled.

"The human body," he said, "will take a lot of punishment without showing it, especially after life is extinct. Take a look at this abrasion, it's fairly typical. You see there has been no true bleeding as the result of this cut. There has been a certain amount of humus, that reddish or pinkish liquid there which has seeped from the wound, but nothing that could rightly be called blood—"

"And so?"

"Upon that I base my conclusion the man was dead before he suffered these abrasions and cuts. See this discoloration here, for instance. A bruise of that size and extent would cause living tissue to turn blue, black and purple and there would be noticeable swelling attendant. Here is simply this softness of tissue and brownish discoloration, another proof the injury was sustained after death."

"Mightn't he have died of heart failure when they shoved him outa the plane? I would."

"It's possible, but I doubt it, Sergeant. You see," the doctor turned the body over and pointed to a wound under the shoulder blade, "this wound was caused by a knife or a similar instrument. It entered between the shoulder blade and the spine at the level of the lower third of the scapula. Tracing its course you can see it pierced the lung and some of the smaller bronchii, penetrating to the pericardium and ventricle of the heart. Death was almost instantaneous, I should say, with little or no external bleeding. From the nature of the wound it is evident that this man was stabbed by a knife with a blade of at least four and a half to five inches long. When he was stabbed the victim was seated with his arms slightly raised and extended. In other words, in much the position he would have been had he been reading or writing at a desk or a table."

"And this knife wound was inflicted *before* the others?"

"Quite a while before. Blood has coagulated in the pleural and pericardial cavities, which would not occur for a half hour to an hour and a half after death. It's hard to say exactly, conditions vary. Then, Sergeant, here is another quite conclusive bit of evidence. Examine the clothes the dead man wore. You will see that his undershirt, shirt, waistcoat and jacket were all pierced by the murderer's knife, but the overcoat was not. Also there are faint, very faint blood stains on the lining of the overcoat which would indicate that it had been put on the body after the stabbing. The victim would not be likely to be in an airplane alive without an overcoat and if he had been stabbed while in the plane his murderers wouldn't have bothered to remove his overcoat before stabbing him, would they?"

"I wonder why they were so careful to put an overcoat on a dead man, and why, if they'd been gonna take him off in a plane, did they stab him at all? Why not just shove him over the edge?"

"That's your job to find out. I can't help you. There are men who would have both stabbed him and thrown him over for the sadistic satisfaction it affords, but in that case I should be inclined to believe that the murderer would have stabbed more than once. This was a workmanlike job, Sergeant. Whoever killed this man knew where to strike and intended to kill him instantly with as little fuss and bother as possible."

"By golly, Doc, I gotta hand it to you. You didn't miss a trick, did you? Now if you can just tell me the color of the man's hair who stabbed him and his general description—"

"I can't do anything for you about hair and eyes, Sergeant, but I'd say the murderer was about medium height and of average weight. Say five feet eight inches tall and weight about one hundred and fifty pounds."

"Well, I'll be—"

"That's almost pure guesswork and it won't help you much. It's all based on the position and direction of the wound."

From behind them in the corridor came the clatter of heels and the door opened.

"Sergeant! Sergeant Tonelli!"

Tonelli swung to the uniformed officer detailed as clerk in Chief Hobson's office.

"Yep!"

"New York Headquarters callin' you on the telephone."

"Where can I take the call?"

"Right in here." The policeman led the way across the hall to an office, vacant at the moment, where there was a telephone on a desk by a window.

"Put that call for Sergeant Tonelli on this wire," he ordered, and handed the receiver to the sergeant.

"That you, Pete?" It was Captain Henessy's voice on the other end. "Glad I got you so quick. Get all you can as soon as you can over there and hustle back here and take charge."

"Is this the big powder and pill man, Captain?"

"Yes, it's him all right. The expert squad is at his apartment right now. Looks like he was stabbed at his desk in his own living room."

"Family been notified, Captain?"

"There doesn't seem to be any family. One nephew and we haven't been able to reach him yet."

"Have you got his address?"

"Certainly we have!" Henessy snapped, "but he's not home. The doorman at his apartment says he's been out all night. Step on it and get over here, will you?"

2

THIRTY-SIX HOURS before his body was flung from the air, an inert mass bringing confusion and notoriety to Newark, a passer-by would have ridiculed the suggestion that Dr. Holstead would live to see only one more sunrise. The chemist strode rapidly along Park Avenue enjoying the sunshine in spite of himself. The spring in his footsteps, the tilt of his head, the eager way he breathed in the nippy air denied the worried creases between his eyebrows. His chest arched itself and his heels thumped the pavement with the certainty and force of fifty-five successful years of endeavor.

As he entered one of the less pretentious apartment houses the carriage man and the porter in the hall greeted him respectfully as an accustomed visitor. Although his mind was a thousand miles away he smiled back at them both with the courtesy that was a part of his abiding charm.

"Is Mrs. Mallor in?" he asked.

"Yes sir, she left word you were to come right up, sir."

Nodding to the attendant in the waiting elevator, Dr. Holstead stepped into the cage. His frown had increased and as they moved upward to the eleventh floor he took a small notebook from his waistcoat pocket and thumbed rapidly through its indexed pages until he found the entry he required. His notebook, with neat entries catalogued each in its place, was a handy reference to the doctor's habits. Everything about him was labelled and filed. His desk at his office was a miracle of neatness. In his apartment the charwoman had yet to find a book unshelved or so much as the corner of a paper protruding from the leather portfolio which lay four-square on the living-room desk.

As with his notebook, files and desk, so with his life. It was well-ordered and annotated for all to read. At nine-fifteen he reached his office. At one he left for the Century Club, lunch and billiards. At four he left the club and proceeded to his home and three hours in his private laboratory. If he had no dinner invitation he dined at either the Century or the Chemists' Club. Rarely, he went to the theatre or to see a highly recommended moving picture play. More often after an hour's chat with his cronies and colleagues at his club he strolled down Fifth Avenue or Park to his apartment and a book. His existence was void of excitement, most people would say, particularly those who could not peer with his seeing eye into the murky depths of a test-tube or a chemical-glass beaker. It was in the laboratory that Dr. Holstead found excitement and to spare.

The one break in routine which he permitted, an unpleasant break he told himself as he scanned the neat entries in his notebook, were these calls. The summons this afternoon was particularly unwelcome. He would prefer to be working or to stay out of doors.

The elevator stopped. Dr. Holstead, memory refreshed, stowed away his memorandum, adjusted his tie and rang the bell of number 11B. A neat maid in cap and apron opened almost at once. With a smiling bow that was half a curtsy, she took his hat and coat.

"Madame will see you in her boudoir."

"Thank you." There was something of irony in the doctor's gratitude. He glanced into the drawing room as he passed and paused, his face lit up with genuine pleasure.

"Frances! My dear!"

The girl, she could have been no more than twenty-two or -three, was sitting sidewise on the window seat, looking down on the traffic streaming along Park Avenue toward the Grand Central Building and the ramp around the station. At his voice her smile of welcome and pleasure matched his.

"Uncle John!" she called and rose to greet him with both hands extended.

"What are you doing moping in the house on an afternoon like this?" He was far more brusque in word than expression.

"Wouldn't you like to know?" she bantered.

"I can tell you. I have the vision. I have second sight!" he boasted. He closed his eyes and spoke aloud in a theatrically deep guttural voice. "I can see a young man. A most worthless young man. He is driving a car, much too fast for city traffic. The car is blue—no—green—dark green with light-colored high-spots here and there. He is coming here he is smiling—happy because he is coming here and pretty soon will have you tucked in beside him and be whirling you away to tea at some expensive place."

The doctor opened his eyes, smiling, and gazed at the girl who, although she smiled, in answer, was smiling only with her lips.

"You're a rotten prophet!" she declared lightly and turned away, the tremor in her voice betraying her gallant fight to keep to the light tone.

"Yes?" The frowning pucker was again between Dr. Holstead's eyebrows. "Isn't Jack coming this afternoon?"

"No. He is not." Carrying on her pretense of nonchalance she moved back toward her place by the window.

"Disgraceful. He neglects you, does he? You'll have to wait until tonight?"

"Not tonight I won't wait. I have another date tonight—*and* this afternoon."

"Look here," there was more concern in Dr. Holstead's voice than a mere lover's tiff warranted, "you and Jack haven't quarreled, have you?"

"No." The reply was muffled. Suddenly Frances flung round and faced the doctor. "We haven't quarreled! I—I wish we had! I could understand then why he stays away." The tears were welling in her eyes.

"Now—now—" The chemist took a step or two toward her, but she waved aside his comfort and blinked back the tears.

"There's nothing at all the matter, you see," she laughed throatily, "except that Jack's always too busy nights and afternoons to come here anymore."

"I was afraid so." The doctor sighed. "I've been wanting to say to you—" he began; a querulous voice down the hall interrupted him.

"Agnes!" the voice called, "didn't Dr. Holstead come in a little while ago?"

"Yes, Madame," it was the maid answering, "he's in the drawing room with Miss Frances."

"O—" there was a world of meaning in that short monosyllable.

Frances giggled.

"Mother's getting impatient. You'd better run along or you'll get a wigging and then *you'll* be weeping."

The doctor sighed again.

"Yes, I'll have to go. But—see here," he took the girl's face between his hands, lifted her chin to look deep into her eyes. "You do love Jack, don't you?"

"More and more and more!" she murmured. There was no mistaking the sincerity of her.

"If he were in trouble, deep serious trouble, would you be willing to help him—even if it involved great sacrifice—perhaps terrible notoriety?"

"Why Uncle John? Whatever? Of course I'd help him. I'd do anything in the world for Jack—"

"You may have to prove that, child. There is something you should know. I believe I can trust your discretion and judgment. Jack is in great trouble, great danger I believe, and you and I are the only people in the world who can do anything for him."

"But what?"

"I can't talk to you here. This is something I'd rather your mother knew nothing about. She—well, you know your mother."

"Poor mummy!" She spoke sorrowfully. "She is so flighty. When can I see you, and where—at the office?"

"No. You'd better give me a ring at the apartment tonight and I'll tell you where. Perhaps we can lunch together tomorrow?"

"That would be glorious. Is it a date?"

"Call me—"

Again the petulant voice sounded through the hall.

"Agnes! Will you remind Dr. Holstead please that I'm waiting for him?"

"I'd better run. I—I wish I could talk to your mother about this but—" He looked steadfastly at her. "I have a great deal of confidence in you, my dear. You're much like your dear father was. Loyal, true, level-headed. A friend and a standby. I think I can trust to your common sense not to be swept off your feet. If, after what I tell you, you feel you can't go on with Jack, don't feel bound by any mistaken loyalty to that scape-grace nephew of mine. Perhaps—who can tell? Perhaps I'm wrong. I have not yet heard the whole story. He may have an explanation for everything. I pray that he may. Anyhow, call me tonight."

"I will, Uncle John, and meanwhile—you keep the old chin from dragging. We've known Jack a long time, we have. I'm betting on him and so are you, you old fraud."

"Yes. I'm betting on him, but I've put a larger wager on you, my dear."

With a final touch of caressing finger on her cheek he squared his shoulders and moved toward the complaining voice in the boudoir.

Mrs. Mallor, the mother of Frances, was one of those women who begin to suffer optical illusion and delusion about the age of forty-five. Beginning then they refuse to believe what their mirror tells them regarding superfluous flesh, lines and wrinkles, grey hair and those other enemies that lie ambushed behind each successive annual milestone. To bolster up whatever slight doubts they may have (and those are caused by ridiculous aspersions of envious contemporaries who really *are* beginning to show age) such women as Mrs. Mallor put a touch of peroxide in the water in which they wash their hair, an extra dab of rouge, until—they come to look as Mrs. Mallor looked. Their eye trouble is not confined alone to their mirrors. They are also incapable of seeing changes in style. The fluffs and furbelows which were the last word the year of their marriage are still the height of fashion to them, and indeed why not? For them the world practically stopped revolving once they had reached that main objective, marriage.

Accustomed as he was to the noxious odors of his profession, Dr. Holstead entered the slightly stuffy, overheated, quite overscented boudoir repressing a strong inclination to hold his nose. To him, a man fastidious to a degree, in this room, underlying every perfume and scent, there clung the faint, rank suggestion of perspiration. Mrs. Mallor was not one of those jewels beyond price among femininity, one of those women who know the value of ventilation as a beauty adjunct.

"How are you today?" he asked with an assumed heartiness. He was somehow a different man from the kindly person who had been so understanding, even tender with her daughter.

Mrs. Mallor was no connoisseur of nuances in sympathy. Any sympathy was better than none, and her symptoms were in direct ratio to the interest displayed in them. Her partridge-like bosom heaved gently beneath her lavender negligee indicating resigned suffering.

"Dear John," she murmured, "it was so sweet of you to come."

She had raised up on her chaise longue at his entrance, but now she sank back as she offered him her hand which invitingly drooped at the wrist. Any romantic would have seen instantly that it was for him to bow low and to kiss the plump digits, but Dr. Holstead's romance was not of that sort. He seized the limp appendage in passing and gave it a vigorous if gentle shake.

"I always come when you send for me," he stated, and sat down on a gilt chair totally inadequate for him and as far removed from his hostess as the room would permit.

"You have been sweet, John. So good to me and my child. I think sometimes that dear Frank, if he is where he can see us, must be so happy to know that his child has found a protector—"

"Frank, my dear Esther, was a sensible, decent and loyal gentleman. I can assure you if he is looking at us he is probably thinking that I'm an old ass to be indulging you in your fiscal idiocies."

"How can you say such things, John?" In her excitement she forgot her invalid role, forgot to rise slowly and gracefully. She jerked upright and in her haste lost one golden mule from a sheer-silk foot and disarranged the billows of violet that enfolded her. "You know very well that I've been as careful as careful can be of the money. I regard it as a sacred trust for Frances."

"Sacred trusts," the doctor remarked dryly, "are locked in safety deposit boxes and consist of Government 3 1/4 percents."

"But it was so pitifully small—I had to get more than that for the money—and I did—you must admit that for a while there I did very well with it. All in all I made over twenty percent on our money in two years—"

"—and lost ninety percent of it in the end."

"But I couldn't know what was going to happen. Mr. Hoover himself didn't know." (That Mr. Hoover referred to was not the ex-President, but a young man of the same name who acted in the dual capacity of broker and financial advisor extraordinary to Mrs. Mallor. It is only fair to say that some of his advice was more singular than extraordinary.)

"You don't have to know what's going to happen if you stick to safe investments."

"But they *were* safe—"

Dr. Holstead was silent.

"And you must admit, John, that everybody—"

The doctor made an impatient movement with his hand.

"Yes, my dear Esther, everybody told you, everybody was telling everybody else—however, I don't suppose you're to blame. What did you send for me for?"

"If you're going to take that tone—" she was petulant and coy at the same time.

"No, no. I only hope you've not been losing any more money. There is none left to lose—"

"No. I haven't. I—John, I do so hate to be coming to you so constantly with my troubles, but you
are the only one to whom I can turn—"

"Yes, Esther, I know all that. What is it?"

"It—it's the rent!" she blurted.

"The rent?"

"Yes. You see we have this place on a yearly basis, the rent is due every six months and—"

"I suppose it's due now and you haven't the money?"

"It's overdue almost three months." Her confession was a wail.

Dr. Holstead drew a long breath.

"And how much is it?"

"Twenty-five hundred dollars."

"Twenty-five hundred? For six months?"

"Yes."

"Do you mean to say that you are paying five thousand a year *rent?*"

"Yes, isn't it reasonable for this location? I think I'm very lucky. The lease still has three more years to run. It was a five years' lease.

It is a comfort to know we're settled here at least until Frances is married—"

"Esther, have you any idea how much money Frank left you?"

"Yes. Of course."

"Do you know that under any sort of decent investment arrangement your total income from that money would not have been much over five thousand a year?"

"But John, while the market was good I made—"

"You made a fool of yourself with paper and pencil like many thousands of others did, but what you made in the market wasn't income."

"Besides," stung by his decisive words, his openly expressed contempt, she was sitting bolt upright now. Her mouth, which she liked to think of as a sulky rosebud, was drawn into a stubborn knot. "—Besides, when you speak of what Frank left you don't count in what he lent to you."

Dr. Holstead studied her coldly for a moment. He seemed to be coming to a decision.

"Esther, did you ever find in any of Frank's papers any memorandum of that money lent to me? Did you ever find any receipt?"

"You know I never did."

"Frank was a pretty careful man, wasn't he? He saved almost every scrap of paper he'd ever received as I understand, didn't he?"

"Yes, he did."

"Then, when you didn't find any note of the transaction between him and me, didn't that ever strike you as significant? Didn't it mean anything to you?"

"But you told me yourself—"

"Esther, think back a moment. It's nearly ten years since you first came to me, as Frank's closest friend, and asked me to advise you on some financial matters, isn't it?"

"It was just two years after he passed away. He was so good. I can never understand why he was taken from me." She was sniffling the easy tears of the self-pitying.

"There is more than one way of getting one's reward," the doctor remarked cryptically, "perhaps he's more peaceful where he is. Anyway, two years after his death your finances were in an unbelievable snarl, were they not?"

"I don't know what I could have done. Everybody takes advantage of a young widow—"

"Tradespeople, Esther, deliver what is ordered, but expect payment. That is not taking advantage."

"But you got everything straightened out for me. You were very good to me, John."

"Better than you think. I'm going to tell you the brutal truth. It's time you knew it. Five thousand dollars a year rent. The idea." The idea seemed to hurt the doctor very much.

"It's really very reasonable for the location and what with Frances's debut and—you certainly wouldn't have Frank's daughter living in some shack on a side street, would you? Our position—"

"Flatly, Esther, your position is that of a beggar, dependent upon charity. My charity."

"*Your* charity?"

"I want to recall to you, Esther, that when I took over the job of getting you straightened out financially I found that Frank had left a comfortable sum, over a hundred thousand dollars."

"Yes."

"It had been in good securities and you had borrowed and borrowed on them until—well—do you recall that at that time I advanced you ten thousand dollars?"

"But you told me—"

"The more fool I. I thought I'd spare your feelings. I thought you'd be backward about accepting aid from a man. I told you that Frank had once lent me some money to invest in my business, a personal loan to tide me over—"

"—and you said that money now represented a share in the business and that you were holding it in trust for me and Frances."

"That's what I said."

"Of course, John, if you hadn't been an honorable gentleman I might never have known about that money, but you had it and I can't see why it's so terrible for me to spend it if I need it. And I do need some now. The real estate man was very rude over the telephone this morning. He—he really said dreadful things—"

"I don't doubt it. I'd like to say some pretty dreadful things myself. Five thousand a year, indeed."

"So," Mrs. Mallor skipped unconsecutively along, "I don't see where any charity comes in, John, grateful as I am to you for all that you've done. We—my daughter and I—are simply using the money her father invested in your business—"

"Esther," Dr. Holstead was very exasperated, yet very quiet, "what you say and think would be perfectly true if it wasn't that it is all founded on a lie. I lied to you, Esther. Lied to spare your feelings."

"I don't understand you, John."

"Don't you want to understand? I lied to you about Frank's lending me money. Since college I can't recall that either Frank or I ever lent or borrowed a cent from each other. He was welcome to all I had and I'm sure I could have had anything he possessed if I'd needed it, but we never happened to need each other that way. Is that clear?"

"Then you mean that there isn't any money? We haven't any share in your business?" Her voice rose into a wail of despair. "You can't mean that! It can't be true."

"It is true, Esther. The money I've advanced you, and it amounts to nearly thirty thousand dollars in these last ten years—that money has come out of my own pocket."

"But you don't mean that, you can't mean that. That leaves us paupers, John—Frances, I—have nothing. The share in your business was all we had to fall back on."

"It's your own fault, Esther. You've killed the golden goose. I got you out of your mess when you came to me first. If you'd let your investments alone in the first place you'd have a nice steady income today, instead of that you have gambled, followed tips on the market from every Tom, Dick or Harry who came along—"

"But Frances had to have things. A girl—you've no idea how expensive a girl is—"

"You needn't worry about Frances. If she marries my nephew she'll be amply provided for, and if she doesn't I'll provide in my will—"

"But that doesn't provide for me!" Suddenly she became vindictive. Her doll's features hardened into a selfish mask. "I know what it is. I can see now. You've decided to *cheat* me out of my share of the business. You think it can all go to your nephew and you're salving your conscience by conniving for Frances to marry Jack— O, I see it all."

"I see a lot myself, Esther," Dr. Holstead, calm in manner, raging inwardly, stood up deliberately. "I've done all I could for you and I told you the truth today in the hope that you'd cease this silly business of trying to live like a millionaire. I will mail you a check tonight for your rent, but that is the last you'll get from me. You've had chance after chance to save yourself, but you're too self-centered, too self-indulgent—"

Fear overcame her at the menace of him.

"You can't, John. You wouldn't. You wouldn't let me suffer, not me. Think of Frank. Think of me. O, John!"

"You'll not suffer, Esther. I can trust you for that, but you might make the rest of us suffer. Frances particularly. I don't want you to do that. I will see to it that you are paid a small annuity for life, but it shall be strictly on the condition that after the marriage of your daughter you leave town immediately. Go South, go West, go anywhere you like as long as you don't stay to poison Frances's and Jack's lives with your whining and your leechlike clinging."

"How can you be so cruel? To hear you—you of all people— you, the man whom I have loved most next to my poor—poor dear hu-usband.—John, how could you talk to me so?"

"There comes a time when plain speaking is necessary. I am anxious that the children be married at once and I am willing to pay— and pay dearly if necessary—that they may be happy. You would always be a burden, might end by ruining them. Jack and Frances are the nearest human beings in the world to me, Esther. I'd like to have had my own children, and these two are the nearest substitute. Now they shall be happy where I failed, if I can manage it for them. That's why I'm willing to pay you an allowance, not for your own sake, for theirs. You're not a bad woman, Esther, not vicious, but you're a fool, which in my opinion is worse. You're a bad mother and you'd be a worse mother-in-law."

"You're sure that you'll be able to spare the money for my allowance, John?" she was bitterly sarcastic in her question, but there was grasping eagerness in it too.

He laughed, strangely gleeful and youthful.

"Yes. I'll be able to spare it. I've won, Esther. I've got the thing I've been working on for years. Soon I shall be able to retire in style. Tonight and tomorrow night I shall finish copying out the formulae and then it remains only to try it in large-scale production, but I've got it—I've got it."

His eagerness, his enthusiasm temporarily overcame her own anxiety for her future comfort.

"You've never told me anything definite about this great discovery of yours, John! Won't you tell me? What is it? What is this great thing you've been working out?"

"That is a secret. A secret, God willing, that is going to pay you your little annuity and keep me in my old age. The children can have the business free and unencumbered and maybe a little over and above that."

He looked at his watch.

"Good Lord, it's after five. I've got to go." He moved quickly to the door trying to forestall any further speech. Mrs. Mallor made no motion to detain him.

"You will send the check for the rent, John dear?" she asked, smiling wanly. The sufferer sank back on her couch of pain again.

"Yes, I'll write it and put it in the mail this evening. You'll have it in the morning. Twenty-five hundred dollars."

"I don't know what we're going to do, what's to become of us," she sniffed. "You're going to get millions out of your discovery, but what have we? You talk about Frances getting married when neither she nor I have a rag of clothes fit to wear—"

"I'll make the check three thousand," he promised hastily, edging through the door, "and don't worry about the trousseau, I'll take Frances shopping myself. Try to forgive me, Esther, it's all for the best. Good-bye." The door closed behind him, hiding from him a startling change in the woman. Her face contorted, almost purple with her fury and the suppression of shrieks of rage, Mrs. Mallor grasped the shoulder of her lacy negligee and tore it into shreds. She stripped it from her body, kicked her golden mules into a corner and, hair disheveled, flung herself face downward on her couch, biting and tearing at the pillows and cushions. There was something doubly horrible in her paroxysm of rage in that it was silent. There was only her labored breathing and the soft, sharp sound of rending fabrics.

Dr. Holstead, manlike, thinking only that an unpleasant job had been accomplished with a minimum of scene and tears, proceeded toward the drawing room utterly unaware of the tempest raging behind him. He paused again at the door and looked in, half expecting to find Frances where he had left her. She was, very nearly, but she was no longer alone. A young man standing beside her looked up as the doctor paused and then advanced with his hand outstretched.

"Good afternoon, Dr. Holstead, I don't know if you remember me or not. I'm Walter Gates."

"Yes, yes, of course, Mr. Gates, you're, let me—"

Frances laughed.

"He's being very formal, Uncle John. Walter may be his real name but nobody remembers it. This is 'Bats' Gates, known also as 'Vee' Gates, and it's a good name for him. He's a terrific glad-hander and you ought to hear the line he has for us poor defenseless girls."

"Yes?" the doctor was evidently still puzzling, trying to place the young man.

"I'm an aviator, Doctor," Gates said pleasantly. "I taught Jack, your nephew, to fly."

"Certainly. Now I do remember. Of course. How are you, Mr. Gates, and how are you and Jack coming along on your radio work? Are you still doing a lot of night flying?"

"Night flying? O, yes, yes."

It occurred to Dr. Holstead that Gates was a very ornamental young man. The sort of youngster who looked his best in sport clothes and was even handsome in the unbecoming round hood of a flyer. He wondered casually if he would care to have a man as good looking and as romantic as this aviator calling on *his* fiancée. Jack must be very sure of Frances and of his own charms. Which, the doctor admitted to himself, was very good. Very good indeed. Frances was the sort of girl upon whom one might depend.

"You can see," Frances was speaking, "what a laggard in love and a devotee to his work Jack is. Vee can get away almost any time to come and see me, but Jack is all tied up with the job."

"I'm a roving bee. You can't blame me for stealing as much honey as I can, can you?" Gates asked. "It won't be long now before you're a blushing bride and then I won't have a look-in."

"O, Mr. Gates," Frances burlesqued her archness heavily, "please don't tell me I'm not going to be a sister to you—*always?*"

"I *hope* not and how!" Gates retorted. To the doctor there seemed a shade of meaning deeper than his manner in the vehemence with which he spoke.

"As a member of the family," there was meaning also behind the doctor's seemingly light statement, "it looks as though I'd better warn my nephew to keep up his fences a little better."

"I don't believe he has any cause to be worried," Gates turned it off.

"What about Frances?" Dr. Holstead inquired.

"You know us women, Uncle John. Fickle, uncertain, weather-cocks in the wind. Now for instance I'm trying to get a very handsome man to take me to lunch tomorrow. Actually begging him to."

"I'll use whatever influence I've got with him to help you out," the doctor promised. "You keep right on trying and in the meantime don't be too rough on my friend Gates here. You don't know your own strength as a heart-breaker, Frances."

Waving gaily he left.

He was frowning his worried frown as he again paced vigorously southward on the Avenue bound for his home. His request that Frances call him at home had not been entirely ingenuous. He had even hinted at more than he really knew about his nephew's affairs, but he reflected as he strode along that the interview which lay ahead of him would certainly solve a great many of his doubts, even if it increased his fears for Jack Holstead's welfare.

And eleven floors above, as he emerged into Park Avenue, the querulous voice called from the boudoir: "Agnes! Has the doctor gone?"

"Yes, Madame."

The storm spent, Mrs. Mallor made sure the door was closed and locked and took up the telephone.

"Is this the Byington Hotel?" she asked when her connection had been put through. "Let me speak to Mr. Gomez, please. Hello? Mr.

Gomez? This is Mrs. Mallor speaking. Does your offer regarding Dr. Holstead still hold good? It does? Five thousand dollars? Very well, Dr. Holstead has just left here. He told me that he would have completed his invention, or whatever this thing is that he is working on, by tomorrow night! Is that what you wanted to know? It is? Then when will I get the money? O, you will? Send it down? In cash? Very well, that is entirely satisfactory. What is it? Of course I'm sure, he told me himself. By the way, Mr. Gomez, what is this great invention?"

There was no answer. Mr. Gomez had hung up, but within an hour a messenger arrived with a packet containing five thousand dollars in currency. Mrs. Mallor was very cheerful at dinner. It never occurred to her that she might have done wrong until the newspapers shrieked Dr. Holstead's murder.

3

THERE WAS NOT MUCH OF AN INTERVAL between Dr. Holstead's arrival at his apartment and the arrival of his visitor. While the doctor was in his dressing room tidying himself there came the ring at the street door. No doormen or flunkies disported themselves in Dr. Holstead's building. Visitors rang a bell in the vestibule and shouted their names or missions into a house telephone and the flatholder might suit himself as to whether or not he would punch the button which automatically unlatched the inside-front door. Dr. Holstead kept no regular servant in his flat. Each morning a charwoman came in, swept, dusted and made beds. The chemist had simplified the mechanics of life as much as possible.

Now, wiping his hands on a towel innocent of monogram or embroidery, a bachelor's towel, but of fine linen nevertheless, he walked hastily into the living room, clicked the button that admitted his guest and returned to run a comb through his hair while the visitor climbed the single flight of easy stairs.

The man revealed in the doorway as the doctor opened the door wore the uniform of an officer of the United States Coast Guard. He was typically a seaman, clean shaven, with blue eyes that habitually smiled but could steady into a glint of purpose. He appeared rather heavy set at first glance, an impression intensified by his broad shoulders and double-breasted coat.

"Commander Betts?" Dr. Holstead asked.

"Yes sir. Is this Dr. Holstead?"

"It is. Come in, won't you, and have a chair?"

31

The two men were sizing each other up without hostility. They were maintaining impersonal courtesy as men will who have serious matters to discuss with unknowns. Their opening remarks showed that they were feeling their way toward estimating a possible antagonist or equally possible friend.

"I—uh—" the doctor spoke first after Commander Betts had been made comfortable. "I'm not a smoker myself, Commander, and I must confess I forgot to provide anything for *you* to smoke. What will you have, a cigar, cigarette? It will only take me a moment to have them sent around from the drug store at the corner."

"Please don't bother, Doctor, I have some cigarettes here and I shall be quite comfortable—"

"Wait just a moment." The doctor rose hastily and passed into the next room, returning with a saucer. "I'm ashamed to say I haven't even got an ash tray in the house, but this will do, will it not?"

"Certainly. It's quite all I need. In fact—if smoking bothers you, Doctor—?" The coastguardsman paused in the act of lighting his cigarette. Dr. Holstead waved him to proceed.

"It doesn't bother me. I used to smoke myself when I was younger, or rather I chewed tobacco more than I smoked. It's inconvenient at times to smoke when you're working in the laboratory. A fleck of ash might ruin an experiment, a spark might mean an explosion. Most research men smoke, but they are nearly all what you might call periodic, or convivial smokers, like the men who will take a glass of beer or a highball in company but would never think of pouring one for themselves when they were alone."

"Chewing," the commander confided with his agreeable smile, "is one of the most comfortable and maligned habits. When I was a junior officer I once went to sea with a commander who was a stern disciplinarian. It was a great comfort, I can tell you, to be able to tuck a small quid of tobacco in my cheek during a long and cold night watch."

Dr. Holstead had placed himself at his desk, his back to the door, facing the fireplace. He leaned forward on his elbows over the broad table, his hands loosely clasped in front of him. It was his favorite posture in conversation.

"There is no use wasting your time, sir," he said abruptly. "I would be glad to hear the whole of what you hinted over the telephone this morning. You can readily understand why I asked you to come here rather than the office. Here we are absolutely sure of privacy. In the office there is always a danger that someone may come in unexpectedly."

"I understand, Doctor."

The coastguardsman cleared his throat, shifted himself in his seat as though this were an unwelcome and more or less embarrassing task he had set himself.

"You appreciate, I trust, Doctor, that our action in coming to you unofficially like this is in the hope that if there is, has been, any irregularity it can be remedied without publicity."

"Then you are sure there has been an irregularity?"

The commander flushed darkly.

"We have no positive proof as I told you on the telephone. We have observed certain things that look suspicious, but we are making no charges. In fact, our orders from Washington—"

The last words were obviously a slip of the tongue and Commander Betts ceased to speak in some confusion.

"You have had orders from Washington?"

"Not exactly orders, sir. Of course the things that we had seen went through in routine reports and your name and that of your nephew were mentioned—this was all strictly confidential."

Dr. Holstead gave a short bitter bark of laughter. "I know how much confidential information in Washington is kept in confidence."

"I can assure you, sir—"

"Don't bother, Commander, I am not casting any reflections on you or your men who are doing their duty."

"At any rate, Doctor, we were instructed from Washington to take the matter up confidentially and directly with you before any action of any kind was taken. Our advice from headquarters stated that the Government, particularly the War and Navy Departments, were under the greatest obligations to you and that everything possible was to be done to aid you in stopping this thing and to keep from making arrests or any other publicity. That's why I called you, sir."

"I see." The doctor stared at the portrait above the mantel in silence for a moment. "And what, exactly, is this that you have discovered? Start in at the beginning and let me have the whole thing."

"I don't know if you're familiar with the way the Coast Guard works nowadays in endeavoring to keep rum-running, alien smuggling and the smuggling of narcotics and other contraband within reasonable limits."

"From the number of speakeasies in operation one sometimes doubts if there is a Coast Guard," the doctor answered caustically, "or Prohibition Enforcement either, but the taxes tell a different story. We pay, so we must be getting something for our money. I'd be glad to know what."

"Our job is something like trying to dam up Niagara Falls, Doctor." The doctor nodded and he went on. "We maintain an off-shore patrol as one of the methods of prevention. A fast ship (usually one of the converted destroyers that have been turned over to us by the Navy), patrols just outside of the Treaty limit until they pick up a known rum-runner or some suspicious character. If the ship they pick up is within the territorial waters they may put off a boat and examine her papers."

"What good does that do?"

"None. Ships, even those carrying contraband, are usually provided with clearances from some port, bills of lading, all the necessary papers. Our men cannot touch them unless they make an attempt to land cargo. It is ironical that in case of a storm a rum-ship has the right to run into an American port, have her hatches sealed and stay in that port until necessary repairs have been completed or the storm is ended and it's safe to leave. In case of distress the Coast Guard would have to stand by the men and ships who are loitering off shore waiting for a chance to break the law."

"A fine situation."

"That's International Maritime Law, sir. Practically all we can do is once we have picked up a rummy we can hang onto him and see that he doesn't land his cargo."

"You mean you place a guard on board?"

"No. We stand by. A full crew and a destroyer has to circle round and round a dirty little craft which is generally hove to and laughing at us."

"You can't keep that up forever."

"We keep it up until the rummy loses heart and puts back to port or goes on to some other port than his home port or, sometimes in a blow or a fog, the rummy can lose us and land his cargo."

Dr. Holstead shook his head denoting his opinion of the futility of such tactics.

"It sounds pretty bad I know, Doctor, but it is one of the only things we can do and do efficiently. I want to say that these tactics of ours have so harassed the rum-runners that they have had to build up an entirely new lay-out to meet the new conditions. In the old days the rum-fleet was composed of ancient tramp steamers, old schooners, riffraff of the ocean; now they are nearly all of a more or less standard design. To begin with they are small boats."

"For ocean work?"

"A ship doesn't have to be the *Leviathan* to be seaworthy. These boats the rummies are using are seventy-five to a hundred feet long with a good beam and Diesel motors or gasoline engines. They have no masts, only low deck houses and they are painted grey or black. At three-quarters of a mile unless the sea is calm and the visibility is good you can't see them at all. The advantage of a ship like that is that it needs only a few men, sometimes only four in the crew. Her construction cost is nothing to speak of and she can carry a respectable cargo of liquor. Frequently these ships pay for themselves in two loads."

"And it takes a destroyer to watch one of these miserable boats?"

"In addition to these specially built boats," the commander went on without answering the doctor, "the rummies have set up short-wave length radio stations on shore and they are using airplanes from shore to the boats. It keeps our shore patrol and our small-boat patrol pretty average busy to keep up with such competition."

"Have *you* no airplanes?"

"Yes, we have, and some more are being built, but it would take a force twenty times ours to really put a stop to rum-running in any kind of an effective way. That's an unofficial statement of course, sir."

"I won't tell anybody you said so, Commander."

"Now then, that being the method in which we operate off-shore, you can see how we came by our information. Several times we have picked up a certain boat—"

"What was the boat?"

"The *Esmeralda* of Nassau."

"The *Esmeralda* of Nassau," the doctor repeated.

"We have held her under surveillance as we know she is one of a string of rum-runners operated by a certain syndicate. Her captain is somewhat of a character. His name is McMurtrie."

The coastguardsman was watching the doctor's face narrowly as he made this statement, but there was no sign to indicate that the doctor had ever heard the name before.

"McMurtrie has a record longer than your arm," he continued. "Once we chased him along the Florida Keys when he was running Chinese. He was known to have eight men, Chinese coolies, in his boat, a small, fast motor-launch, but when the revenue cutter over-hauled him (it was a nasty day with a high sea running) his boat was empty. Only himself and his partner, a big black fellow aboard. We know he tied those poor coolies back to back and dumped them overboard, but we can't prove it. Time after time he has run in liquor. He's the slipperiest cuss in the water. He's like an eel. We understand he has a record, a criminal record in England and we know he's a hijacker, practically a pirate. Last, but not least, he has been the center of a dope smuggling ring for years."

"Sounds like a pleasant sort of fellow."

"Funny thing is that he *is* pleasant. He looks and acts like a gentleman. His uniform is always as spruce and trim as a Royal Navy man's. In fact they say he was in the Royal Navy during the war and did splendid service."

"I take it he's Scotch from his name?"

"He's not Scotch and that isn't his name."

"Quite a character, as you say, Commander."

"He is." Betts was grim. "But we'll get him yet and when we do we'll go the limit to put him where he belongs—in Federal prison for a good long stretch. Between you and me and the binnacle, the British authorities find him somewhat of a thorn in their flesh but they are powerless. As far as they are concerned he's always within his rights and within the law. Anyhow, we've been watching Mac and the *Esmeralda* and four times now he's been in communication with the shore by means of an airplane. Four times that we know of. We've never yet caught him in the act of transferring contraband and until we do our hands are tied."

"It's this airplane that led you to come to me, isn't it?"

"Yes. Three times we've, or rather our patrols, have had a searchlight on this plane. It always comes out at night."

"And you have identified the plane?"

The commander took a slip of paper from his pocket.

"Yes sir. We have never been able to get the license numbers of the plane but we have a good description. It is a three-seater sport-model amphibian. Biplane with a single motor. The distinctive mark is a figure painted on the side. At night and in a searchlight it's hard to distinguish colors exactly, but this mark seems to be painted on in red. It is the figure of a devil, with horns, hoofs, tail and a pitchfork."

"A devil!" Dr. Holstead repeated slowly.

"Yes sir." Commander Betts awaited further comment but there was none. Dr. Holstead was lost in thought. He spoke after a considerable interval.

"Well, go on. Is that all?"

"No. We aim to co-operate with the shore authorities and the police as much as we can. There is no official connection between our service and any other but—we try to help each other out when we can without conflicting."

"So you informed the police about this plane?"

"Yes, in a semi-official way. We found that there has been a considerable amount of cocaine coming into the city of New York. More than usual and the police believe that a new gang is operating."

"How are they operating?"

"To tell you the truth they are suspected of getting their supply through your company."

The doctor did not seem staggered by the statement.

"In other words, you have come here tactfully to tell me that I am smuggling in cocaine and selling it illicitly?"

Commander Betts laughed embarrassedly. "Not exactly that, sir."

"Then what?"

"There is no suspicion that you, personally, have anything to do with this business, Dr. Holstead, but yours would not be the first respectable organization to be used for the distribution of drugs."

"Then you think that somebody in my employ—"

"Dr. Holstead, I'm a seaman and used to saying what I mean and what I think. I see no use in taking a long tack in a fair wind. What we suspect is that your nephew, Jack Holstead, is getting cocaine from the *Esmeralda* in his airplane, is flying it ashore, and he or someone else is distributing it through your company. That's the plain fact."

"But you said that you had not seen anything loaded or transferred from the boat to the airplane."

"The point about drugs is that there is a lot of value in very little bulk. I don't have to tell *you* that, Dr. Holstead. The stuff is worth very much more than its weight in gold to an addict. A comparatively small parcel could be tossed from the deck of a boat into the cockpit of an airplane without anybody seeing it even though a patrol boat was within plain sight and had the binoculars turned on them."

"In that event why wasn't the plane stopped and searched?"

"We have only recently found out to whom and where the plane belongs. We have had to search every flying field within fifty miles and do it secretly. Besides, we hadn't facilities to pursue a plane."

"I see," the doctor spoke his thoughts aloud. "The thing that impresses me about your story is that you think my nephew must be an extraordinarily stupid young man. I don't think he is and it grieves me to find it out, if it is true."

"I'm afraid I don't follow you."

"I mean, Commander, that my nephew is far from stupid. He is, on the contrary, a more than ordinarily clever youngster. He has had a scientific training and has rather a keen analytical mind. I can't see why, if he were to engage in smuggling, he would take the trouble to decorate his airplane in such a manner that it could only be a question of time before he was caught. I have seen his plane, have ridden in it with him and I may say in passing he is a good pilot. It is quite true that his plane has the figure of a red devil painted on the fuselage. The machine was, I believe, originally designed and decorated to the order of a friend of his, another flyer, the man, in fact who taught Jack to fly. Jack never took the trouble to erase the emblem, although it was not exactly to his taste. Nevertheless it is a comparatively simple matter to buy a little paint and obliterate such a disastrous identification mark and I'm disappointed that Jack, if he is breaking the law, is doing it so badly."

Commander Betts smiled in spite of the gravity of the situation.

"I don't blame you for feeling that way," he admitted, and we've thought of the same thing—only—we've checked up. Your nephew spends a great many of his evenings away from home and does a lot of night flying. On the dates that his plane was seen he was out flying somewhere. At least he informed the telephone operator in his apartment that he was on his way to the flying field and told her to take his messages."

"Worse and worse," Dr. Holstead lamented. "He not only marks his plane so that it will be recognized but he actually leaves word that he is going to be flying in it. Now I put it to you, does that seem reasonable? Would anyone other than a moron do such a thing?"

"It does seem foolish, but what is the explanation?"

"Were you entirely frank when you said that I was not suspected of being implicated in this affair? You really think I'm a victim and am not using my business for criminal purposes?"

"Quite, sir. We have every reason to be confident of your personal integrity."

"Thank you. Then you actually are coming to me for aid and not simply to pump me, to find out all you can?"

"We would welcome any assistance you can give us."

"That's good. I think I can be of some service to you. The analytical mind has been subjected to a great deal of what I believe is called 'hooey' in the modern parlance, but the man who is in the habit of thinking from effect to cause and from cause to effect has a slight advantage over the average man who thinks more or less at random. I believe that I can see some faint glimmer of light and reason in this business and if you will allow me a day or so I may, I probably will, be able to give you information of value to you."

"We came to you in the hope you'd take this attitude. That's all we ask, Dr. Holstead." The commander rose and again stood as if hesitating to speak. "We—our principal desire in this case is to stop the leak—"

"Yes, of course, Commander."

"If we can stop this stuff from coming in we will be glad to forget anything that has happened—"

"In other words, in your own blunt sailor way, if I can make my nephew be a good boy you'll not send him to Atlanta. Is that what you're trying to say?"

"Well, something like that. I am not, of course, authorized to offer immunity, but in view of your services to the Government—and if you can assure us that this thing will not occur again and that the plane with the red devil will stop prowling over the twelve-mile limit—if you can assure us of that I think it is safe to say that the matter will be dropped."

"You mean well, Commander, and I thank you. Now hear what I have to say. *I* am quite sure that my nephew has nothing to do with this thing or that if he has he is in some way a victim. I am so sure of it that I say to you that I will do nothing to help you unless you give me your word as an officer and a gentleman that regardless of *whom* is discovered to be guilty of this damnable business you will prosecute that felon to the full extent of the law. If my nephew has been engaged in smuggling cocaine he is best out of the way. I love the boy dearly, but I would infinitely prefer to have him dead right here at my feet than to be engaged in such a business. He knows how horrible and fiendish it is. A layman might be excused on the score of ignorance, but Jack has studied chemistry. He knows the effect of drugs on the human system. He knows what groveling beasts drugs make of men. If he has been engaged in this traffic, penitentiary is too good for him. That is my position. Is it agreed?"

"Why—yes sir. We will of course prosecute if we are provided with evidence and it comes within our scope. It was only out of consideration for you—"

"I want no such consideration. I do *not* believe that Jack is guilty. I *will not* believe it unless he confesses it to me or it is proven to me—rather if I prove it myself. But if he is, then he must pay the penalty."

"May I say I admire that spirit, Doctor? If we had more of it there would be less work for us."

"I am not talking for applause. It would be my death if the boy were to prove to be both a fool and a criminal."

"For your sake and for his, I hope there is an explanation."

"Yes—" the doctor had fallen into deep thought again and answered absently. Commander Betts took up his cap and walked toward the door. "Yes—ah—thank you, Commander, you have been most kind."

"My thanks are due to you, sir, for being so patient and understanding. Will you let us know what you want us to do and what you have found out?"

"Yes. It may be several days—say a week from today?"

"That is all right. Take your time. Of course we will continue on the look-out and if anything comes up to alter the situation we will advise you. Good day, sir. We will expect to hear from you next week."

"You'll hear from me." The man who was to die in little more than twenty-four hours made the promise serenely.

Alone, he paced the floor, thinking, thinking. Once he glanced at his watch.

"Too late now," he murmured half aloud, "the office will be closed. But maybe—"

He took up a Manhattan telephone book and began to turn the pages looking for a number, found it and dialed swiftly.

"Hello," he said, "I'd like to speak with Miss Pierce, Miss Sheila Pierce. O, hasn't she come in yet? Will you tell her that— Never mind, I'll call her later."

Before he could be asked any more questions he broke the connection and once again resumed his pacing up and down the floor. He halted after a time, went into his laboratory, opened the light safe that stood in one corner and took one of the large notebooks it contained. This he carried over to his work table where he began a chemical experiment, stopping from time to time to make a neat notation in the book.

4

EVEN THOUGH HE HAD PUSHED HIMSELF and the Newark police to the utmost, the chimes in the Metropolitan Tower recorded noon as Sergeant Tonelli's taxi skidded from Fourth Avenue into Twentieth Street and stopped at the southwest corner of Gramercy Park. There was no need to search for street numbers; the uniformed officer lounging in front of a house on the west side of the square was ample indication of Tonelli's goal.

"Where is it?" the sergeant snapped. The patrolman saluted.

"One flight up, front, Sergeant!"

"Thanks."

Tonelli took a swift but inclusive glance at the building before he dived inside.

It was one of those well-built brick and brownstone fronts which were the pride of the Knickerbocker families in the Nineties and now, shorn of porches and stone stoops, have been remodeled into apartments for those rare Manhattanites who still yearn for a modicum of quiet and dignity.

First Class Detective Michael Moran, Tonelli's running-mate, waited at the head of the stairs.

"Jeest!" he commented, "we thought you was gonna spend the week-end in Jersey!"

"I didn't have the weak-end over there," Tonelli growled back, "I left you on this side."

"O yeah?" Moran fell in behind his superior officer's advance toward the front of the apartment. "What happened anyhow? What'd ya see?"

"I seen a lotta Jersey cops and a man that was dumped out an airplane into a mess of plate glass, that's what. Whatcha got here?"

"See for yourself."

Dr. Holstead's apartment occupied what had been the parlor floor of the old mansion and in the remodeling of the building the rooms had been allowed to retain their original magnificent proportions. What was formerly the drawing room had been used by the chemist as a combination living room and study. Three large windows overlooked the park and beneath them was placed a long and wide table covered with an orderly mass of books, magazines and papers mostly technical in character. A flat-topped mahogany desk stood almost in the center of the floor, placed so the user would face the fireplace, which was of white marble in a simple, lovely Georgian design.

Normally the desk was austerely bare. It held a blotting pad with morocco leather tabs, a large old-fashioned silver ink-pot, and, placed meticulously square on the blotting pad, a morocco leather portfolio which had neatly tabbed compartments wherein had been filed current correspondence and memoranda on personal matters requiring immediate attention.

This neatness had been destroyed by a ruthless hand. Invitations, personal notes, memoranda and bills had been pulled from their places and scattered helter-skelter, or hastily thrust back any which way. Some had strewn over on the floor and where it had fallen on the litter there lay a pipe, its ashes spilling from its cold bowl.

The desk chair with its high, upholstered back and comfortable bucket seat had been thrown on its side and by its position told the story of an inert body, lifted and dragged from where it had slumped across the desk.

Tonelli stooped and picked up the pipe, sniffed at the tobacco and looked around as though in search of a place to lay it.

"Finger-print men been here I see," he remarked as he noted white powder still clinging to the briar.

"You're the last one in. Everybody else is through," Moran said. "Soon's you've seen it as it lays they'll cart away the evidence."

Over the mantel hung a three-quarter-length portrait of a woman whose face reflected the inner strength of a sweet and simple nature. She was dressed in the costume of the Eighties. A companion portrait of a man of the same period hung at the end of the room away from the windows, over a row of built-in book shelves. A man whose wedge-shaped, long and narrow face and whose curiously set eyes gave him a vulpine appearance.

Tonelli strode over and closely inspected the portrait.

"This must have been the doc's father," he remarked to Moran. "They look enough alike to be brothers." He swung back and looked up at the woman's face. "And yet— Say, Mike, didja ever notice how a fella can look enough like his father to be him and yet look a lot like his ma too? This Doctor Holstead was a dead ringer for his old man up there, but he had a look of the lady here too. He looked a lot like her."

"Whatsa idea? What do you care who the doc looked like? You better get busy and find out what the guys that bumped him looked like and why they did it. Looka here. See? Here's where they found blood."

"Yeah?" Tonelli didn't seem concerned with the blood on the rug, nevertheless he inspected the floor at the place Moran indicated. The floor was covered flush to the baseboards with a thick velvet carpet of a taupe shade. The occasional furniture was chosen more for comfort than artistic effect, yet it was in the main Georgian in feeling. Chairs were wide and generous, soft and easy. It was a room meant to be lived in.

"This furniture must have cost plenty," Tonelli remarked.

"Whadda you care? You ain't goin' in for art now, are you?"

"No," Tonelli straightened up. "I was just noticing."

"Yeah, all the wrong things," Moran grumbled.

Tonelli led the way out of the room without answer.

"Say, ain't you even gonna give a look 'round?"

"I seen all I wanna see. What's the rest of the place like?"

The rest of the apartment, like the living room, reflected the personality of its owner and was adequately luxurious in its simplici- ty—the quiet home of a quiet, middle-aged man of taste and discern- ment. There was a bedroom at the rear looking out over a walled-in garden plot in which flourished one of Manhattan's too-few trees. The bed was an antique four poster with a strictly modern mattress and box springs. Here too, in the bedroom, the floor was completely carpeted. There was another fireplace, and the same general air of spaciousness, leisure and bachelorhood. A dressing room separated the bedroom and the bath, and in the dressing room and hall were several closets and built-in clothes-presses, two of which were lined with cedar. There was also a small kitchenette with a mechanical refrigerator. The larder was sparse and the stove gave no indication it had been used much, if at all.

It might have been any man's dwelling except that what had originally been a hall-room at the front of the house, opening by a door into the main hall and by a second door into the living room, had been converted into a small but perfectly appointed laboratory. Here was a stone-topped table with shelves laden with racks of test tubes and bottles, a sink cluttered with unwashed porcelain receptacles, some of which were stained by a black sticky substance which Tonelli afterward learned was coal tar. A second bench held a delicate set of chemical balances in their glass case. Retorts and a battery of Bunsen burners stood beneath a hood to carry off the fumes; distilled water in wash-bottles was handy.

"The old boy certainly musta done a lotta homework," the sergeant remarked. His attention had been immediately attracted to the corner by the window where stood a light office safe with a combination lock. The door of the strong-box stood open, its riffled contents strewn about in the same disorder as the papers on the desk in the living room.

The principal contents of the safe appeared to be a number of black, cloth-bound loose-leaf notebooks. Tonelli picked up one at random and opened it, shaking his head in bafflement as he tried to make sense of the long strings of formulae and algebraic equations. Another and still another of the notebooks yielded the same results. The only thing that held meaning for the detective was the meticulous dating of the pages and the fact that each page was initialed "J.R.H." If the dates were an accurate indication the experiments noted in the books ran back over a period of twenty years and there were easily a hundred of the books.

"Did Doc Helm have anything to say about these?" the sergeant asked. Dr. Helm was the Police Department chemist and all-round scientist.

"He said they was notes on chemical experiments," Moran answered.

Tonelli shook his head, dropped his book back on the pile and wandered into the living room, through into the bedroom and back out into the hall.

"Ain't yuh gonna nose around? Didja see how that rug was scuffed? There where the blood is and how this chair lays. The head-quarters men left everything like it was so's you could see it."

"What of it?" Tonelli demanded. "I ain't no scientific shark. There could be a million clues right here under my nose and I wouldn't see none of 'em. That's the experts' job. When we get downtown there's gonna be a report waiting for us with the whole story. They'll be able to tell us the first name of every guy that's been in this room for a month and what brand of tobacco there is in that pipe and—"

"Dr. Helm took the knife away with him," Moran volunteered. "He hadda take it to the laboratory but he said you could see it when you came downtown."

"Knife? What knife?"

"Looks like the one the murder was done with, all bloody and everything. They found it laying right here on the floor."

"What kinda knife was it?"

"It was one of them we usta call Swedish knives. You know—it was like a regular pen-knife only bigger, and it didn't have no bone or pearl handle pieces like a pen-knife. There was a gadget like a little wooden barrel with a slot through it. When you opened up the knife you had to pull it all the way through the handle, then pull the blade out and slide it back into the barrel—"

"What the hell are you talking about?"

"I'm talkin' about this Swedish knife the murderer used. They build 'em like that so's they won't close up on you when you're usin' 'em. Sailors use 'em a lot."

"I remember now. They're like a regular knife, a paring knife, only heavier than a paring knife. The blade is held into the handle with a spring. When you want to close the knife you hafta pull out the blade, fold it into the two brass strips that hold it and slide it back into the handle again. When it's closed the whole knife ain't no bigger than the handle and you can carry it in your pocket."

"Yeah, that's it. Funny thing though, there wasn't nothing here except the blade. The handle was gone."

"Humph! That *is* a funny one. Like you said, people use them knives for heavy work because they can't fold up on you like a jack-knife, yet here's a guy that uses one to stab another guy and goes off without the knife, but with the handle—"

Tonelli broke off his musing.

"Well, what do yuh say? Shall we get downtown and see what the sharks have found out with their magnifying glasses?"

"You all through here?"

Tonelli glanced at the room, still neat in spite of the ugly litter of papers on the desk and floor.

"I wonder what they were looking for? Not money. Some paper or other—"

"When you gonna talk to the dame?" Moran asked, apropos of nothing.

"What dame?"

"The dame that walked in on me this mornin' when I first got here." Moran seemed marveling at the sergeant's ignorance.

"Say, listen, Mike, do me a favor, will you? Tell me something about this case. Not that I care, only Henessy's gonna ask me questions and it won't seem right if I don't know something."

"She certainly gimme a big surprise."

"What do you mean surprise?"

"I'd just got to the flat, see, an' I was nosin' around when all of a sudden I hears a noise and looks up an' there was a dame comin' in the door."

"Was the door open?"

"Naw! That's what gimme this shock like I'm tellin.' ya. The door was closed an' it locks with a spring lock."

"Then how'd this dame—?"

"Gimme a chance. She hadda key."

Tonelli herded his partner into a corner by the front windows.

"Now," he said, standing over Moran threateningly, "tell me about it. All about it, don't leave out nothing. Begin at the start. She had a key and you was scared."

"Who said I was scared? I gotta shock, that's all. You don't expect nobody breakin' in on you without warnin' at seven in the mornin'."

"So she came right in, did she, like she was used to it?"

"I'll say, an' when she seen me she sorta jumped—"

"If she saw your mug she musta thought it was the boogy man."

"O yeah! Well, anyway I sez, 'Hello, sister, who are you?' She's a pip, Sarge, you wait'll you see her. I could go for her."

"And anything else in skirts. What did she say then?"

"She sez, 'O!' sorta startled like, 'where is the doctor?' Then she sees the things all over the floor and the chair turned over and she says, 'Has something happened? Has Jack been here?'"

"Jack who?"

"That's what I ast her. I says, 'Who's Jack, sister, was you expectin' to see him here?' An' then she says, all confused, 'Why yes! No, I mean.' An' I says, 'Well, when you make up your mind you can let me in on it. Who are you?'"

"Great work, Mike, you were certainly using your head."

Moran missed the sarcasm in his superior's voice.

"Sure I was. The old bean was clickin' like a watch. So she says, 'Who are you?' Right back at me."

"And then it all came out," Tonelli murmured.

"You oughta seen her eyes pop when she seen my shield—"

"I betcha—"

"She sorta screeches, 'O my God! What's happened? Is he hurt? Did he hurt the doctor?'"

"This is getting exciting, Mike!"

"Yeah, that's what I thought. I says, 'I'm afraid the doctor's dead, Miss!'"

"You would! What did she say to that?"

"She didn't say nothin'. She began to shriek an' carry on an' then she fainted."

"And then what?"

"Doc Helm and his bunch an' the medicos come in from headquarters an' that was all. They fixed her up and sent her home."

"Didn't she make any explanation at all as to why she was here at that time in the morning?"

"Yeah, she said the doc asked her to come. Said he had a special job for her."

"What kind of a special job?"

"I dunno, and I guess she don't neither. He wasn't here when she got here."

"That's funny, ain't it, seein' as how he was on a marble slab over in Newark at the time?"

"Say, I don't get you this mornin', Pete. I ain't never seen you in no mood like this before. Whatsa matter? I know I ain't no Sherlock, but jeest, I'm doin' my best, ain't I?"

"You said it. Ain't we all? And ain't we gonna catch hell just the same?"

"What do you mean catch hell?"

"We always do. This guy was a big shot, see? He had lotsa friends. Here he goes getting bumped off like a mobster. Where does that leave you and me?"

"In the soup like always."

"An' why not?" Tonelli demanded. "Why not? If I was the chief I wouldn't take the rap, would you? We ain't got a Chinaman's chance of gettin' the guys that did this job—"

"We could hang it on somebody."

"I don't play like that and you know it. When I send a guy down he goes down because I got the goods on him and I don't finger him 'til I do get him with the bundle in his arms."

"Which leaves me an' you holdin' the bag."

"It does if we don't produce the guy that did the dirty work," Tonelli agreed grimly.

From the corner of his eye through the front window he saw a car draw up to the curb. A magnificent car. A Packard roadster with a custom-built body painted a dark green with cream trimmings. Mechanically he made a mental note of the license number. 4 Y 75-59.

"We've got visitors," he remarked.

A tall young man, hatless, his fair hair disheveled, his dark top-coat open showing a crumpled shirt front and sadly mussed dinner clothes, sprang from the car, leaving it projecting out into the street on an angle of thirty degrees. Without pausing to shut off the engine he dashed for the steps to be stopped by a brawny arm in blue.

"What's the idea, buddy?" the officer on guard in front growled. "Hadn't you better park that car right before you leave it?"

"Get out of my way! I've got to get in here!"

"Who're you?"

"I'm Jack Holstead! I'm Doctor Holstead's nephew! A policeman was waiting at my apartment, he said—"

Tonelli swung open the casement window and leaned out.

"Let the gentleman come right up here," he ordered, "and then park that car and lock it and bring the key up."

The officer stood aside and Tonelli closed the window.

"You didn't by any chance find out who the lady was who came in this morning, did you, Mike?" he asked as he crossed to the hall doorway to admit their visitor.

"Whadda you think? Sure I did!" Mike spoke indignantly. "She was—" He dug in his pocket for his notebook. "She was Miss Sheila Pierce, the doctor's sekkatery!"

"Sheila? What has Sheila to do with this?" The disheveled young man on the threshold demanded. "Where, where is my uncle?"

5

"You better come in and sit down," Tonelli invited. "Your uncle—the body is still over in Newark."

"Then he is—it's true—he's dead?"

Tonelli nodded.

"Murdered! His body was dropped out of an airplane in Market Street, Newark, early this morning?

"But—that's impossible. Are you sure it's my uncle?"

"Sit down and get yourself together," Tonelli advised. "It looks like it was your uncle. There may be some possibility of a mistake. Later on you'll have to go over and identify the body, that is unless he has some other kin—"

"He hasn't. I'm all there is. He—he was a bachelor."

Holstead slumped in a chair and gazed wide-eyed at the havoc that had swept the room. "What's happened here?"

"As nearly as we can make out, now watch yourself—maybe you're too upset to hear any more right now?"

"No. No. I'm all right. I—I'll pull myself together. You can tell me everything. I'll be all right. What happened here?"

"It looks like he was murdered in this room."

"But—" Holstead sprang to his feet, "but you said he was in Newark! You said he'd been dropped out of an airplane."

"I said his body. He was dead when—before he was thrown over the side."

"Have they got the plane? What are you doing about it?"

"Everything's being done that can be done. We haven't got the plane yet, but we've got a good description of it. Good enough anyway."

"What did it look like? Where—?"

"Now you calm down and I'll tell you all we know about it. Would you like a drink? Did your uncle keep any liquor in the house?"

"There's some around here somewhere, but I don't want it. Tell me what you know."

"This morning early, about five o'clock or a little before, a night watchman named Pazco was making his rounds in Market Street, Newark, when he heard an airplane flying low overhead. The thing dived down and your uncle's body was dropped from it."

"My God!"

"It landed on top of the glass dingus in front of a store and the plane flew away."

"But the watchman saw it? Saw the plane?"

"Yes, he saw it all right."

"How do you know my uncle—if it was my uncle—was dead before he was dropped out of the plane?"

"Coroner says so. He'll tell you all about it if you want to hear. Your uncle, we're pretty sure it was him, was stabbed, with a knife, right here in this apartment. We have the knife and you can see for yourself what has happened here."

"Was it thugs? Burglars?"

"Don't look like it. Did your uncle have enemies?"

"Enemies! Certainly not. I don't think he had an enemy in the world."

"What could he have had here that anybody would want?"

"Do you mean money? Jewelry?"

"No. Some valuable paper or document."

"I haven't any idea what it could be. My uncle was a chemist. He—he was a research man—a scholar—I'm sure there couldn't have been anything—"

"Did you see much of your uncle? Did he talk to you, tell you things about himself, what he was doing? You're sure there wasn't nothing valuable here?"

"He told me as much as he told anybody, I suppose. It never occurred to me that there could be anything—"

"Nothing of value seems to have been taken," Tonelli stated. "Look around. Do you see anything gone?"

"No. Everything seems to be as it was, but then I couldn't say exactly. He had a good deal of valuable chemical apparatus, but I can't conceive of anyone doing murder for that. Besides I wouldn't know if any of it was missing."

"How long has it been since you saw your uncle to talk to?"

"Last night."

"You were here last night?"

"Yes."

"What time?"

"Why, fairly early in the evening. I should say about nine o'clock. Right after dinner."

"Did he act all right then? I mean was he the same as he always was?"

"Certainly. He seemed normal to me."

"Nothing preying on his mind?"

"Nothing except me, as usual."

"Was he worried about you?"

"Not exactly worried. You see, he has always wanted me to come into the business and I'd rather not— Then there was another matter we disagreed about—"

"You quarreled last night?"

"Why no—not exactly—that is—"

Holstead was confused. He almost stammered. Tonelli turned away from him.

"I don't like to dig into your family business if I can help it," he apologized. "Tell me anything you want to tell me. Anything you think would help."

"I can't see how this would help you in the least."

"O.K. That's up to you." The detective walked over to the window and looked out. Below the policeman on watch had wheeled the car into the curb and as the sergeant stood there a knock came at the door.

"See who that is, will you, Moran?" he ordered.

It was the officer with the key to the car.

"Thanks," Tonelli took the key, "that's all. Go on back to your post and let me know before you let anybody in."

The man saluted and left. Holstead had regained his poise.

"This airplane?" he asked. "You say the watchman saw it? What was it like?"

"Just an ordinary two-wing airplane, except that on the side, on the body—"

"You mean the fuselage?"

"That's it. On the side there was some sort of a red figure."

"What kind of a red figure?" Holstead's eyes had widened. He gripped the arms of his chair and leaned forward intensely. "What kind of a red figure was there on the fuselage?"

"Well, it wasn't very light and Pazco was too excited to take a good look I guess, but as near as he could remember it was something that looked like a man."

"A red figure of a man? Could it have been a red devil—with—with a pitchfork?"

"It might have been from what Pazco said. Why? Do you know anything about a plane with a red devil on it?"

"I—" Holstead started to speak and then obstinately shut his lips in a tight line. "I think I'll not say any more just now, if that's all right with you."

"It's all right with me," Tonelli shrugged, "only you know that everything you hold back, all you keep from us is gonna make it harder for us to find out what this is all about. We're gonna need all the information we can get if we're gonna find your uncle's murderer."

"I know," Holstead was firm. "I know I shouldn't keep anything back but—this—I want to think it over and make a few investigations on my own before I say anything. I'll tell you all I know as soon as I've looked up one or two things."

"O.K."

There was a short silence.

"What was it that you were talking about when I came in?" Holstead asked. "Didn't I hear someone say something about Sheila Pierce?"

"She was here this morning."

"The police sent for her?"

"No. She just came in. She came in while my partner was here looking around. That was before anybody had been notified."

"What did she want? Did she say?"

"She said your uncle asked her to come in early this morning. For some special job he wanted done."

"My uncle *asked* her!" Holstead's tone was incredulous.

"Yes. Wasn't she in the habit of coming here?"

"Certainly not. Didn't I tell you my uncle was a bachelor?"

Tonelli made a deprecating gesture.

"But she must have come here often to take dictation, didn't she? Wasn't she your uncle's secretary?"

"Of course she was, but I don't think she's ever been across this threshold in her life, that is until this morning."

"No? Then how come she had a key to the apartment?"

"A key? A key to the apartment? Are you sure?"

"She let herself in with a key, didn't she, Mike?"

"I'll say she did, and she acted like she was used to usin' it too," Moran declared.

Holstead was bewildered. He passed both hands over his forehead and covered his eyes with his palms for a long moment.

"I don't understand it," he said.

Tonelli regarded him indulgently.

"You was out sorta late last night, wasn't you?"

"Why—yes."

"Maybe had a drink or two, huh?"

"Why yes, at dinner. I had nothing afterward."

"Sorta tough, coming home from a party and running into something like this," Tonelli condoled.

"Party? I wasn't on any party."

Tonelli winked.

"I getcha. I won't say anything about it. No use dragging in a lady's name. The newspapers might get hold of it."

"A lady? What are you talking about?"

"Why," Tonelli was embarrassed, "I guess I got it wrong. I was just putting two and two together, see? Your clothes, and then you didn't get home until after noon—I just thought—"

"I suppose you did. Anybody would, but you're wrong. I—all I've been doing is riding around."

"Riding where?"

"Up through the park, out to Westchester, I don't know. Anywhere and everywhere."

"How long have you been riding?"

"Why—ever since I left here last night."

"You've been riding around ever since nine o'clock last night?"

"Pretty nearly. A little after that, anyway. I stopped once in a back road, I don't know just where, somewhere near Armonk I think, and I must have fallen asleep. It was daylight when I woke up."

"Was there anybody with you, Mr. Holstead?" Tonelli's voice had taken on an edge.

"No. Nobody."

"You musta stopped for gas or oil, or maybe a sandwich or something?"

"No. I wasn't hungry and the tank was full. I just rode around."

Tonelli leaned forward earnestly as he stood over the young man.

"Mr. Holstead," he said, "are you sure you didn't quarrel with your uncle last night?"

"Quarrel? *You* might call it that, but I wouldn't."

"Whatever you call it, Mr. Holstead, it musta been pretty serious to drive you out at night in your car in such a state of mind you didn't know or care where you were going to."

Holstead straightened up in his chair. His jaw set and he met Tonelli's eyes. He even smiled slightly, ironically.

"I see what you mean," he announced, "and from the looks of things you're right. It was serious, my talk with my uncle, damned serious, but it was strictly personal and private. And, for your peace of mind, I'll say this. I didn't murder my uncle, if that's what you're thinking. I didn't murder him, but I'm going to find out who did."

"I'd like to know myself," was the only answer Tonelli made, and he spoke very mildly.

"I'll tell you when I find out," the hint of a boyish grin that accompanied Holstead's words robbed them of offense.

"Thanks," Tonelli said dryly.

"What do we do now? Do you mind if I look around a bit?"

"Help yourself. You're the boss here now."

The careless words struck Holstead hard. His face twisted into a grimace of pain, but he said nothing, examined the living room with one long continuous, searching glance and moved into the bedroom.

Moran, his eyes blazing with excitement, stood midway between the sergeant and the door through which Holstead had passed.

"Whatcha gonna do? Nab him, Pete?"

Tonelli shook his head.

"Why should I?"

"That's an awful funny story he tells about drivin' around all night."

"Yeah. People do funny things when they're worried," Tonelli commented easily.

"Then you ain't gonna take him in?"

"Not for a while anyway."

Holstead reappeared.

"Nothing out of the way in the bedroom," he said, "and it couldn't have been robbery, ordinary robbery. Nothing has been touched."

"Have you been into the workshop there?"

"The lab? No."

"Better take a look," Tonelli walked with him into the laboratory and stood watching him casually. Holstead went over to the safe and picked up a notebook from the pile.

"Did your uncle keep anything valuable in that cabinet, anything but them books?"

Holstead turned with the notebook in his hand. "These were pretty valuable," he said, "valuable

to him. They are the notes of years of research. They couldn't be replaced at any price. He kept them in this fire-proof cabinet for that reason and as far as I know that's all he did keep there."

"Would them notes be any good to anybody else?"

Holstead considered.

"They might have a value to the right people." The attractive boyish smile that persisted in spite of his worry broke through again. "But I can hardly think that the head of the department of chemistry at Columbia University or a former President of the Chemical Society would murder my uncle for his notes. It would be easier and simpler to ask for them."

Tonelli grunted.

Back in the living room once more Holstead wandered about for a moment or two with his hands in his pockets.

"You said something a while ago about my having to identify the body?"

"Yes, I guess you'll have to look at it. It's a necessary formality."

"It is over in Newark?"

"Yes."

"How soon do I have to go over there?"

"The sooner the better, I'd say."

"Am I in custody here?"

"What?"

"Am I under suspicion of anything? Can I do as I like, go where I please?"

"I don't see any reason why not."

"I wasn't sure. You were so perturbed at my not having any way to account for my time last night."

"Yeah?"

"Yeah." Perhaps unconsciously Holstead mimicked him. "What I'm getting at is, I don't want to go over to Newark looking like this unless I have to. I'd like to get uptown and have a shave and a bath before I go."

"That's all right by me. How're you going over to Jersey?"

"I'll drive, I think."

Together the two detectives and the nephew of the murdered man walked downstairs and stood for a moment at the curb.

"Any more information you get I'd be pleased to have," Holstead said as he stepped into his car. "You aren't going uptown, are you?"

"No. I'm past due downtown. I wouldn't be surprised if the chief didn't have a couple of men on *my* trail by now."

"Well—thanks for your courtesy." Holstead put out his hand hesitantly but there was no hesitation on the part of the sergeant in grasping it.

"Watch your step," Tonelli warned, "and don't stay out all night tonight without knowing where you are."

"I'll know where I am tonight," the answer floated back from the moving car. "Don't let that bother you."

"You gonna let him go off like that, nobody tailin' him nor nothin'?" Moran expostulated.

"Just like that," Tonelli snapped. "Ain't I a damned fool?"

"I'll say!" His partner's tone was bitter in belief.

The two men crossed the street, skirting Gramercy Park, and crossed again on the south side to the line of taxicabs that waited in front of the Players' Club and the National Arts Club.

"Centre Street!" Tonelli ordered, following Moran into the cab at the head of the line. "And make it snappy."

6

Captain Henessy, formidable behind his desk, looked up with a scowl as they entered. "Time you were reporting!"

"Yes sir."

"Well?"

"It's all wet. Lousy. If you can make sense out of any of the stuff I've got you're better than I am."

Henessy teetered back, bouncing lightly on the spring of his swivel chair.

"What made you think I wasn't better than you are? Where you been all day? Picnicking?"

"No sir. I been over to Jersey."

"Didn't you find anything at all?"

"Nothing that makes sense."

"Let's hear the fairy tale then."

"It is a fairy tale, and it's got my goat! Here's this guy, this Dr. Holstead, bumped off like a gangster. He was taken for a ride like as if he was a big mobster that had pulled a cross on the gang. When the mobs pull a stunt like this they're advertising what will happen to guys that crosses them."

"So what?"

"I bite. So what? This Holstead wasn't in on no rackets that I ever heard about, was he? Why should any killer want to advertise that he'd killed him?"

Henessy took a typewritten report from the file at his elbow and looked it over.

"Holstead's record, all we can dig up, is clean as a whistle," he admitted. "Not a murmur against him here, except—have you talked to the Narcotics Squad about him?"

"How could I? I ain't had a chance. I just got back from Newark. Say, you're in bad with the Chief of Police over there and I don't mean perhaps."

"I am? That's too bad. He's sore, is he?"

"Sure. He wants to know can't we bury our own dead over on this side and if the Chief of the Detective Bureau is too busy to work on a murder case."

"Aw, tell him to go run up a rope."

"That ain't diplomatic. Your orders was to be diplomatic and maybe I didn't strain a button obeying orders."

Henessy grunted.

"Anything about the doctor's nephew, Jack Holstead, on that blacklist of yours?" Tonelli asked.

"Just his name. Why?"

"Well, I did something just now. Maybe you'll ride me for it, but it's done and I had my reasons."

"What'd you do?"

"Let young Holstead get away—"

"And never even put a shadow on him," interposed Moran.

"That's right, Chief. I let him get away clean—if he wants to run."

"Why should he want to run?"

"Things don't look so good by him, Chief. He was in his uncle's house last night. Had a quarrel with the old man about business and something else—he won't say what—and then he goes off, couldn't be located this morning. He says he was driving around all night in his car. He don't know *where* he was driving, nobody *saw* him and he wasn't *with* anybody."

"And you *let* him go?"

"Yeah."

"Why?"

"In the first place I don't crave to put the finger on these Park Avenue boys until I know where I'm at. If I locked him up he'd have three fancy mouthpieces to spring him inside of a half an hour—"

"What was the real reason, Pete?"

"Well, Chief, the airplane that dumped Dr. Holstead in Newark belonged to Jack Holstead."

"What?" It was Moran who shouted, but the captain sat up straight.

"Come again, Pete?" he commanded, his moustache bristling.

"I said that Dr. Holstead, the guy that was bumped last night, was dropped out of his nephew's airplane."

"And you let the kid go?"

"I let him go."

"What for? So he could get a nifty alibi ready?"

"He might but I don't think so, and if he does, what of it?"

"I don't get you, Pete. If you know that this kid dropped his uncle's dead body out of his air—"

"Hold on, Chief. You're going too fast. I didn't say nothing like that."

"No?"

"No!"

"Then what did you say?"

"I said the old guy took a tumble out of the kid's bus but I didn't say the kid was in it."

"Naw," Moran was mightily sarcastic, "the kid was riding around the Bronx River Parkway all the time and if you don't believe it ask him. Nobody seen him, he was just riding around."

Tonelli's jaw set obstinately while Henessy looked long and silently at his star sleuth.

"All right, Pete," he said at length, "you win! Now what's the picture? How did you find out about the airplane?"

Tonelli laughed.

"Asked," he explained. "Maybe you ain't never heard tell of it, Chief, but there's a big airport near Newark."

"Yeah, I've heard of it. I've heard of Lindbergh and Byrd too."

"They wasn't there this morning, but the night service man was. He was there with a wallop."

"Yeah?"

"I took Pazco, the night watchman, and the patrolman on the beat, they was the ones that saw the old gentleman take his nose dive, and I loaded them into a police car with the compliments of the

Chief of Newark and we went out to the airport. What I was looking for was a plane with a big red splotch on her side."

"And you found it?"

"And how! The first thing we saw in front of one of them big garages they call hangars. As soon as he sees it Pazco lets out a yell, 'That's it!'"

"Do you think he was on the level? How could he identify the plane? Do you think he got a good look at it this morning?"

"Maybe yes and maybe no, I wasn't taking any chances. I goes and gets hold of the operations officer of the field, a nice little bimbo in a cap like a navy officer, and I asks him who the bus belongs to. You coulda bought me for a nickel when he says it was Jack Holstead's."

"You can't beat that for a hot one!"

"Jeest, if you ain't shot with luck!" Moran contributed.

"I'm lucky at that. Anyway I asks this operations officer what the plane was doing out there and he says it was being serviced and inspected after being in flight. 'When was it in flight?' says I. Mind you this was before the noon papers was out and they didn't know nothing about the murder out at the flying field."

"Ain't they got no telephones in Newark?" Moran asked impertinently. "Couldn't somebody have called the field and tipped off them guys?"

"It's a chance, but why?" Tonelli demanded, and Moran subsided.

"Anyway," Tonelli continued, "I asked the guy when the plane had been up. 'You'll have to see the night service man about that,' he says, 'I'll go get him for you.' He come back after a while with a fella they'd got outa bed and they tell me he's the night service man on duty from midnight to eight A.M. 'What time did this plane leave the field and when did it get back?' I says to him. He come right back at me. 'It went out at'—(we was in the office by then and this night man dug out a sheet of records to back him up)—'at four twenty-five A.M. and it come back in again at five-three A.M.' That checks pretty close, you see, because the body was dropped at four-fifty A.M. 'Did Mr. Holstead himself take it out?' I asks. The night fella said yes, but when I asked him if he was ready to swear to it he sorta hedged.

He finally admitted it was darkish and he was sleepy when what he supposed was Jack Holstead came rolling up in his car. 'I'd know that car anywhere,' the fella says, 'you can't mistake that big Packard with that green paint and that yella trim.'"

"He's near to right, too," Moran declared. "We seen the car this morning and you couldn't forget it."

Tonelli nodded agreement.

"Anyway the night man said the car drove right up to the hangar and two men got out leaving one man sitting in the seat. Jack Holstead, or the fella the service man thought was Jack Holstead, got into the plane and began to fiddle around. He put on his helmet and goggles and told the service man to open up the hangar door.

"'Wasn't it sorta funny for Holstead to be there at that time in the morning wanting to fly?' I asks, but it seems that it wasn't. Holstead has the night-flying bug. Almost any time he's likely to show up and want his plane and he's liable to have anybody with him, so this didn't strike the service man as anything out of the ordinary. Anyhow he was too busy opening doors and things to think. The pilot gave a lot of orders and kept him busy and finally, still wearing his helmet and goggles, the pilot climbed down out of the cockpit after he had started the engine. The propeller was turning over slowly but the machine was chocked and everything was all jake and safe. Then the pilot and the man that came with him helped the third man out of the car. Both fellas laughed some and said something about their friend being tight and that they had to get him to Boston in time for work in the morning. The service man says that the third man was so helpless they practically had to carry him to the plane and boost him up into it. His feet dragged along the ground. The service man came to help them as soon as he could, but by the time he got to them they had him in the plane."

Tonelli paused. "'What would you say if I told you that third fella was dead?' I says to the service man. He laughed. 'Dead drunk, you mean,' he says, so I didn't argue with him.

"According to the service man's story, after they had the fella in the plane the two that had brought him hadda little argument but he couldn't hear what they said. Anyway, the fella in the helmet and goggles climbed back into the cockpit, give her the gun and off he went with the supposed drunk while the other fella got back into the automobile and scooted toward the road for New York.

"The only funny part of the whole business to the service man was when the plane came back. It came back so soon he thought it had engine trouble and he come out on the jump to meet it. It came into the field, landed at the far end, a quarter of a mile at least from the hangars, and instead of taxiing down to the hangars it stayed there at the end of the field. The service man started out to it on the lam. He saw the pilot tumble out of the plane and go over toward the road. He kept on out there and when he arrived found the plane empty.

"He didn't know *what* to do. He walked back to the office thinking that maybe Holstead would come along but he didn't, so this service man, who seems to be kinda dumb, didn't do nothing.

"'What did you figure happened to the passenger,' I asks. He didn't know. He said all aviators were crazy and he'd seen drunks act funny before. It wasn't any of his business so he just put the bus down on the mechanics' schedule for a thorough test and overhauling and let it go at that."

"You mean to say," Henessy demanded, "that mechanic out at the airport saw a plane take off with two people in it and come back in twenty minutes with only one person in it and he didn't ask what had happened to the other person?"

"I told you what he told me, Cap. There wasn't nobody to ask. As soon as the plane lit the pilot jumped over the side and ran over to the road."

"And the mechanic didn't go over to the road to see what became of the pilot?"

"He was pretty dumb, Cap, like I said. I asked him all those things and by the time I was through and the field authorities found out what it was all about there was a hullabaloo around there. It ended in the mechanic getting scared and confused and then I couldn't get anything out of him. He told three different stories in ten minutes after he found out there'd been murder done. The way I figure it he told most of the truth the first time I asked him. I figure this mechanic is a little thick anyway, like I said, and he was sleepy when the three men came driving up. He just did what they told him to do in a sort of daze. You're liable to do anything at four o'clock in the morning when you've been up all night and are getting your first sleep."

"The guy didn't have no business being asleep on the job," Moran declared virtuously.

The sergeant turned on him savagely.

"Is zat so? I suppose you never snatched a snooze on the beat when you was in harness?"

Moran growled in his throat.

"So," Tonelli sat back in his chair and looked his superior in the eye, "I let the young fella go. What else could I do? What would you do?"

"Damned if I know. The same thing you did, I guess. Pass the buck to the chief like you're doing."

Tonelli grinned.

"I *am* sorta passing the buck, ain't I, but this is one of the times when I gotta do it. There's no use getting tangled up in these society cases unless you know where you're at."

The skin on Henessy's cheek-bones flushed darkly, throwing the network of tiny broken veins that covered his face into sharp relief and turning them purple.

"I'll tell you where you're at," he snapped. "You're at New York Police Headquarters and you're talking to the Chief of the Detective Bureau and you're a flattie under orders. One of those orders is for you to go out and get me the guys that bumped Dr. Holstead. I don't care who they are nor where they come from or who their friends are. There may be politics in the police department, but politics stops at murder. This wasn't a gangster killing. This was a respected and respectable citizen and by God they're the fellows we're here to protect. Now do you know where you stand?"

"You bet!" Tonelli's acknowledgment was immediate and sincere. "I just wanted to know if there was any more in this thing than I saw on the surface."

"If *you* can see anything, what is it?"

The sergeant laughed ruefully.

"I told you it didn't make sense. It don't add up to much, does it? It's all so sappy. If young Holstead killed his uncle, why didn't he leave him lay in the apartment? If young Holstead didn't kill his uncle why did he take him for a ride in his skywagon? And if somebody else killed the old man why did they get young Holstead to take him for a ride, and if they didn't why did they go to all the trouble to take him themselves and make it look as much like the youngster as possible?"

"You got *me* dizzy," Moran said.

Tonelli only looked the obvious retort.

"There's worse and more to come," Henessy promised. "I forgot to tell you. You and me is due at the commissioner's office at five o'clock."

"What for? It's after two now and I gotta—"

"I know. Do all you can and be at the commissioner's office at five. Somebody's going to be there that we've got to hush-hush about. I don't know who or what, but somebody pretty important. Important enough to have the Mayor call up and make an appointment anyway."

Tonelli groaned.

"I knew it. I knew, it was coming. We're gonna get all tangled up in red tape over this thing and then when we don't get anywhere we're gonna get another panning for being so dumb we can't catch a murderer."

"I get the panning," Henessy reminded him. "You've got it soft. All you've got to do is to figure out who killed the old man and then go and make a pinch."

"That's all."

"Where do you go from here?"

"I thought I'd better drop in and see what Doc Helm has made out of the stuff he collected at the apartment this morning—"

Captain Henessy agreed by nodding slightly.

"—and then I thought I'd run over to Pearl Street and third degree Dr. Holstead's office force a little bit. There might be something there, you never can tell."

"Don't forget the Narcotics Squad."

"I won't. I'll see them before I go around to Pearl Street."

"And don't forget that you're due at the commissioner's office at five."

"Fat chance."

"What about that Newark gang, are they all right?"

"Yeah, I'd say so. The chief was a little rattled this morning, but so would you be if somebody dropped a dead man in your rose bushes."

"Think they could play foxy if we put it up to them? And would they?"

"Sure. They'll be all right that way."

"What do you think of calling them up and telling them to keep a quiet eye on young Holstead when he gets there to identify the body?"

Tonelli consulted his watch, large and open-faced like himself.

"The way that boy moves I'd say he was over there now."

Henessy reached for the telephone.

"Get me Newark Police Headquarters.

"Hello. Captain Henessy, New York Police Department, speaking. I'd like to talk to Chief Hobson please. Hello, Chief? Henessy speaking. Sorry I couldn't get over there this morning. Well, I'm sorry anyway. I know you handled it fine. Tonelli told me you were fine to him. Thank you. Any time we can do as much for you, call on us. By the way, Chief, we expect young Jack Holstead, the nephew of the doctor, will be there soon to identi— O, he has. Has he gone yet? I was going to ask you to sort of keep an eye on him— O, you did? Is that so? He did? Where to? What? Well, I'll be damned. Thank you, Chief. That's what I call first-class detective work. I don't know how we can ever thank you enough but you can bet that I'll see that credit is given where credit is due when this thing is all washed up. Good-bye."

The captain pushed the 'phone away from him as though he were chewing on something very, very bitter.

"What's the bad news?" Tonelli demanded.

"Plenty. Your friend Jack showed up fifteen minutes ago."

"He musta broken a couple of speed laws getting there."

"He identified the body and didn't tarry about it. He asked a few questions and then left Newark Headquarters. Hobson had him tailed."

"The hell you say. I didn't think he had it in him."

"He did. Jack went to a drug store around the corner and called a number. They traced the call. He called the Newark Airport."

"What do you know—"

"Jack's on his way out to the airport now."

"Hobson still tailing him?"

"He is."

"What do you want me to do?"

"Go ahead with your check-up on this end. Hobson will call back and tell us what the kid does."

"Suppose he takes his plane and flies away?"

"Hobson's given orders that the kid is not to be allowed to escape. He'll be arrested if he sets foot in a plane."

"That's O.K. by me."

"Me too. Get on your way and don't forget five o'clock."

7

TRAILED BY THE FAITHFUL MORAN, Tonelli, after leaving Captain Henessy's office, climbed two flights of stairs and walked to the rear of the building.

They found diminutive, wizened Dr. Helm looking more worried and puzzled than usual, although his pleasantest known expression was a frown.

"Didja find out anything about that knife in the Holstead case, Doc?" Tonelli asked.

"Something," Helm admitted. "Almost all contradictory."

"How so?"

"There are a number of finger prints on the brass of this knife," Dr. Helm produced it, "some of them fairly clear, some blurred but easily identifiable as those of the same man."

"I don't suppose we got a record of the prints?"

"Yes," Dr. Helm spoke slowly, "we have."

"Swell!" Tonelli was jubilant. "That makes it easy. Then this was a professional job?"

"On the face of it, yes."

"Whose prints are they?"

"A man known as Samuel Ertz, alias Slim the Sailor."

"Slim the Sailor?" Tonelli was astounded. "The dope peddler!"

"According to his record, yes," Dr. Him agreed. "Convicted twice. Committed once to the Island for observation and treatment as an addict—"

"Fat lot of good that did him. It don't do any of them any good that I ever heard of. You're dead sure about those finger prints, Doctor?"

"I'm sure the prints on the knife are those of Slim the Sailor," the expert reiterated patiently, "but I'm not sure those finger prints are the prints of the man who committed the murder. For one thing," he explained, answering Tonelli's unspoken question, "none of these prints are in blood. They are all on the brass; none on the blade except those which underlie the blood. In other words, they are old prints, prints made through the daily handling and usage of this knife."

"And the handle was gone?" Tonelli mused.

"There was no trace of the handle, and, as you can see for yourself, this knife is useless as a weapon—useless for almost any purpose without the handle."

"Are you sure this is the knife used in the murder?" Tonelli demanded.

"Either this one or an identical one," the expert stated. "I think, however, an identical one."

Tonelli made no effort to conceal his surprise, and Moran snorted.

"Because," the expert spoke as if he were saying something very momentous indeed, "the blood on this knife is not human blood."

"Not human?"

"No. The blood on this knife is that of a guinea pig."

"A guinea pig?"

The chemist nodded.

"Then what the—?"

"This may help." Dr. Helm held out a bit of white waxed paper that had been twisted into a ball.

"What's this?"

"We found it near the blood stain on the floor, ostensibly dropped by the same person who dropped the knife."

The chemist smoothed out the piece of paper. It was of the same shape, but a trifle larger than a cigarette paper.

"Looks like the wrapper of a shot of coke," Tonelli said.

"Precisely what it seems to be," Dr. Helm agreed. "In fact this paper has contained cocaine."

"Slim the Sailor's knife and a twisted coke paper— Jeest! There was a lotta careless guys in on this killing. Clues everywhere," Tonelli thought aloud.

Dr. Helm said nothing.

"You say the killing was done with this knife or an identical one, Doc?"

"The measurements of the wound and those of the knife are very close, remarkably close." Tonelli came to an abrupt decision.

"We better pick up Slim quick while the picking is good. Moran, go pick up Slim the Sailor and bring him in."

"What charge?"

"Spitting on the sidewalk, fat-head. What do I care? Think up a charge on the way over to West Street, that's where he used to hang out—and say, Mike," he called as his partner turned to leave, "I guess you'll find the handle of Slim's knife on him when you find Slim. Don't let it get away from you and don't smear it all up. Bring it in to Dr. Helm here and let him see what he can make of it."

The sergeant spoke again to the chemist as Moran departed.

"Guinea pig blood? What do you know! Was the blood on the floor pig blood too?"

"No," Dr. Helm spoke positively, "it was human blood. Dr. Holstead's blood. I've checked with the chemist's report in Newark by telephone. The haemoglobin test of Dr. Holstead and the blood stain check. The blood spots on the carpet in Dr. Holstead's study probably dripped from the assassin's knife."

"Then you think he was killed there?"

"We think so." The expert took up a diagram from his desk. "Here, you see, was the doctor's desk facing the fireplace. He sat probably with his forearms resting on the desk, his back to the door. He always sat hunched up over his desk. It was a characteristic attitude—"

"Then you knew Dr. Holstead?"

"Almost every chemist or scientist of any standing in the country knew him," Dr. Helm explained. "He was one of the greatest of the research men in the synthetic organic field. Usaki, the great Japanese chemist, and Berliski at the University of Chicago have both called him in consultation—"

"I don't know who those fellows are, but the way you talk about them makes me know they was big shots, Doc."

"Yes?—Well, all that, I suppose, is beside the question. As we see it he was seated at his desk when the assassin entered and stabbed him. He was then lifted from his chair and partly carried, partly dragged across the room and down the steps. We found two more small spots of blood on the marble of the stairs near the bottom. From then on we can find no further trace of him. The one thing that so far has been in our favor is the thick carpet."

"How so?"

"Heavy pile carpets under microscopic examination reveal almost as much as soft earth will. For instance, we know that someone, a person with flat feet and run-over heels, a woman probably about fifty years of age, weighing about one hundred and forty pounds was in the apartment early in the day, before Dr. Holstead returned. The caretaker, I deduced by the evidence of the vacuum cleaner and broom over some of the tracks. Inquiry proves that to be true. We have located the charwoman, an honest soul who knows nothing and finished her work in the apartment before noon, when she left everything in order."

"I told Moran I needn't look around much," Tonelli murmured, "that you'd tell me all there is to know."

"Then," Dr. Helm continued with no trace of satisfaction at this praise, "Dr. Holstead came in. Peculiarities of his shoes identified *his* marks. We checked with shoes of his we found in the clothes closet. Later, a man, I should say a young, fashionably dressed man came in who was smoking a pipe."

"You sound just like Sherlock Holmes."

"I'm using somewhat the same method he is supposed to have used. The tracks show shoes of an exclusive and fashionable last and tobacco ash spilled and walked on as the man stood beside Dr. Holstead's desk. He paced up and down. Probably stamped, was angry or excited."

"I'm listening, Doc. I'm alistening."

"This man left, leaving his pipe on the desk, as minute traces show, and then later, considerably later, as the pile on the rugs had had a chance to regain some of the elasticity and go back into place, *two* men entered."

"Were they—?"

"Yes. The murderers. And—I can't be sure if just before they came in or if she came with them, there came a woman."

"Why can't you be sure?"

"Because of confused tracks. The woman was Dr. Holstead's secretary, Miss Sheila Pierce. She entered the apartment again, later, while Moran was there—"

"Yes, he told me."

"So it is practically impossible for me to say exactly when her first footprints were made. Certainly they were made prior to her entry while Moran was there. And her first tracks were probably made prior to the entry of the murderers. It looks as though she was in the room before the murderers were or at the same time, but probably before."

"Then she was there sometime between the man with the pipe and the murderers, you think?"

"O yes. Some of her prints distinctly underlie those of the murderers."

"Why are you so sure the two men were the murderers?"

"First, because it would have taken a man's weight and strength to drive the knife, a knife of that sort, home. Second, because Dr. Holstead went from his desk to his laboratory after his first male visitor left. Overlapping footprints again. And third, because I can show you from the prints just how the murderers crept in, how one waited near the door while the other stabbed, and the prints show how the man stood who did the stabbing. I think there is no doubt."

"I betcha there's no doubt if you say so," Tonelli spoke emphatically.

"Now as to finger prints, I have those on the bowl of the pipe which, from the New Jersey police description, are not those of Dr. Holstead, and I have a faint, very faint, print of a right hand, made by one of the murderers who leaned on one of the papers on Dr. Holstead's desk. This is the paper, this sheet of blue with a memorandum of a meeting of the Society of Chemical Engineers, and some notes for an address. This print does not correspond to the prints on the pipe. The murderers, I may say, were of about ordinary height and weight—"

"So the Jersey medical examiner said—"

"—and that's about all I can give you to work on."

"No finger prints on the wax paper?"

"If there were, they were obliterated by the crumpling up of the paper."

"Have you any trace of what the murderers were searching for, or maybe the murderers didn't make all that mess with the papers?"

"I think they did, but I have no idea what they were looking for."

"Did you know anything about Dr. Holstead's habits or friends?"

"Only that they were very quiet, both his habits and his friends."

"How old was Dr. Holstead?"

"About sixty, I believe."

"He was a bachelor?"

"Yes. His nearest relative was his nephew, his younger brother's son. The boy was named for the doctor, and when the father died Dr. Holstead took the boy and educated him. He had him trained in chemistry and the boy went to the same schools his father and uncle had attended, Westminster, Yale, then the University of Bonn. However, I think the younger Holstead branched off from chemistry into some physical research, something to do with flying—"

"Did you know that young Holstead owned an airplane, Doctor?"

"No. But it is very likely."

"Were the Holsteads rich?"

"I couldn't say. Certainly the pharmaceutical business of the laboratories was good, and I'm sure Dr. Holstead spent very little."

"Have you ever heard that the boy was wild?"

"I really know nothing of their private life. Dr. Holstead was only an acquaintance. I knew him professionally and I used to see him at Chemical Society meetings and at the Chemists' Club. What I've told you is more or less gossip, things I've gathered from mutual friends—"

"Who knew the doctor well?"

"Several of the men at the Chemists' Club did. Dr. Steeple was his best friend, I guess, but he died a year or so ago—"

"How should I go about getting the dope on the doctor?"

"You could start in *Who's Who*. There's quite an article about him there— Nothing I've not told you, however, as far as I can remember."

"This ought to give me a start. In the meantime I'll get over to his Pearl Street office. They might have turned up something there.

You sure you didn't get any names or addresses from the footprints and things?"

"No." There was no humor in Dr. Helm's denial. There was no humor in Dr. Helm. "What do you expect to find at his office?"

"It won't hurt to talk to his people."

"They can probably tell you all there is to know. Holstead was a solitary man, his habits were retiring. There is probably little or nothing available anywhere else that would help you, Sergeant."

"Thanks, Doc. I'll be seeing you."

The little man only grunted and turned back to his work.

8

LITTLE WORK WAS BEING DONE that afternoon in the old-fashioned building in Pearl Street that housed John K. Holstead, Inc., manufacturing chemists. Even in the shipping department on the ground floor of the five-story plant, employees had a tendency to gather together and murmur to each other about the strange death of the boss. A general air of excitement pervaded the whole place.

One flight up, where the business offices were located, everything but the absolutely essential routine had been frankly abandoned. On the third floor and the fourth where girls with deft fingers wrapped, packed, bottled and tended pill-compressing machines, there was the same buzzing undertone of conjecture that disturbed the lower floors. Only in the laboratories at the top of the building, under the keen eyes of Dr. Vincent Kramer, the chief chemist, the laboratory assistants went about their work as usual.

As if infinite leisure were at his command, Tonelli sauntered into the reception room on the second floor and, leaning over the oak rail which separated the office from the reception room, spoke casually to the telephone girl, Miss Sarah Klein. She was pert, pretty, twenty or so and combined the duties of receptionist with operating the switchboard.

"I'd like to see Dr. Holstead's secretary?"

"I don't know if you can," the girl spoke hesitantly, "we're so upset here today—"

"Maybe she'd see me anyway," the sergeant smiled. "I'm from Police Headquarters and I'm working on this case."

"Gee!" she was frankly awed. "I'm awful sorry but she ain't here. It was an awful shock to her. She's home in bed."

"That's tough!" Tonelli remarked. He leaned on the rail in an easy familiar fashion and spoke conversationally. "What do you people around here think about it?"

"You know," she told him confidentially, "I wasn't surprised in the least!"

"No? Why not?"

"I had a feeling—you know how it is when you have a feeling something is going to happen—"

A call came and she plugged in her lines, snapping her keys with a businesslike and efficient air. "Holstead and Compnay!" she chanted, "good afternoon!" and then: "Just a moment, plee-uz!" She completed a circuit and smiled up at Tonelli.

"Yes sir," she resumed where she left off, "I had a feeling. The minute Dr. Holstead walked in the door I felt something, I can't quite explain it, but you know what I mean—creepy like."

"Nope," the detective answered her with a minimum of courtesy, "I don't see what you mean. I don't never feel creepy myself." Which was a downright lie, but justified at the moment.

Tonelli had his own methods of questioning. He was a pretty keen judge of men and women, this large, beefy man. He had worked his way up from the gutters of Bleecker Street to the blue and brass of a "cop." From the lowly status of a "harness bull" he had toiled to the lofty heights of the Homicide Squad and special pet of the "Chief" by sheer hard work, horse-sense applied and main chance seized. It meant something to be the special pet of Captain Henessy. It meant hard work, long hours, constant responsibility and danger and practically no thanks, but most of all it meant a chance to do honest, solid police work.

Tonelli was keen because he followed his instincts and his reactions toward people. Born in the big city, of city bred and reared parents (Neapolitans they were), he was a highly specialized animal. His speedy appraisals, the accuracy of his judgment of human beings, were as much a product of special training and inbred aptitude as the instincts of any other jungle brute. However inept the parallel between city and jungle, it is still true that nowhere else is life more precarious, nowhere else is death more swift to strike and nowhere else do their denizens reap so instantly the award of special adaptability to extra special conditions than in the streets of big cities and in the trails of the jungle.

So without knowing or caring how or why he knew, Tonelli knew without probing that the girl who "felt creepy" on the morning before the murder had probably felt nothing of the kind. She had developed that idea of creepiness and mystery by dint of a thousand rehearsals of the events of the day. Every member of the office staff had contributed to that feeling. Every visitor had been told about it and had questioned:

"How long before he was killed did you see him? Did you see him yesterday? The very day? Tell me, did he look just like he used to look—you know, just like ordinary? Didn't you sorta feel something was wrong? Gee, I bet it must be spooky to sit in this office even in broad daylight. I'd be scared to death to stay here. He might come prowling in any minute. Aren't you a *tiny* bit afraid?"

Tonelli knew the kind of questions she was being plied with by her friends. He was protected from the same kind of queries only by the fact that his fellow citizens, those who knew him at all, knew they would receive short answers to any such questions directed to the sergeant. Short answers and no information.

Now he said to the telephone girl:

"Nope! I don't never feel creepy. What made *you* feel so creepy?"

"Well, I don't know, it was kinda in the air."

"The air was swell. It was a nice sunshiny day."

"Well, you know how it is, when you've got a feeling—"

The office boy "kinda had a feelin'" too, and the two girls who worked adding machines and typewriters admitted, when stimulated by questioning, that they had "noticed something kind of queer" about the place.

Jovial, never losing his temper, maintaining the air that it was all a lark and didn't really matter, Tonelli questioned and probed.

There was no reason for any premonitory feeling and he was equally sure there had been no premonitions. Dr. Holstead had come in as usual, about his usual time. Business had gone on as usual. After nearly twenty minutes during which Tonelli, to an uninformed observer, would have seemed to have been loafing—and flirting slightly with a pretty telephone girl—he got his first hint of importance. Two men had been to call on Dr. Holstead yesterday morning, she let drop. "Who were they?" Tonelli demanded in bantering tone. "Some druggist friends of the doctor who wanted some headache pills?"

"Nuh-uh!" she shook her head negatively, "these were rough-looking men. I never saw them before and they gave phony names. They called themselves Mr. Smith and Mr. Jones."

Her answer severed Tonelli's jocular vein. "What made you think they were rough looking?" he asked seriously.

"Why—I don't know. They just were."

"Were they dirty?"

"No."

"Did they wear good clothes?"

"Yes—I guess they were good enough."

When boiled down, the statements indicated only that they were men nobody in the office had ever seen before and they were of an out-of-doors type. "Not exactly foreign looking, but—"

"Did they look like seafaring men? Sailors?"

They might have been. She was sure only of one thing. They weren't druggists or doctors, chemists, research workers or business men such as might be calling on Dr. Holstead without arousing comment.

They came in at nine o'clock and had waited, sat quietly enough on the long bench by the door and they hadn't seemed to know Dr. Holstead nor he them. He came in and passed them by without speaking and went into his office before one of the two, the taller and burlier, approached and asked the operator if that wasn't the boss who had just gone in.

"That's what he said," the telephone girl assured Tonelli, "I remember his very words. He said: 'Ain't that the boss?'"

"What did you tell him?"

"I told him yes, that was the boss, and then he said: 'Tell him we're here an' we're gettin' sorta tired of waitin'.'" She imitated the hard tone of the man, drawing down her mouth in one corner as she did so.

"Did you tell the doctor that?"

"No. Not exactly. I told Miss Pierce that the two gentlemen waiting to see Dr. Holstead said they were getting tired of waiting."

"Had they been waiting long?"

"About fifteen minutes. They came in right after nine o'clock."

"What did Miss Pierce do?"

"I guess she told the doctor because after a minute or two she came out and told them they could come into the office. The doctor would see them."

"And they went in?"

"Yes."

"What happened then?"

"Nothing. They went in and they stayed there for a while and after a while they came out."

"You didn't hear anything they said to Dr. Holstead?"

"No. You can't hear anything that goes on in his office from here where I sit."

"That's too bad. Then the men came in and saw him and went away quietly."

"No. That wasn't all. They had been there a few minutes—"

"How many minutes?"

"I don't know, I didn't time them. But after a few minutes Dr. Holstead called me—"

"He called you into the office while the men were there?"

"No. He called me on the telephone from his extension."

"What did he want?"

"He asked me to call Dr. Kramer."

"The chief chemist?"

"We've only got one man of that name."

"What did he want with Dr. Kramer?"

"I don't know. He asked me to have Dr. Kramer come right down to his office."

"Did you notice anything unusual about him? I mean Dr. Holstead?"

"Yes. I told you he was sorta—"

"Yeah, I know. He was sorta creepy. But outside of that. Was there anything peculiar about the way Dr. Holstead spoke to you?"

"Yes there was. He sounded like he was mad."

"Was that peculiar?"

"Yes. Dr. Holstead was never mad."

"Never?"

"I never saw him angry once and I've been here over a year."

"So you were surprised when he spoke as if he was mad?"

"I was. I said to Miss King, she's that girl over there with the dark hair, I said to her as she passed by, she was just leaving the office for a minute, I says: 'I bet Dr. Kramer is going to catch it over something. Dr. Holstead is awful mad.'"

"And what did Miss King say?"

"She said: 'I don't care if he does.'"

"What did she mean by that?"

"She don't like Dr. Kramer very much."

"Why not?"

"She takes dictation from him a lot and she says he's awful fussy."

"How do you mean fussy?"

"He uses a lot of big words. Chemical words, and he don't like it if she can't spell them properly."

"I see. What happened then?"

"Then Dr. Kramer came down."

"Came down?"

"Yes. He stays up in the laboratory on the top floor most of the time when Dr. Holstead is here. Of course when Dr. Holstead is away he works in Dr. Holstead's office."

"In other words he's the boss when Dr. Holstead is away?"

"Yes. Him and Miss Pierce."

"Miss Pierce?"

"Yes. She takes charge of the office and Dr. Kramer does anything about the laboratory or the drugs or that part of the business that's necessary, but Miss Pierce does all the rest."

"Was Dr. Holstead away much?"

"O, lots. He was always going someplace. Chicago or down to Washington or somewhere abroad. He was hardly ever in the office."

"Then Dr. Kramer and Miss Pierce ran things most of the time, did they?"

"Most of the time. Even when he was in town Dr. Holstead only came down to the office in the mornings. Afternoons he was always out."

"Out where?"

"I don't know. Miss Pierce could tell you."

"I suppose so. Now what happened after Dr. Kramer came down from the laboratory and went into Dr. Holstead's office? He did go into the office, didn't he?"

"I should say he did. He came flying downstairs and into the office in a hurry."

"Why? Did you tell him that Dr. Holstead was mad?"

"No sir."

"Then you told him that there were two men with Dr. Holstead?"

"No. I didn't mention them. I only said: 'Dr. Holstead wants you right away, Dr. Kramer.'"

"What did he answer?"

"He said: 'All right. I'll be right down.'"

"Nothing else?"

"Nothing else."

"But he came right down?"

"I'll say he did. His coat tails were flying."

"What did he say?"

"He said: 'Where is Dr. Holstead?'"

"Yes? Was he pleasant?"

"Well—yes. He looked sort of anxious."

"Did that surprise you?"

"Why, I didn't think of it at the time because I knew Dr. Holstead was mad—"

"O yes, I'd forgot Dr. Holstead was mad. So then what?"

"Then he went into the office."

"You didn't hear anything?"

"No. I told you I can't hear anything away out here."

"That's right, so you did. How long did Dr. Kramer stay in the office?"

"Say listen, Mister, I got plenty of work to do on this switchboard. There are twenty-two extensions and four trunk lines and

I've got other listening to do besides trying to hear what goes on in Dr. Holstead's office and I've got plenty to do without watching the clock. Why sometimes it comes five o'clock without me knowing it even. Only the other day Miss King stopped on her way out and she had her hat and coat and everything on and I didn't even know it was time to go home and she said to me, she said—"

"You win, sister. You're no clock-watcher. You don't know how long Dr. Kramer stayed in the office, do you?"

"Yes— I think— No, I'm not sure. I remember them going—but I'm not sure when Dr. Kramer left the office—"

"He musta left sometime."

"Sure he left, I saw him go, but I don't remember if it was just before the men left or if he stayed in there until just before Dr. Holstead put in the call for the University Club."

"Dr. Holstead put in a call for the University Club? Who did he call there?"

"He called his nephew, but he wasn't there."

"The nephew wasn't there?"

"No, because the doctor called me back and told me to leave word at the club to have his nephew call him as soon as he came in and that if his nephew called I was to tell him to come right downtown and I wasn't to forget it. My, he snapped me up."

"Then he was still mad?"

"I'll say he was. His words sounded just like he was breaking sticks—you know, snappy like."

"I know. And he called his nephew right after the men left? You did say that, didn't you?"

"Yes. I remember that because the men left and the doctor came to his office door and he called out, 'Miss Pierce, would you come here please!' and then Miss Pierce went into his office and closed the door and then came the telephone call."

"Was he sore when he called Miss Pierce?"

"Well, he didn't act like it was anything she had done. He just seemed sorta irritable and cross generally—"

"Where does Miss Pierce sit?"

"Over there by his office door."

"How does he generally get Miss Pierce when he wants her?"

"Like he did then. He just comes and— My goodness! Here I am talking like he was still alive and would come walking in any minute—"

"Don't let that get you. How did he call Miss Pierce?"

"Like I told you. He comes to the door and calls her or sometimes he just hollers from his desk—"

"Then Miss Pierce can hear what goes on in his office from where she sits?"

"I guess so, I don't know. Her back is right against the partition and it's only thin boards—"

"I see. He seemed pretty particular about getting his nephew, did he?"

"My lands, yes. He was very particular about everything that morning. Every time he gave me a call he repeated it over and told me it was important, that is, almost every time. Goodness knows he needn't. Like I said, I've been here over a year and I haven't forgotten to deliver a message once, anything important, that is—"

"You say he put through a lot of important calls?"

"He always put through a lot of important calls. Why once he called up the White House in Washington and he was always talking over long distance to Generals and Colonels and Cabinet officers and there were so many doctors around here, you'd hardly believe—"

"I don't mean generally, I mean right then, yesterday morning. Did he put through a lot of important calls yesterday morning before he was killed?"

"I don't know how important they were, but they were important enough to him if you could tell anything by the way he was so anxious about them—"

"Who were some of the people he called up? Have you got a list of the calls he made?"

"I've got a list of all the numbers called all over the building, but I haven't got the doctor's calls separate, if that's what you mean."

"That's what I meant all right." The sergeant seemed disappointed. "Have you got the list?"

The girl took her pad from the desk at her side and turned back the pages.

"Here they are. Three pages of numbers."

Tonelli studied them in silence for a moment.

"How many of these numbers do you know? You get me? I mean how many of these numbers are old stuff to you? There must be a lot of them that your departments here call every day, business calls—"

"O, there are. I guess I know more than half of those numbers by heart."

"I tell you what you do then," Tonelli suggested, "you take this list and go over it and mark off every number that was called by way of regular business. See?"

"You mean like calls from the shipping offices, the express company and the railroad offices?"

"Just what I mean. Then, you see, we'll be able to get to the calls that Dr. Holstead made—"

"I can pick out most of them now—"

"That's the stuff. You mark them too. You go all over the list and—maybe you'll get your picture in the papers before you're through as the girl who furnished the principal clue to the murder."

"Do you think so? Honest?"

"Why not?"

"Wouldn't that be grand—to have my picture in the paper and—and what'll I do with the list when I'm through with it, got it all marked?"

"Give it to me." The sergeant half turned as though he had finished with her, then changed his mind and asked another question.

"By the way, did you ever get in touch with Dr. Holstead's nephew?"

"O yes. Almost right away. He called here in a few minutes after his uncle tried to reach him. I gave him the message and he said he'd come at once."

"Did he come?"

"Yes. He must have left the club quick, too, because he was here in a little while."

"How little a while?"

"About half an hour or three-quarters of an hour."

"Did he go right into his uncle's office?"

"Yes—well—"

"You don't seem to be right sure."

"Well—you see he stopped to speak to me—"

"You can't hate him for that. I'd stop myself. What did he have to say?"

"O nothing, just his kidding."

"What kind of kidding?"

"He's always kidding me about my boyfriend."

"Does he know your boyfriend?"

"No. He doesn't know him, but he's always kidding me about him. He's always asking me when I'm going to be married. He's got a great line, Mr. Jack has. He says as soon as they get a decent telephone girl here she up and gets married on them."

"Are you going to be married?"

"Not until the boyfriend gets a raise. You see he works at the electric light company and—"

"Swell. I hope he gets his raise soon. Tell me, did Jack go right into his uncle's office after he left you?"

"Well—he stopped and spoke to Miss King and then he stopped a minute at Miss Pierce's desk—"

"Jack must be quite a fella with the ladies."

"He's awfully handsome. You ought to see him. He has the darlingest curly hair—"

"I guess I'll see him all right. He did get to see his uncle, didn't he—after he had visited around among you girls?"

"Don't get a wrong impression about him. He's not like that at all. He's very nice. He's never said a thing out of the way to any of us here. We all like him—"

"Don't worry about that, sister. What I want to know is, did he see his uncle?"

"Certainly he did. Didn't I tell you he went right into the office the minute he got here?"

"That's what I've been trying to get at. How long did he stay?"

"Not very long."

"Was the doctor mad when he talked to him?"

"I didn't hear anything that was said, all I know is that when Jack came out of the office the doctor came to the door with him and as near as I can remember he said: 'All right, young man. I'll take your word for it, but you'd better come around to the apartment this evening anyhow. There are several things I want to talk to you about.'"

"What did Jack say?"

"He said (he's always awful nice to his uncle, never talks back or anything), he said: 'Just as you say, Uncle John. You don't mind if I don't come until latish, do you? I've got a dinner date.' I remember that just as plain, because I wondered who the dinner date was with—"

"Yeah?"

"That's what he said, and his uncle made one of his cracks, he was always doing it, he said: 'I hope you'll settle down soon and stop this running around. You ought to be married. I need you here.' Mind you, they might not be his exact words, but something like that."

"What did Jack say to that?"

"He said, kidding like: 'We don't have to worry about that right now, do we? We can talk that over this evening.'"

"That didn't sound like his uncle was very mad with him, did it?"

"You couldn't ever tell about Dr. Holstead if he was kidding or what. He was awfully stern."

"He was, was he? Stern with Jack, do you mean?"

"With everybody. He used to say he could excuse anything but stupidity. He was dreadful if anybody made a mistake. Sarcastic. But like I told you, that once, that morning on the telephone, was the only time when I ever heard him when he was real mad and I *know* he was mad then."

"Well, you've been a great help, sister. You look over that list and mark those calls for me and I'll be back in a while to get the whole thing. You're sure you know what I want?"

"You want me to mark all the calls and who made them."

"That's it. Now how do I get upstairs? I want to see Dr. Kramer for a few minutes."

"You go right out of that door there and take the steps. There isn't any elevator except a freight elevator at the back. Dr. Kramer is on the top floor at the back. Anybody will tell you where. You ask for the laboratory."

"O. K. sister, I'll be seeing you."

The girl cut her flippant wave of farewell in midair. Suddenly she became quiet, demure, or rather put on that frigidly insolent courtesy that seems to be demure to the unobservant. Tonelli, glancing behind him for the cause of this sudden change, found himself gazing at a girl. An extremely attractive and smartly dressed girl. He stepped back a pace as she approached the receptionist.

"Good afternoon," she said. "Is Jack—I mean Mr. Holstead here?"

Tonelli, observing closely, listening with all his ears, decided that this girl had recently been through an emotional crisis. Although she was pale and strained, she had not been weeping. Her eyes, seeming larger and more luminous because of her pallor, were the soft, deep grey of a summer storm cloud. Rather taller than average, her slim figure was graciously rounded in the right places and she held her head well, Tonelli noted, even as he noted the gleam of golden tints in her hair, which was not, however, blonde. Her nose was short and straight, her skin firm and even in texture. The oval contour of her face squared somewhat at the jaw line before rounding into her chin, but it was her mouth that at once kept her from striking beauty and gave her character and individuality. It was a bit too wide, and even in her present mood held the promise of a quirk in the corners that would match a sparkle in the grey eyes. Although held in check by the square jaw and the firm chin, the fullness of the lower lip made discreet promises.

"Mr. Holstead isn't in, Miss Mallon" The telephone girl was needlessly and overly polite.

"They told me at the club," the visitor was plainly surprised and disappointed, "that he could be reached here. I was in the neighborhood, at the bank, and I thought I'd come in and see him. This dreadful thing— The newspapers—"

"Sorry, but he's not here." The telephone girl centered herself squarely before the switchboard, closing the discussion. Miss Mallor held her ground.

"Is Miss Pierce here?"

"No. She's home ill."

Tonelli stepped forward.

"Maybe I can help you."

Miss Mallor glanced from Tonelli to the telephone girl in swift inquiry. Miss Klein deigned to explain the sergeant's presence.

"This is the detective from police headquarters who is here finding out about Dr. Holstead."

"O," Miss Mallor neither started nor shrank from Tonelli. She was pretty direct and sure of herself, for a woman, the sergeant thought.

"Mr. Holstead had to go over to Jersey too—for some necessary formalities," he explained, "but he ought to be back soon."

"It doesn't matter." She hesitated and spoke again to the telephone girl. "Will you please tell him, when he comes in, that I was here? And you might tell him I'll be home all afternoon and evening if he wants to call me. I've cancelled my appointments."

"I'll tell him." The reply was grudging.

Miss Mallor started to say something more, thought better of it and, pausing only to throw Tonelli a brief, faint smile of acknowledgment and thanks, hurried out. Tonelli looked after her until she was out of earshot.

"Snappy dame!" he remarked. "Who is she?"

"Stuck-up thing!" the lady of the switchboard sniffed. "She's Mr. Jack Holstead's fiancée."

"O? Where does she live?"

"Park Avenue, of course. Where else *could* she live?"

"You don't seem to like her very much."

The lady of the wires sniffed again.

"She and that mother of hers! They haven't got a nickel to their name. They shook down Dr. Holstead something scandalous. Always getting money from him, the old lady was. She won't get any more now—or else she'll get it all."

"How come?"

"Why else should Miss Frances Mallor be marrying Jack—except for his money?"

"You seem to know a lot about the Holsteads' private business. How do you know all this?"

"It's common talk around the office. If I was Sheila Pierce I'll bet you I'd say a thing or two."

"What could she say?"

"I wouldn't let Jack Holstead hang around *me* all the time and be engaged to a regular old gold-digger too if I was her. You bet I wouldn't."

"I betcha wouldn't too," Tonelli remarked, and set off in search of Dr. Kramer.

Jack Holstead *must* have a way with the ladies, the sergeant thought to himself. And how deceptive these gold-diggers were. He'd have taken an oath from her appearance that Frances Mallor was a fine girl, good sport and regular fellow. Looked like she *couldn't* do a thing like marry a guy for his money. Tonelli sighed as he climbed the steps. You never can tell. He chuckled to himself then. That telephone girl was a spiteful little cat. Probably had her own cap set for Jack.

9

IF TONELLI HAD ANY KNOWLEDGE of such things he would have seen that even though the laboratory over which Dr. Kramer presided was not filled with up-to-the-minute gadgets it was still a most complete and workmanlike plant for analysis, control and minor research. As it was he gained and carried away with him an impression of efficiency, not only from the look and feel of the laboratory but also from the manner and personality of Dr. Kramer.

The doctor dominated the scene. His force and color made his two assistants mere lay figures. One of these busied himself in weighing minute quantities of what looked like ashes; the other bent endlessly and intently over the delicate adjustment of a Bunsen burner which kept a dark liquid in a glass flask churning at some high and exact temperature as shown on a long, straight thermometer held in the neck of the flask by the cork stopper through which it passed.

Like his assistants, the chief chemist wore a white overall coat belted at the waist. He advanced to meet the sergeant with a pleasant smile of enquiry.

"You're Dr. Kramer?" the detective asked.

"Yes. Is there anything—"

"I'm Detective Sergeant Tonelli, Homicide Squad. I'm in charge of this case of Dr. Holstead's murder and I'm trying to get as much information to work on as I can."

The doctor shook his head sadly.

"It's a terrible business. Won't you come into my little den here and sit down?"

He led the way into a cubicle separated from the laboratory by half-glass partitions, pulled out a chair for the detective and, seating himself, leaned over and rummaged in a lower drawer of the desk for a box of cigars which he opened and placed conveniently, waving an invitation to the sergeant. He kept up an almost constant stream of comment all the while.

"A dreadful business and a great loss to the scientific world. There are too few men of Dr. Holstead's caliber and attainments. I simply cannot bring myself to the belief that he is gone. He was so necessary—"

Tonelli lit his cigar and, through the first clouds of smoke, leaned back studying the man seated before him. There was strength and power in the face. The nose was firmly aquiline, pinched somewhat thin near the end with a square, definitely divided cartilage. The jaw was longish, the lips thin and the chin firm, the forehead high and broad, surmounted by rather sparse hair combed straight back from a parting on the left side. The hands were well kept, long, strong and slender with tapering yet spatulate fingers. The beautifully creased trousers, fine lisle socks and expensive shoes which showed under the white overall denoted something of a tendency toward dandyism in a quiet, altogether cultured manner. The chemist was a trifle above average height with a well-knit athletic body, although his skin had the pallor of the indoor worker. A man close to forty years of age, Tonelli judged, a person who took the best care of himself without indulgence or pampering.

"Everybody tells me the doctor was a great man," Tonelli agreed, "but nobody has yet told me why. I don't know nothing about scientific men. Who was the doctor and why was he so great?"

Dr. Kramer smiled.

"Perhaps we exaggerate a trifle from the layman's point of view when we say that Dr. Holstead was a great man. He has done an enormous amount of research. None of it spectacular from your angle, perhaps. During the war, for instance, he was an advisor to the Chemical Warfare section of the War Department and one of the principal experts at Edgewood Arsenal. He has done a great deal of work with arsenicals and in the phenol groups—but I have here a complete set of his talks and reports to the American Chemical Society if you'd care to see them. They describe in detail, technical detail that is, some of his work—"

"I wouldn't understand it," Tonelli waved away the proffered documents.

There was a twinkle in the chemist's eye.

"Many of his colleagues might say the same with more than a degree of truth," he reassured the detective. "Dr. Holstead spoke in terms that only the most advanced students could follow, but that does not in the slightest degree alter the value of his work. He has laid the foundations from which untold things may come in the future—"

"What, for instance?"

"That would be hard to say. His work was general, scientific. After he had finished would be time enough to talk of practical results. We have gone so far in the synthesis of materials—"

"What do you mean 'synthesis of materials'?"

"Well, you have seen the various synthetic leather products, for instance. The seats of these chairs we are sitting in are upholstered in synthetic leather made from coal tar—"

"Is that what Dr. Holstead was doing? I thought he made drugs and serums and things?"

"*We* make the drugs and serums," Dr. Kramer put a slight emphasis on the "we". "We make them here in this laboratory, at least most of them. By that I mean that we do what is known as control work here. Our raw materials, of course, we buy in quantities, and our manufacturing laboratories are over in Jersey. However that doesn't quite answer your question. Dr. Holstead had passed beyond the point where he was at all interested in anything as simple as the manufacture and compounding of drugs for the wholesale trade. This business was for him simply a source of income—"

"His meal ticket?"

"Precisely. His meal ticket. He took little or no interest in what went on here. In the beginning he undertook to make a few products in demand and the business grew rather in spite of him than because of any great effort on his part. Latterly he has given most of his time and certainly all of his brain power to his research. This plant is run almost entirely by me."

"His nephew wasn't in the business?"

Dr. Kramer considered before he answered, then spoke with caution.

"I hope that you will not misunderstand anything that I say, er— Mr.—"

"Sergeant Tonelli is the name, Doctor."

"Yes, of course, Sergeant. I have the greatest sympathy, I might almost say affection, for Jack Holstead and I regret as much if not more than anyone else that he has been such a disappointment to his uncle. But then, on the other hand, I can understand that this business would not attract a young man who has no interest in chemistry. The manufacture of drugs is a confining business, there is very little adventure or romance—"

"Young Holstead wouldn't come into the business then?"

"I don't know that he ever actually refused, he simply failed to show any interest or enthusiasm—"

"And that was a disappointment to Dr. Holstead, you say?"

"Naturally. Jack being the person closest to him, the person who would presumably inherit his property, the doctor had hoped that he would come into the business and carry it on."

"Did the doctor ever say anything to you about this?"

"Not directly, although I have often heard him speak to Jack about it. As a matter of fact, I was in the doctor's office yesterday morning when he sent for Jack to talk to him about this very thing."

"Did they quarrel?"

"Now listen, Sergeant. I told you when I started that there must not be any misunderstanding between us. There was no such thing as a quarrel in Dr. Holstead's office yesterday morning. Dr. Holstead was a man who did not quarrel and Jack has too much love and respect for his uncle to quarrel with him. They had their differences of opinion, but there was nothing—er—acrimonious about it—"

Dr. Kramer's voice trailed off doubtfully and he sat looking out of the window for a time. Tonelli sat back in his chair smoking his cigar, watching the chemist's face.

"Anyhow," Tonelli said, "they did have some sort of a discussion, didn't they?"

Dr. Kramer continued looking out of the window without reply.

"I've got myself into a rather embarrassing situation, Sergeant," he said at last, turning and facing the officer squarely. "You came here and got me to talking and I've said too much or too little, haven't I?"

Tonelli nodded.

"My position is rather delicate. Superficially I would seem to have an axe to grind," the chemist went on. "In a way it would appear that if Dr. Holstead stepped out of the business I would be the logical one to carry on here and that therefore I might resent the introduction of Jack. That, however, is not the case. It would have been and would be very much better for me if Jack had come into the business. I have plans for expansion here that requires capital, and Jack could have induced his uncle to invest that capital. He was the heir and his uncle would have listened to him. Also it happens that I am on the very best of terms with him. He has even said he would put me in entire charge here. If he had become the controlling head of this business, he would undoubtedly have given me carte blanche to go ahead with my plans."

"Which Dr. Holstead did not do?"

"Exactly. Dr. Holstead was, for one thing, a conservative. He confined himself to a few lines of manufacture although he was willing to admit to me that there would be a large profit, even greater profits in some other lines we could add without affecting our efficiency or the present quality of our goods."

"Then why—?"

"Inertia principally, Sergeant. Dr. Holstead had reached the age where he was content to continue to do that which he had always done in the way he was doing it. He didn't want to make a change of any kind, even an improvement. He was content with this business. He, like it, was a trifle slow and old-fashioned. He was content to keep it small, to go his own way and leave the active management to me until he could turn it over to Jack."

"Is that what he had proposed to do? Turn it over? You speak as if that had been proposed."

"Yes. I *know* that he offered to step out completely if Jack would come in and take hold. Give Jack the whole thing, lock, stock and barrel."

"Then there would be no real advantage to Jack Holstead in his uncle's death, would there? If he could have the business anyway, why should he have anything to do with killing the old man?"

"That, Sergeant, is why I asked you to listen carefully to what I had to say about the relationship between the two men before you drew any conclusions."

"Well, I'm listening."

"In many ways Jack is of a similar disposition to his uncle. He is not to be sidetracked from his own hobbies."

"What are his hobbies?"

"Aerodynamics and aerial communication."

"Flying, huh?" Tonelli acted as if this were news to him.

"Something more than flying. Jack is an excellent pilot, but flying to him is merely incidental to his work, or rather his hobby."

"Yeah?"

"He has done a great deal of experimenting with airplanes and radio used together. I believe he has helped in some measure to solve some of the problems that they have had in setting up wireless telephonic communication between a pilot in the air and an observer on the ground."

"Where's he been doing this stuff?"

"Several places. Out at Newark Airport, down in Staten Island at the National Guard flying field there—"

"He's working with the Army?"

"Not officially I believe, but he has been given some help and encouragement by the War Department—"

"I should think the old man would have been pretty pleased instead of peeved at that. The kid might have a lot worse hobby than that, mightn't he?"

"He was pleased to see Jack's mind taking such an inventive turn, but— Look here, this is all gossip, nothing more, and I don't believe that we are getting anywhere with it. There is something that you should know. Something more important than this—"

"Let's have it."

"Two men came here to see Dr. Holstead yesterday morning. Two men who, as far as I can tell, were total strangers to him—"

"Yeah?" Tonelli gave no sign he had ever heard of the two men before.

"They—I wasn't there in his office when they arrived—but they *threatened* Dr. Holstead, from what he told me and what I gathered after I was called into conference."

"Threatened him? Why? What for? How?"

"It seems that the gentlemen were what I believe are called racketeers, I think that's the term."

"Yeah? What were their names?"

"They called themselves Mr. Smith and Mr. Jones, but quite obviously those were not their names."

"No? What about this threatening?"

"Perhaps I'd better tell you the story as I got it from Dr. Holstead."

"I'm waiting."

"It seems that these two men arrived here before Dr. Holstead came down to the office. They asked for him, were told he was not here yet and they said they'd wait. Dr. Holstead came in, but not knowing the men passed them by and went into his office. In a few minutes Miss Pierce came into the doctor's office and said that the two men waiting had been there for some time and that they had sent an impertinent message to him. He said, after some deliberation, that he'd see them at once."

"Did he say *why* he saw them?"

"He didn't tell *me* why. Simply said he decided to see them."

"Uh-huh! Go on."

"I must say to you that I don't believe Dr. Holstead was quite frank with me about the visit of these men."

"How do you mean not frank?"

"I may be wrong, but it seemed to me that he was not telling me everything. He had the air of telling me only what he wanted me to know. I can't explain to you how I knew this—"

"I guess you knew the doctor well enough to know when he was lying. By the way, how long *did* you know the doctor?"

"I came here about five years ago. Dr. Holstead was looking for a man who could relieve him entirely of the routine of this business and I have had many years of experience in manufacturing chemicals and medicinals—"

"I just wanted to know how well you knew him. Go on about the two men."

"Parenthetically, I may say that I knew Dr. Holstead very well. One does get to know a man very well in such a confidential relationship as existed between Dr. Holstead and myself."

"Sure. I can see that."

"Which is what astonished me all the more when I noticed that the doctor was holding something back regarding this interview with the men. However— He said that these men came in, that they were rather rude. One of them sprawled in a chair by his desk; the other, with his hands in his pockets, wandered around the room saying nothing for a time and eventually came and sat on his desk, leaning over him in a manner definitely threatening."

"Yeah?"

"They were in this attitude when I came into the room. The one man seated in front of the doctor's desk chewing savagely on a cigar; the other perched on the edge of the desk dominating the doctor."

"What about this threatening?"

"Dr. Holstead told me the spokesman came to the point very roughly as soon as the two visitors were admitted and seated. The spokesman said to Dr. Holstead: 'How much coke do you people handle?'"

"Coke?"

"That was precisely what Dr. Holstead said to him, Sergeant. He echoed the fellow's words. 'Coke?' Dr. Holstead said and laughed, 'We are not fuel dealers, sir,' he told him. The man brushed aside the doctor's words brusquely. He explained, once he found out that the doctor was really mystified, that he meant cocaine. Dr. Holstead was astonished even more. He asked the man what possible difference to him it could make how much cocaine the firm handled. As a matter of fact, Sergeant, we handle a minimum of the stuff and then only as an admixture in some other products, or as we are obligated to supply the needs of a good customer."

"This fellow didn't know that?"

"Evidently not. He was under the impression that we handled a large volume of cocaine and that moreover we handled it illicitly. He insisted upon it, so much so indeed that Dr. Holstead sent for me to come and try to convince the man that we were perfectly honest dealers in medicinals."

"Where's this threatening come in?"

"I did rather leave that out. The men did not actually threaten the doctor while I was in the office, unless the manner and tone can be construed as threats."

"They can sometimes."

"The doctor told me that before I entered these men had said that they were in complete possession of information to the effect that this concern was engaged in illicit narcotic business, that we were connected with a group of smugglers of narcotics and that they, the two visitors, represented a rival ring and that they intended to 'cut in' on Dr. Holstead's business. If the doctor did not agree to this 'cutting in' process they would do something drastic."

"Why didn't you tell this story immediately, Dr. Kramer? Why didn't you or Dr. Holstead call the police yesterday morning? You must know we'd want to get this dope stuff as quick as we could. Why didn't you kick through before this?"

"To be frank, Sergeant, the whole episode was so fantastic, so little to be taken seriously—"

"What do you mean fantastic? A couple of guns come in here and practically stick the place up, they get hold of the head of the works and put the boots to him, and you think it ain't to be taken seriously? Come on, Doctor! Why didn't you give us this information before? What you holding back about?"

"I assure you, Sergeant, I've not been holding back. If I'd thought this information was of any value to the police—"

"O.K. Don't let's waste any time arguing. That's your story and you'll stick to it. Let's go on from there. What happened after you came into the room?"

"It was rather curious. The atmosphere was very strained. The doctor said: 'Come in, Dr. Kramer. Will you please assure these gentlemen that we do not handle any volume of cocaine, heroin, morphine or any other habit-forming drug and that certainly we have no hand in unlawfully smuggling them into the country?' I was, astonished, as you can imagine, and I said that of course we didn't handle a great quantity of the drugs, practically none in their pure form and that most certainly we had no hand in any smuggling. That man who was seated growled at me: 'O yeah? Well I know different, see, and we're gonna cut in on your game.'"

"What did you say?"

"I was flabbergasted and rather helpless. What could I say? I looked at Dr. Holstead in amazement and he stood up. 'I will trouble you gentlemen to leave this office,' he said. I greatly admired him at that moment. He was a man of splendid courage who made no compromises with what he conceived to be right. 'If you dare to return here and bother me or any member of my staff or family,' the doctor told them, 'I shall notify the police at once.'"

"And these guys left?"

"They muttered and glowered but they did get out. The one who did the talking, however, stopped in the doorway for a final shot. 'You win, buddy, for now,' he said to the doctor, 'but we hold aces at that. Your whole family's flying pretty high, but we'll bring you all down.'"

Dr. Kramer stopped short and bit his lips in vexation. Tonelli gave no sign that he saw the by-play. He leaned forward intently when he asked the next question.

"What did Dr. Holstead do when they had gone?"

"He was very much agitated. He paced the floor. 'This is a dreadful business, Kramer,' he kept saying, 'what are we to do about it? Do you suppose these men are serious?'"

"Didn't either one of you make any move to call the police?"

"I suggested it, Sergeant, and Dr. Holstead agreed with me. 'You're right, Kramer,' he said, 'we should notify the police at once and I will. I'll call them at once.'"

"But he didn't call."

"I couldn't say about that. After we had talked a while about the strange visit I left the office and came back up here to the laboratory."

"What was the doctor doing when you left?"

"If I'm not mistaken he was putting in a call for his nephew at the University Club."

"What do you suppose Dr. Holstead wanted with his nephew, Dr. Kramer? Did he tell you why he was calling him?"

"Why no. He didn't tell me."

"But you can guess why the doctor was calling him?"

"No— No. I can't say that I can."

"Have you any idea what the tough guy meant when he was talking about high-flyers?"

"Why—why—"

"You can guess all right, can't you, Doctor?"

"Why I—"

"Tell me, Doctor, did these men say anything at all to Dr. Holstead about his nephew?"

"Dr. Holstead didn't tell me—"

"You admitted a few minutes ago that Dr. Holstead was holding back something. Was that what he was holding back?"

"I can assure you, Sergeant—"

"You could assure me a lot of things if I'd be assured, but I wouldn't. Why were you keeping back this stuff about the dope racket? What did you have to hide?"

"*I* have nothing to hide, Sergeant." The chemist snapped his statement and put a great emphasis on the "I."

"Then who has?"

"I—"

"It would be to your advantage if young Holstead came into this business with some fresh capital, wouldn't it?"

"I rather think it would."

"And it would be to your advantage to shield him if he was in serious trouble so he could stay free to come into the business, wouldn't it?"

"In a way, perhaps, but it seems to me—"

"Why not admit that the reason you've kept this stuff to yourself was to avoid implicating Jack Holstead more than you have to?"

"I will admit nothing of the sort."

"But that's the way it looks, don't it?"

"Why— I hardly know what to answer—"

"Yeah. Well hold your breath or you'll lose that when you hear what I've got to say. I'm going to take Jack Holstead down to head-quarters and find out what he knows about dope smuggling. What do you know about that?"

"I know very little about it, as I have told you, but it occurs to me—"

"Yeah? What?"

"That I would be careful if I were you. Jack Holstead is a young man with many and powerful friends—"

"What's that got to do with it?"

"Only that it seems to me if you are going on what I have said your information is very meagre and slender, to say the least— In fact—"

"I suppose you'll lay down on me, go back on what you said if it comes to a show-down?"

"I'd not go that far, perhaps, but I would certainly stand on my constitutional rights and say no more than I could swear to of my own knowledge—and that, as you can see, is practically nothing."

"I see. All right. I'll hold off. You win, but I'm going to see if I can't find out something somewhere else—"

"Thanks for the warning, Sergeant. I'm going to call Jack Holstead and his attorney and also my own. Good-day to you!"

10

"I WONDER," TONELLI WAS SAYING to himself as he left the offices of Holstead & Co., Inc., "what kind of a person this Miss Pierce, the doctor's secretary, is?"

He had every intention of finding out as soon as he could, but at the moment he had to make the best speed possible in order to be in Commissioner Francis X. O'Rooney's office by five o'clock. An old sidewalk pounder himself, the commissioner was something of a martinet. Yet the force felt him solidly behind them, and because of this confidence in the head of department their morale had tightened up in the last few years. There was no foolishness about the commissioner. He was a cop himself and knew what a cop had to contend with. At the same time it was difficult to put anything over on him, as some of the time-servers and grafters had found out.

Captain Henessy was ahead of the sergeant although Tonelli reached the office two minutes before the hour. The detective chief, pacing up and down, growled a greeting to his subordinate.

"What kind of a partner is that you've got?"

"Who, Mike? He's a swell guy. The most careful, painstaking detective I've ever worked with. Thorough, that's Mike—"

"Lay off the bologny," Henessy snapped. "He must be crazy."

"Not Mike," Tonelli stoutly and loyally maintained. "You just don't get him right, Captain. What's the matter?"

"He called in to the office an hour or so ago and I thought he was going to cry over the telephone."

"If he did he had good cause," Tonelli declared. "What did he say?"

"He said you'd sent him out to gather in Slim the Sailor and he was having a time finding him. He can't dig up but one or two of Slim's old pals and they all swear that Slim has gone ritzy on them and they haven't seen him for weeks."

"Yeah? I don't see anything—"

"Wait a minute! Wait a minute! You haven't heard anything yet. After he gets this bleat off his chest what do you suppose that big boob says to me?"

"I can't guess. You gotta tell me."

"He says 'Cap'n, there's a fellow tailin' me, I think.'"

"Yeah?"

"And I says to him 'You think? A first grade detective and you don't know if you're being tailed or not? You find out or come on up here and turn in your shield and I'll pin it on the first boy scout I meet.'"

"So what?"

"He says: 'What'll I do? Bring this guy in? Tonelli never said nothing about bringing in no guys that was tailin' me.' So then I lit into him. I said—"

"The commissioner says for you and Sergeant Tonelli to come right in," the clerk announced at that moment.

"Did you get anything else from Mike about this shadow, Chief?" Tonelli enquired anxiously as he followed the captain toward the inner office. "Did he say where the tailer picked him up and how?"

"No, I didn't get any of that. I told him to save it for you and that he could call back to the desk after five o'clock and you'd leave instructions for him then."

"O.K." Tonelli sighed.

He was so much preoccupied with his thoughts and worried about his slightly thick-headed but loyal and, as he had said, painstaking partner that his salute to the commissioner was a trifle absent-minded. The commissioner's opening words, however, swept the cobwebs from his brain and brought him sharply to the present, all attention.

"Captain Henessy, Sergeant Tonelli, I want you to meet Mr. Henri le Mai. Mr. le Mai has something very interesting to tell us regarding Dr. Holstead. I told him that you were handling the case, that I have every confidence in your ability to run down the murderers if they can be found, and have offered him the complete co-operation of the Police Department. I hope that you will do everything you can to reassure Mr. le Mai and that you will tell him all you know and keep him posted up to the minute on any and every new development in the case."

It was a long speech for the commissioner, excusable because it was not every day that Henri le Mai in person had a request to make of an official of the city.

Tonelli, acknowledging the introduction, took stock of this man who had become almost a legendary figure in American finance and international trade. This was the man who had done the impossible. He had broken the German domination of the chemical trade of the world. Almost overnight, when during the war American and British and French textile manufacturers had been unable to procure German dyes they had used for years, the le Mai Company, spending millions like water, had risen to the need and to the real emergency. They had produced usable dyes. Barely usable substitutes at the very first, but increasing in quality as they progressed until when the Armistice came and the Treaty of Versailles was signed the German Dye Trust found to their dismay that not only could le Mai make as good dyes as Germany had ever made, in some cases le Mai had bettered the product. In the manufacture of the cheaper and more generally used colors, such as indigo and blacks, the le Mais' adaptation of the manufacture of dyes to large scale methods of American fabrication so lowered the cost of production that they were able to meet the German companies and undersell them in the great markets of the Orient, China, India and Japan, as well as in Europe and America.

Tonelli didn't know any of this. Like most other Americans of his age and education, to him the le Mais were a name. They were a powerful family. Their name had been synonymous with the manufacture of gunpowder and dynamite before the war, but, imperceptibly, since the war the name crept into public consciousness through thousands of imprints on every kind and sort of article and commodity. From automobiles to hair combs "le Mai" was a trademark to be conjured with.

Perhaps Henri le Mai was used to that first awed shock which almost invariably followed the announcement of his name. He was entirely at his ease under the gaze of the two policemen. He nodded to them in turn, pleasantly, his dark, lean face lighting up when he smiled.

"The commissioner has spoken very highly of you two gentlemen," he said. His voice was deep and cultured. If he was strained or excited his excellent training enabled him to cover it. "Particularly you, Sergeant Tonelli," he went on. "The commissioner assures me you are the best man he could have detailed to this case, this sad and tragic murder of Dr. Holstead."

The big detective sergeant grew awkward under the praise. He reddened and fingered his hat.

"We're doing our best," he mumbled.

"I'm sure you are," le Mai agreed, "and I have come to urge you personally to do better than your best if it should be necessary. It is vitally important, not only to my company, but also to the United States Government, Sergeant, that the murderers of Dr. Holstead be captured. Not only that, but they must, if possible, be taken alive and documents of the greatest and most vital interest be recovered."

"You had better give Captain Henessy and the sergeant all the information you just gave me, Mr. le Mai," the commissioner interposed, seeing the look of bewilderment that overspread Tonelli's face. The sergeant, taken entirely off his guard, was gaping at the great magnate as if he were an exhibit in the Zoo.

"With the greatest of pleasure, Commissioner, but perhaps we are intruding on your time. If there were some place we could talk in privacy—"

"Stay right where you are," the commissioner urged. "Pull up a chair, Henessy, and you, Tonelli. This is important enough to take all of our attention for as long as it is needed. Go on, Mr. le Mai."

"As a starting point," le Mai said as the two officers drew up chairs, "Dr. Holstead has been in our, I mean the le Mai Company's, employ in a consulting capacity for several years. About six years ago he came to me and showed me one of his experiments. I won't go into the technical details, but I can only emphasize the importance of what Dr. Holstead showed me by reviewing a little history. Probably both of you gentlemen are familiar with the great strides that have been made in chemistry in this country in the past decade. Ever since Perkin, the English chemist, discovered his first coal tar dye, which he called mauve, and that was in the latter part of Queen Victoria's reign, the most wonderful and remarkable development has taken place in the field of synthetic organic chemistry, principally in coal tar products.

"Up until the time of the World War, Germany, England and France, with Switzerland, had each built up a coal tar industry, but over here we had none. This was largely because in this country we were wasting our tremendous wealth of coal tar. Coal tar is one of the principal by-products of coke, and we were using millions of tons of coke each year in the manufacture of steel. However, we were converting our coal to coke in a most primitive manner—" he broke off and laughed. "I hope I'm not boring you by what seems to be ancient history, but I can assure you that what I am saying has a direct bearing on this case."

"You're not boring me," Tonelli declared.

"Nor me," said Captain Henessy. "Take your time and tell your story in your own way."

"Thank you!" Henri le Mai smiled slightly, probably at the thought of being given permission to speak. He who was constantly being importuned to give his opinion, to say anything he would. "Here in the United States we were converting our coal to coke in the easier, and wasteful manner. Furnaces that were open and that allowed all of the precious by-products of the coal to be dissipated. For that and other reasons we had no dye industry. We bought all of our dyes abroad. With the beginning of the war we were faced with something like a dye famine and we had to do something about it. We did. And my company was one of those who saw a great opportunity and grasped it.

"I won't go into all of the details, but by the time the war was over the United States was independent of Europe in the matter of dyes. But not only in dyes—" he paused impressively, "dyes are only a part, a small part of the products that can be manufactured from coal tar. Coal tar is the basis of the modern chemical industry. From it we make artificial leather and celluloid and these transparent damp-proof papers that everything is wrapped in today. We make synthetic resins and a host of drugs and chemicals. The headache tablets you buy in any drug store are coal tar products. I could go on for hours. It is magic, wonderful, the things that come out of that black sticky mass.

"The building up of this new chemical industry here in America was not done easily. It took toil and brains, the brains of thousands of trained technicians, and it was all accomplished against the very earnest endeavors of our European competitors to keep us from gaining a foothold in this field. We have had to contend with all sorts of trade wars. Congressmen and officials in Washington were misled, even bribed to attack us. There was sabotage in our factories—"

"Yeah, I know something about that. I was in on some of the war stuff here in New York and after the war too," Henessy volunteered. Tonelli kept silent. He had been in France wearing the Orion constellation as a shoulder badge.

"Then I don't have to enlarge on that. Now gentlemen, here is something I haven't mentioned in spite of its great importance. Warfare as it is fought today is chemical warfare. The same ingredients that go into dyes and synthetic leather and headache tablets also go into high explosives and war gases. For instance, T.N.T. is produced as one of the by-products of a very common dye. You can see, then, how very much interested not only the United States Government, but every other government is in the production of coal tar and other chemical products. New discoveries of a military nature are being made every day and I can assure you that there are no lengths to which some of the foreign manufacturers will not go to discover these secret formulae."

"I betcha," Tonelli murmured.

"The notes that Dr. Holstead brought me interested me exceedingly. He had been doing independent research in one of the branches of coal tar and had discovered what seemed to him, and to our chemist after we checked his work, to be what looked like synthetic rubber."

Both Tonelli and Henessy failed to be impressed.

"I don't know whether or not you gentlemen appreciate the importance of that statement. It is a fact that the Central Powers during the late war might have held out for a great deal longer, might even have won the war had it not been for the lack of certain raw materials, and one of the principal items in that list of necessary things was rubber. If they had been able to synthesize rubber in 1914 it might very reasonably have happened that you and I would be subjects of a Prussian Emperor today."

"And the doc found it?" Tonelli burst forth.

"Not quite. He had only some preliminary notes and experiments that seemed to pave the way toward the discovery of a commercially possible product. It is very frequently the case that we can do things in a laboratory under ideal conditions and in small quantities that are absolutely impractical, if not impossible, in large scale manufacture."

"I can see how that is," said Henessy. Both he and Tonelli were fascinated by le Mai's story. They sat with their eyes glued to his face and never missed a word. His explanations were opening wide vistas of conjecture and they waited breathless for the link that would connect this terrific commercial epic with the murder of Dr. Holstead.

Le Mai wasted no time in getting to that point now that he had laid a groundwork of comprehension in his auditors' minds. They now would appreciate the importance of what he was telling them.

"Ever since the day Dr. Holstead laid his preliminary notes before me he has been working on this problem. We have maintained the utmost secrecy. As he has worked out a portion of his experiments, got to the point where we could carry out some part of the work in our own laboratories or in the plant, he has sent us, or more usually, brought us his notes. Only our chief chemist, who is one of the vice-presidents of our company, and myself know the whole of the work that has been done up to date. The experiments we have carried out for Dr. Holstead, the notes of his that we have checked have been carefully distributed so that no one man might know exactly what was going on. It is not that we do not trust our men, but this was a secret that was too vital to take chances with.

"Six months ago I had a conference with Dr. Holstead in Washington with the head of the Chemical Warfare Division of the Army and with the Chief of Staff. Only we four were at that conference and none of the details of the work was discussed even there. Previously our sole mention to the government that we were working on this problem had been made two years before when Dr. Holstead himself, with my permission, had told the Chief of Staff.

"In spite of that intense secrecy I found out only a week ago that the secret had leaked out. Not only had it leaked out, but a very powerful and wealthy group of foreign manufacturers, subsidized by a foreign power, was carrying on a series of experiments paralleling those of Dr. Holstead.

"We were worried, and I at once communicated with Dr. Holstead. I talked with him at his home over the long distance telephone and, making no mention of the thing to which I referred, I warned him that his work was being duplicated abroad—"

"How did you find out it was being done abroad?" Tonelli asked thoughtlessly, and then bit his lip and flushed darkly when le Mai smiled cynically.

"One fights the Devil with fire," the industrialist said softly. "If the foreign groups have their secret sources of information, we also have ours."

"What did Dr. Holstead say about your warning?" the commissioner put in the question largely to give Tonelli time to recover his poise.

"Frankly, he laughed at me. 'A week ago,' he told me, 'even day before yesterday, what you've told me would worry me, but it doesn't today.' Naturally I wanted to know why he was so easy in his mind and then, unwisely I'm afraid, he told me. 'In my last experiments,' he said, and I think I can remember almost his exact words. I remember because he was as jubilant as a boy who has found a bag of marbles, 'in my last experiments I have found what we've all been searching for. I've checked and rechecked all of my work and I've found where we have gone astray. The whole success of my formula depends upon one small thing, a small matter of timing, the blending of two ingredients and the temperature at which they must be blended. Whoever has copied my work up to date will have a hard time if they follow on where I've led. Nothing that I have done has been wrong except this one thing. I have almost finished checking my observations and by the end of the week I shall be able to bring you complete notes for a practical process.'"

"Did he?" the question burst from Henessy.

"Gentlemen, that is why I am here. Yesterday Dr. Holstead telegraphed to me. Here is his telegram."

Le Mai spread out the folded message so that they all might read:

> NOTES CHECK STOP PROCESS COMPLETE STOP UP ALL NIGHT STOP VERY TIRED STOP WILL COPY FORMULAE AND INSTRUCTIONS ON METHOD TONIGHT AND BRING THEM TO YOU IN MORNING STOP EUREKA AND GLORY HALLELUJAH ANOTHER STEP FOR THE CONQUEST OF UTOPIA HAS BEEN MADE.
>
> HOLSTEAD

"Jeest!" Tonelli marveled, "and this morning he was dead."

"And his secret formula with him?" the commissioner's question was half a hopeful statement.

Le Mai shook his head sadly.

"His secret is not dead!" he announced positively. From his pocket he took a radio message. "I show you this in utmost confidence," he said as he unfolded it. "Nothing under any condition is to be said about this. To tell of it would involve a great many people here, and abroad in at least three countries, in the greatest difficulties. It might even lead to their deaths."

The three police officers leaned forward eagerly as they read the message:

> FAMILY HERE ADVISED BY CABLE ORIGINATING NEW YORK EARLY THIS MORNING CHILD BORN DETAILS BIRTH WILL BE MAILED
>
> WARREN

"Is this code?" Tonelli asked.

"A very simple one," le Mai explained. "Translated it means that the secret formula is in the hands of foreign agents in this country and will be transmitted to principals abroad as soon as it is safe for them to do so."

"But this radio was sent from London?" Henessy said.

Le Mai smiled again.

"London may be reached by telephone from Paris, Berlin or Basle as easily as you can call Philadelphia," he said simply.

Tonelli sighed.

"And now what?"

"That," said le Mai pleasantly, leaning back in his chair, "is for you to tell me. I am willing to place myself and all the facilities at my command at your disposal. For obvious reasons I would prefer to keep out of this personally, but if worse comes to worst I will get into it as far as may be necessary. Also I can promise you that all of the facilities of the Federal Government will be placed at your command if you need them—"

Tonelli and Henessy glanced at the commissioner who took the lead. He spoke slowly.

"Would you rather that this matter be handed over to the Department of Justice or some other branch of the Secret Service?" he asked.

"Not unless the New York police feel that it is an undertaking too big for them," le Mai answered significantly. "It would be far better for all concerned if we can keep the Federal authorities out of it. It might become an international issue if it is not handled carefully, and that is not desirable from anybody's point of view. Personally, I have all confidence in your men, Commissioner. If the murder of Dr. Holstead can be handled as an ordinary crime; if nothing is said about this formula publicly and if the notes of Dr. Holstead can be recovered and the criminals brought to justice here in the regular course of your local police work, it would relieve us all of a great burden and lessen the danger of international controversy. It is one thing to apprehend a murderer here in the city of New York and bring him to justice, and quite another to have to go beyond the territorial limits of the United States in an endeavor to recover lost property or to avenge Dr. Holstead's death."

The commissioner nodded agreement.

"And another thing I want to say here and now," le Mai added. "I am more interested in bringing about the vengeance of Dr. Holstead than in recovering the notes of his secret process, valuable as that process is. I have known and admired, I might almost say I've loved Dr. Holstead for years. I will spare no expense, leave no stone unturned to bring his assassins to justice and to see that they suffer the full penalty for their crime."

"Mr. le Mai, did you ever suspect that Dr. Holstead might be a dope fiend?" Tonelli asked the question bluntly.

Le Mai's eyes flashed.

"That's ridiculous! A wanton slander on the memory of a great and noble man. A man who gave everything, even his life, to his science. A man who thought always of the public good, never of himself. How do you dare to make such an insinuation?"

"It's not an insinuation, Mr. le Mai, it was a question. I have discovered, as far as I've been able to investigate, that some way, somehow, Dr. Holstead was involved with a gang of dope smugglers. It looks like they were the ones that killed him."

"You'll have to look farther than a mere gang of smugglers for Dr. Holstead's real slayers," le Mai stated positively. "There is no question that Dr. Holstead was an honest, upright man. He had no vices that I or any other of his close associates were aware of, and we would have known. The le Mai Company, Sergeant, is not in the habit of casually employing men of no reputation in its work, particularly in work of this delicate character. We are careful to investigate fully the past history and the present habits of every man in a responsible post, and I can assure you that Dr. Holstead was blameless. A man of the highest integrity with no entangling alliances."

Is that true of his nephew too?" Tonelli asked.

"His nephew?"

Tonelli nodded.

"I am not acquainted with his nephew," le Mai answered, "I cannot vouch for him. Have you any reason to suspect that he may be a party to this matter?"

"Some," Tonelli spoke laconically. "I'll know better later. Do you know anything about Dr. Kramer? The chemist in Dr. Holstead's company?"

"There I'm on ground as sure as that of Dr. Holstead's past and present record," said le Mai positively. "Kramer was with us before he went to Dr. Holstead. Holstead and I personally selected him from among the more brilliant of our younger men when Holstead found that his research work on his formula made it essential that he neglect his own business. I recommended Kramer for his present position and from what Dr. Holstead has told me he has filled it admirably."

"That's a clean bill of health for him," Tonelli admitted.

"Was it Slim the Sailor's finger prints that put you on this dope lead?" Henessy asked Tonelli.

"Partly, Captain, and partly some other stuff. I got a pretty hot lead that Tom and Jerry (you know the pair, Commissioner), Groban and Braily, I mean, I got a tip that they were in to see Dr. Holstead yesterday morning and that they tried to ring him in on a dope-smuggling racket. I'm not sure it was Tom and Jerry, but it sounds like them and their methods."

"Have you brought in Slim the Sailor yet?" the commissioner queried. "He might have something that would help."

"Moran's out after him."

"He should have called in to the office by now, too," Henessy spoke up. "Maybe we'd better go see, if there isn't any other lead you or Mr. le Mai can suggest, Commissioner."

"Call your office from here," the commissioner ordered. "See if you can get a report on Moran or from him."

"Him having a shadow don't look so good now," Tonelli lamented. "I wonder if Mike's all right."

"We'll see and if he's not we'll make him right," Henessy commented grimly.

"I might suggest," le Mai said as Henessy took up the telephone, "that you investigate the employees in Dr. Holstead's organization. It is possible that the leak is in some way through that channel."

"We'll do that," the commissioner promised.

Henessy was talking over the telephone.

"Yeah? Is he? Well get him and have the call put through here to the commissioner's office."

The captain disconnected and explained:

"Moran called in from a drug store at Pell Street and the Bowery. He said he had a line on Slim and was waiting for instructions from you, Tonelli."

"Maybe you better let me talk to him when he calls back," Tonelli suggested diffidently. "I know Mike pretty well and maybe I can get more out of him than you or the commissioner could. He might get sorta scared if you go at him."

All three men smiled.

"You take the 'phone call, Tonelli," the commissioner agreed. "We don't want to scare Mike Moran." He made himself clear to le Mai. "Mike," he said, "has been decorated three times for conspicuous bravery in the discharge of his duty, Mr. le Mai. That's the reason we're all so careful not to frighten him."

"You can't scare Mike with a gun," Tonelli protested, "but he does get in a dither if the captain here starts to ride him. I know Mike, he's a swell dick but you gotta know how to handle him."

The telephone cut short his defense of his friend and at a glance from the commissioner Tonelli answered it.

11

"SAY, WHATSA IDEA OF ALL THIS RUN-AROUND," Moran demanded on his end of the wire, completely unaware Tonelli was in the commissioner's office. "Where are you and where you been all this time?" Mike was patently angry at being shifted about and kept waiting by the headquarters' operators.

"Keep your shirt on!" Tonelli admonished, "I got work to do just the same as you have. Where *you* been and what *you* been doing?"

"I see," le Mai spoke softly not to disturb Tonelli, "that the sergeant knows exactly how to handle Mr. Moran. I admire his tact and diplomacy."

"Pete's a great diplomat!" Henessy laughed. *Sotto voce* he told le Mai and the commissioner the result of Tonelli's mission to New Jersey and what he had said and done with the Chief of Police on the other side of the river.

Meanwhile Moran was tumbling out his tale of woe to Tonelli.

"This is a swell chase you sent me on," he complained.

"Have you caught up to Slim yet?"

"Now, not yet, but I just buzzed a pal of his and he says Slim has been awful flush the last two or three days. He's all coked up, this pal says, and Slim told him last night he'd struck it rich. He showed him a big package of snow he had with him. Slim told this fella he was gonna go home and go on a real jag with this happy-dust."

"Didja find out where he lives?"

"Sure I did, whatda ya think I am? He lives in a dump over on Forsythe Street."

"What about the shadow on your tail?"

"I lost him—easy."

"What do you mean lost him?"

"I give him the slip. Dodged up into the Chatham Square El Station, went through the turnstile and then dodged out under the chain and across the bridge to the uptown side. It was easy."

"Yeah? Do you know who he was?"

"No, who was he?"

"I'm asking you, bunny. Did you ever see his mug in the Gallery?"

"Naw, an' I ain't never seen him in any line-up neither."

"Nothing on him, huh?"

"Nary a stitch."

"I thought you told Captain Henessy you'd wait for orders? And the shadow's gone. Slipped you."

"You mean I slipped him. I'm after Slim. Besides, you oughta heard Henessy gimme the works. Jeest! After the pannin' he give me I hadda do somethin' to show I wasn't dumb."

Tonelli gave it up.

"O.K., Mike. I tell you what you do. Meet me in front of Slim's house. I'll be along there in about ten minutes. What did you say the number was?"

Moran gave him the number and added, "Don't keep me waitin'."

"Ten minutes," Tonelli promised.

"You didn't by any chance have any of your men on our tails to-day, did you Mr. le Mai?" the sergeant asked as he faced the group in the office again.

"Why no, certainly not, Sergeant."

"What's the matter, Pete?" Captain Henessy asked.

"Mike's lost his shadow and I wish he'd kept him in tow. I'd like to have a quiet talk with that shadow and see who set him on Mike's tail."

"Mike should have had sense enough—" The commissioner began, but Henessy stopped him. Henessy, like Tonelli, went on the tried and workable principle that it was all right to give a subordinate hell yourself, but you must stand between the man who *took* his orders from you and the one higher up who *gave* orders to you.

"It's my fault, Commissioner. I gave Moran hell for letting the man tail him and told him he was a lousy dick if he couldn't shake a shadow. Moran was only obeying implied orders."

"Too bad," the commissioner commented. "What's your idea of the next step, Tonelli?"

"I'm going to meet Mike and gather in Slim. He's the only definite lead we've got to date and it won't do no harm to hear his chatter."

"I don't suppose it will," the commissioner granted, and the sergeant stood up.

"That being the case I'd better be on my way. Mike will be waiting for me and I told him I'd be there in ten minutes. Pleased to have met you, Mr. le Mai, and I hope I can produce for you. I'll do my best anyway."

"You can depend on that," the commissioner backed him up.

"And we don't have to worry too much about that shadow Mike lost," Tonelli continued, speaking to Henessy and the commissioner.

"No?" said Henessy.

"No," said Tonelli, "I got a little shadow of my own. He picked me up as I left Holstead and Company's office and he brought me down here. I shouldn't wonder if he didn't have the same boss Mike's man had."

Here the sergeant made an effective exit.

MORAN WAS GLOWERING as Tonelli joined him before the tumbledown house on Forsythe Street. "Ya call this ten minutes?"

"Stow your yap," Tonelli admonished him. "Have you found out anything since you called me?"

"How could I find out anything warming up this curbstone?"

"Seen your shadow again?"

"Naw, I lost him all right, all right."

Tonelli didn't answer. He gazed up and down the squalid block, peered into the shadows of the basement delicatessen and inspected the dusty display windows of the first floor shop from which block gold letters were peeling. A battered brass samovar and several consumptive pieces of furniture were disconsolate behind the dirty glass tacitly supporting the claim of the blistered lettering: "M. Markovitz, Antiques," but lending more verisimilitude to the smaller legend: "Second Hand Furniture Bought and Sold."

"No use standing here," the sergeant decided, convinced that the man who followed him was not in sight. "Let's go in."

A smudged and ragged sign tacked over the bell-push gave the information, "Neatly Furnished Rooms To Let." Tonelli pushed the button and waited. After an interval he pushed it again.

"Why'n't ya send him a wire ya was comin'?" Moran asked. "With all this noise it's a cinch Slim will make a getaway."

In the bowels of the house there was a scraping clatter, and presently the door was opened by a slattern. Her run-over high-heeled shoes rocked on her feet; her lumpy, uncorseted body blabbed under a grease-stained cheap silk dress. She eyed the officers without malice, her face blank. It might have been modelled in lard.

"We're looking for a fella called Slim. Slim the Sailor. Does he live here?"

"Yeah. He lives here." She pondered the matter a moment. Somewhere in her vague mind an idea had connected. "Slim's gettin' a lot of friends all of a sudden," she volunteered.

"Yeah?"

"There was a fella here about ha'f or three-quarters of an hour ago for Slim."

"Did he see him?"

"Sure he did, whadda ya think Slim is? The King or somethin'?"

"Is he still here?"

"Naw. He lef' right away."

"How long ago did you say that was?"

"Ha'f hour or more."

"Slim's still here ain't he?"

"Sure he is."

"What did this fella look like that come to see Slim?"

"He was a little guy with a cap. Say, who're you anyhow?" Suspicion flared at last. "Are you guys cops? What's Slim done now? Is this a pinch?"

"No, we just wanna see him."

The woman laughed sneeringly and stood back to let them pass.

"If he's up there you ain't gonna get much outa him," she predicted, "not after the way he was last night."

"Was he here last night?"

"I'll say he was and he had a snootful too. He was Rockefella and Morgan all rolled into one last night. I seen him hopped up before, but last night took the cookie. I wisht to Gawd you would put the bee on him. I'm sick of the sight of him—" She turned on her lodger with the virulence of her kind. In the shadow of hunger and constant threat of prison there is little loyalty.

"Where's his room?" Tonelli advanced toward the stairs.

"Two flights up in the back, and if you take him outa here keep him out. Gawd knows there ain't nothin' in this furnished room racket no more. Even if a fella don't pay his rent on time he could be decent now and come in like he was a white man and not stay hopped all the time. I said to my husband—"

Her garrulous whining pursued the two officers up the worn and filthy stairs. A pin point of light in a gas jet made the passage on the second floor darker and damper than it need be. There was a smell of generations of coarse cooking and unwashed bodies mixed with dead but unburied cabbage and very much alive garlic.

"What a sweet dump this is!" Moran grumbled, close on Tonelli's heels.

"How'd you like to be the star boarder?" the sergeant jibed.

"Like Slim?"

"Yeah, like Slim."

They creaked up the second flight of steps onto a landing that was black as a coal-heaver's hat. Tonelli fumbled in his pocket and struck a match.

"This must be the door," he said, and rapped.

There was no answer. Moran laid his ear to the panel.

"I don't hear nothin' inside."

The sergeant rapped again, pounding with the clenched knuckles of his fist.

"Hey Slim! You in there? I wanna talk to you a minute."

"I guess he's asleep, spending that million dollars he hop-dreamed last night," Moran decided. "Whadda ya say? Shall I push the door in?"

From below winged a querulous wail from the landlady. "If you break anything up there you gotta pay for it. I run a respectable house, I do—"

"Aw dry up!" Moran's mutter could hardly reach her. "Whadda you say, Pete?"

"Slim! This is the police!" Tonelli made a last effort to arouse the occupant of the room. "You better let us in or we'll come in anyway."

"Nuts! He ain't there, and if he is he ain't gonna let us in. He's dead to the world. Far away in cokey's Paradise, that's where he is. Whadda ya say? Shall we go in?"

"Go on."

Gripping the knob firmly, lifting up on it and at the same time applying his shoulder to the upper panel, Moran threw his weight against the door. There was a splintering rip of dry-rotted wood as the lock tore out of the pulpy frame. Moran spun into the room as the door gave way.

"Jeest! You could push the whole house over with your little finger," he sputtered.

Tonelli, on the lintel behind him, stared into the room.

"You gotta pay!" the landlady's voice came up to them.

The room was narrow, dingy, dark. What light might have come through the cracked panes of the single window was stopped by the grime. In the gloom, yellow-white curlicues and loops, the frame of a narrow iron bedstead, embossed themselves. The sour bedclothes were tumbled in a heap, a varnished chair and a dilapidated washstand fought for what small space the bed left; the cracked window shade hung askew.

"Slim ain't here," Moran spoke.

The sergeant reached above his head and snapped on an electric light bulb that dangled from the ceiling on its unadorned cord.

"He's here," he corrected his partner, and stooped over the slight figure huddled in the deep shadow cast by the bed on the floor. "Nope." Tonelli stood erect and pushed his hat back on his head as he made a further correction. "You was right the first time, Mike. He's gone."

"Whadda ya know!" Moran marveled.

"How long ago did you lose your shadow, Mike?"

"'Bout an hour ago."

"Was that before or after you found out Slim's address?"

"It was after." Moran suddenly saw the trend of Tonelli's questions and burst into vehement defense. "But say—that guy couldn't 'a' been the one that was here. He wasn't no little guy with a cap, he was a sorta tall fella with a soft hat on."

"Yeah?" Tonelli seemed absent-minded as he bent over the corpse. "Well, anyway I betcha Slim hasn't been dead for more than a half an hour and—" he retrieved from the floor beside the body an oblong piece of white wax paper, about the general shape of a cigarette paper but larger. The sort of paper that is frequently used to contain a "shot" of cocaine. "—and," he continued, carefully folding the paper, "I'm going to take this over to Doc Helm right now and find out what is what. Maybe he can tell me something. You go call up headquarters and make a report. I'm in a hurry."

The sergeant tore down the steps and raced to the corner, where he hailed a taxi, then his hurry seemed to abate. He hung on the step of the cab carrying on a senseless argument with the driver for what seemed ages to him, but when his cab did at last get under way for Centre Street, by peering out of the back window he had the satisfaction of observing that his own particular shadow had had opportunity to summon a second taxi and was following. Evidently the man had been waiting out of sight for the detective to come out of Slim's lodging. It was necessary to Tonelli's happiness at the moment that he have his shadower where he could put his hand on him if he wanted him—and if he could catch him.

The last proved to be fairly simple. Tonelli's cab turned the corner into Centre Street and the driver swung open the door on the pavement side. Tonelli didn't come out there. While the car was still in motion, the sergeant dropped out on the far side, and, as he had expected, the pursuing taxi slowed up and swung wide in the street to pass. Without hesitation he leaped onto the running board by the side of the driver, swaying outward to allow the door to open as he wrenched at the handle. He was barely in time to snatch at the man inside before he dived through the opposite door.

"No you don't," the sergeant snarled, "you're coming along with me."

"What do you want with me? I ain't done nothing." The wretch in Tonelli's hands did not dare to squirm, although his eyes shifted and darted like those of a rat looking for a hole to slide into.

"We'll see about that," Tonelli promised. "If you ain't done nothing I'll apologize. You've got nothing to worry about."

"Yeah, but *I* have." It was the taxi driver protesting. "Who's gonna pay my fare?"

"Maybe you better come along too," Tonelli suggested. "How'd you like to answer some questions?"

"Don't get me wrong, boss," the driver reached for his gear shift as he spoke, "I didn't have nothing to do with this fella. He called a cab, that's all. He's just a fare to me."

"Pay him." Tonelli emphasized his command with a shake of his victim's arm.

Sniveling, the rat-like captive paid his driver.

"Thanks, Cap!" With a waved salute the cab was gone.

Tonelli fished in his pocket as he crossed the pavement in front of headquarters and flipped a coin to his own driver, who pocketed it in haste and scuttled away. Court proceedings are long and drawn out; fares are few and hours long if a driver is to make a living. These taxi-men, like their many brothers, prefer to squelch their curiosity rather than be even remotely involved in police work.

Bunting his captive along in front of him, figuratively if not literally, Tonelli deposited him with Captain Henessy's clerk for safe-keeping and hurried along to Dr. Helm's room.

It was getting late, but the chemist was still at work. The scientific force of the New York police, like that of any other force in any other city of the world, is too small for the work it must do. Hours mean nothing. Overtime is unheard of by the pay clerk and taken as a matter of course by the enthusiasts. Tonelli had yet to enter the chemist's room by day or night and not find the wizened little man bending over a laboratory table or painstakingly making entries in his card file. It was a police legend that the man never slept.

"Take a look at this, Doc," Tonelli came straight to the point.

The chemist took and carefully unfolded the paper the detective had found beside the dead body of Slim the Sailor.

"Is that the same as the other one? The one you found by Dr. Holstead's body?" Tonelli asked eagerly.

With an exploring fingertip the chemist felt gingerly in one of the folds of the paper where a tiny quantity of the white powder it had contained was lodged. His face assumed an expression of intense interest and he cocked his head on one side in his own particular small-dog fashion. Somehow he reminded Tonelli of an extraordinarily intelligent, eagerly sniffing fox-terrier. He was sniffing. Sniffing tentatively at his finger first and then at the paper, he crossed to his table and held it under the strong light there, examining it carefully with a magnifying glass.

"This paper looks to be about the same as the other one," he said at last.

"Then—" Tonelli began.

"But the contents were very different. Superficially they may have seemed to be the same, but the paper found beside Dr. Holstead had contained cocaine. This one, unless I'm much mistaken, and I don't think I am, contained cyanide of potassium."

"The poison?"

"The most rapid and deadly poison I can think of off-hand."

"That accounts for it then," Tonelli remarked.

"For what?"

"For Slim's position. He looked like he'd slid down from the edge of the bed, face first. Tell me, Doc, this poison is strong enough to kill a man if he snuffed it up his nose, ain't it?"

"If enough of it to cover the head of a pin was swallowed or got into the throat it would cause practically instant death."

"Thanks." Tonelli edged toward the doorway. "Will you look this paper over and find out all you can about it please?"

"Is this part of the Holstead case?"

"Yeah, up to now. Up until we hear what the medical examiner has to say anyway; then, unless I miss my guess, it's the beginning of another murder case coming out of the Holstead case."

The little man nodded as Tonelli clumped out and down the hall going toward the stairs and Henessy's office, then crossed to the sink and carefully washed his hands before setting about examining the paper Tonelli had brought him.

But, halfway to Henessy's sanctum, Tonelli changed his mind. "I think I'll drop in and give the Narcotics Squad a buzz," the sergeant murmured to himself. It was a short conference from which Tonelli emerged very thoughtful.

Henessy was walking back and forth like a caged tiger as the sergeant entered his presence.

"Well," he said in his most unpleasant tone (and he had a wide assortment of unpleasantries), "you and that dumb partner of yours are making a fine hash out of it, ain't you? How come you let Slim bump himself right under your noses?"

"We didn't," Tonelli answered grumpily, flopping down in the nearest chair without dignity or formality.

"He's dead, ain't he? The medico just reports to me by 'phone that he inhaled cyanide. That's the hell of a way to kill yourself, but that's what he did. The stuff's all over his upper lip and in his nose. He died so quick he toppled over flat on his face from where he was sitting on the edge of the bed."

"Yeah, I seen all that," Tonelli's voice was ineffably world-weary. "And still you're wrong. Slim didn't kill himself, poor mutt."

"No? Was he accommodating enough to snuff cyanide because somebody come in and told him he wanted to kill him?"

"Nobody had to tell him to snuff it." Tonelli ignored his chief's elaborate sarcasm. "Slim was a hop-head. The stuff was handed to him as cocaine and he snuffed it up. He didn't have to be coaxed to do it. He did it of his own free will."

"By God he would at that, wouldn't he?"

"Yeah," said Tonelli, and his weary tone was more and more bitter. "He would and that makes me and Mike bigger saps than even you thought. It woulda been bad enough if we'd let Slim get away with suicide. What we did was to let somebody step in and murder him in cold blood right under our noses."

For once Captain Henessy forbore to "ride" his prize flattie. Nothing that he could say could make Tonelli feel any worse for what the big sergeant knew to be an irreparable blunder. Something like pity for the suffering man before him made Henessy ask:

"What're you going to do with this rat you brought in with you? Shall I have him brought in here and give him the works?"

"He won't need much works," Tonelli said, "but let's get started on him. I let one lead slip through my fingers in this case, from now on I'm tightening up. What's the latest on young Holstead?"

It was Henessy who betrayed guilt now. He could hardly bear to look the sergeant squarely in the eye.

"That's one on me, Pete," he said. "I put too much faith in the Jersey cops, or maybe it wasn't their fault, just one of the breaks of the game. One of our men might have made the same slip."

"Slip? What slip?"

"Just that. A slip. Young Holstead took the Jersey cops for a chase, took them out to Newark Airport, hung around there a while and talked to two or three people, then left the field driving that fast car of his, the Jersey men keeping tabs on him with a motorcycle man and a police car. Somehow (they wasn't so lavish with details), he gave 'em the slip over by Bayonne and he's gone."

"Gone? Bayonne?" Ideas were connecting up in Tonelli's head fast. "He'd have to go that way to cross the bridge to Staten Island wouldn't he? That's where he's headed. That flying field down there at the end of the Island."

"Yeah?" Henessy was making swift strides for his telephone. "Get out a general alarm and have one of the airplanes stand by for orders," he commanded.

Tonelli snapped his fingers.

"That's an idea," he exulted, "I forgot all about them fancy flying cops. Them babies will come in handy."

12

ONE HABIT TONELLI had which differentiated him from most of the men with whom he worked, which in fact set him aside from most other people. If, when, and as Tonelli felt the details of a situation become so numerous as to be confusing, he deliberately sat down regardless of hurry and stress about him to think the whole thing through. Tangled threads begin to assume at least a sense of direction under such treatment, he had found. Now, while headquarters seethed with the turmoil of orders, while Henessy pushed buttons, barked orders and shot messengers in every direction, Tonelli sat beside the captain's desk and marshalled his thoughts.

Clarity came with his recognition of the course events had taken and with his clarity of mind came decision. There was no use, he knew, in trying to confer with Henessy at the moment. The captain was hardly in a position, or in a condition of mind to listen to calm discussion of possibilities and probabilities. The intrusion into the Holstead murder of Henri le Mai had at once the effect of placing the commissioner and Captain Henessy on their mettle and flustering them to the degree where they felt they must make motions of action to satisfy the great industrialist even if action without knowledge were useless or at the best ornamental. Tonelli approved that course. He knew that only inaction spelled defeat in police work. Wait he could and would, but only when he waited, ready for anything, any opportunity to act.

The sergeant, seeing all of these things, calmly pulled toward him a scratch pad and, while Henessy went through his gyrations, made hasty notes. Finished with his written reminder, he stood up

silently commanding attention until Henessy snatched a moment
to say:

"Well?"

"I think I better be getting in touch with this Coast Guard man
next. This Commander Betts they was telling me about down in the
Narcotics Squad," Tonelli explained. "It oughtn't to take me long to
find out all I need from him and then I can slide along uptown and
see this Miss Pierce. I gotta feeling I'd oughta see her as soon as I
can."

"Yeah? Well, go to it. I s'pose you got a feeling young Holstead
is going to think better of it and walk in here any minute too, huh?"

"Nope. I don't think that. But I do think young Holstead is right
where we can put the finger on him if we want to. Looka here. I made
out this list for you. These are the things I wanna get a line on and
any flattie can do them as easy as me. Will you give the orders while
I'm getting hold of Betts and having a chin with the lady?"

Intent on his own thoughts, Tonelli's tone was a shade peremp-
tory. Henessy bridled.

"They just made you head of this Bureau instead of me?" he
enquired, but he took the list and looked it over. Neither he nor
Tonelli found it necessary for the sergeant to apologize or explain
his brusqueness. "What makes you think young Holstead might
be at the flying field in Staten Island?" the captain grunted, seeing
Tonelli's note on that point.

"I don't think he might be there. I'm dead sure he ain't there
now," Tonelli hastened to assure his chief. "It looks to me like Jack
went to Staten Island Flying Field to cop a plane. If we getta line on
what sort of a plane he got and flew away with, if he got one—"

"I getcha—" Henessy was already flinging orders over the telephone that would galvanize the precincts from New Brighton to Tot-
tenville. That done he went back to the sergeant's notes.

"I see you wanna make a round-up too," the chief spoke again.

Tonelli snickered to himself at the acerbity Henessy contrived to
load into his statement but outwardly he gave no sign.

"Yeah. It won't do no harm to see what Tom and Jerry gotta say
for themselves. And why don't you put the boots to this punk that
was tailing me? There's a coupla more people I'd like to work over

too, but maybe we better wait till after I've seen Betts and maybe hadda talk with Miss Pierce and this Mallor skirt. I—"

"Yes, Inspector!" There was a real bite behind Henessy's words now. "Yes, sir. I'll see if I can carry out your orders—"

"Aw for the luva Mike, Chief!" Tonelli pled with him. "Don't go gettin' that-a-way. You know I ain't getting no swelled head. I ain't trying to horn in on anything— Jeest, I wouldn't have your job on a bet."

"Yeah. I know, Pete," Henessy sighed. "You get sorta haywire when you're tied to a desk like this and there's things breaking all around. I wish to God sometimes I was out on the street again with nothing on my mind but a cap and the only authority I had to wield was a night-stick. Get out of here and do your stuff. Everything's under control."

In the outside office Moran was waiting, shuffling from one foot to the other and looking miserable. Conscious that he had bungled over Slim the Sailor, Moran had the hang-dog expression of a man who merits a stiff going over on the carpet and while hoping that it will happen and be done as soon as possible, yet would give his arm if it were not to go through with.

"Come along!" Tonelli accompanied the words with an emphatic jerk of the head which mentally yanked Mike out of his vacillating mood and brought him, eager and happy, pounding at Tonelli's heels. That was the place for Moran. He would rather be there than anywhere else, although if you asked Mike he'd name almost any number of pleasures he believed he preferred.

"Where ya goin'—"

Ignoring the question, Tonelli dropped into the nearest chair and reached for a telephone.

"I wanna get hold of Commander Betts at the Coast Guard." The sergeant spoke into the instrument. "Do you know how to get him?"

Tonelli's face was a study as the answer came back to him over the wire.

"What's that?" Moran heard him say. "You say he's been trying to get hold of Captain Henessy and me all afternoon? Why didn't some-body say something? What? Well you could have got through some way. What's the matter? Ain't there enough harness bulls sleeping in squad rooms all over town? You could have found somebody to send to me. O.K. O.K. Get me Commander Betts now.

"The dumb clucks!" Tonelli growled to Moran as the operator worked on his call. "Can you beat it? Commander Betts has been trying to get me or the chief almost all day and this bozo says we been so busy he ain't been able to get the message to us. What do ya know—"

"Hello?" he broke off, transferring his interest to the telephone. "That you Commander Betts? This is Tonelli, Homicide Squad, in charge of the Holstead case. I understand you have something— I know, Commander, and I'm sorry. I didn't get the message until— Well, just as you say. Where are you? Huh? O, I see. Well, why don't you meet me— I tell you what, I gotta stop in at 47th Street between Second and Third Avenues on my way uptown. You could meet me there. Will you do that? It'll save me a lotta time and I need all the time I got now. Thanks, Commander."

"Who you stopping to see on 47th Street?" Moran demanded as they sped uptown.

"That little twist, Sarah Klein, the telephone operator at Holstead's office. She's getting me a list of telephone calls and she'll have it for me by the time I get there."

"Whatcha gonna do with a list of telephone calls? Ain't they in the book? I can't see how that's gonna help you."

"It might not. You never can tell." Tonelli was content not to argue with Moran.

Miss Sarah Klein hadn't dreamed that Tonelli in person would call for her telephone list. Taken wholly by surprise by the great man she was as flustered as she was flattered. Here he was and her in the same dress she wore at the office, hardly even time to powder her nose and dot at her lips, but, all important to Tonelli, she had the list ready.

"I didn't think you'd come for it yourself," she gushed. "I just got it finished before I left the office and I says to Miss King, I says: 'Do you think he'll come for it himself?' and she says: 'No. He'll be too busy. He'll send somebody for it.' And then here you are—"

"Where's the list?" Tonelli refused to be drawn into conversation. Ostensibly alone, he knew the entire Klein household had ears glued to keyholes and door panels.

"Here it is," she produced it, "like I promised."

"H'm!" Tonelli ran his eye down the record of calls. She had not only marked them off, but had also copied the unusual numbers on a separate sheet of paper with the names of the persons and places called neatly tabulated in columns under the names of the persons making the calls. On the previous morning Dr. Holstead had called his club, Mrs. Mallor and his bank, in the order named. These were early calls, and from their position on the list were made before he had received his two men visitors. After the visit he had called his nephew and then, Tonelli's eyes grew round, he had called Commander Betts at Coast Guard Headquarters.

"It's a good thing I stopped here before I saw the commander," he muttered. "This might save me from some dumb cracks."

Watching for coincidences in point of time, Tonelli saw from the list that Dr. Kramer had apparently gone immediately to the telephone after he had left the interview with Dr. Holstead and the two mysterious men visitors and called the Hotel Byington.

"Who lives at the Hotel Byington?" Tonelli made his question quite casual.

Miss Klein shook her head.

"I been racking my brains," she confessed, "and I can't seem to think. You see," she reached over the sergeant's arm and flicked the pages, "Miss Pierce called that number twice the day before and Dr. Kramer did too. It must be some out of town customer."

"Yeah, I guess it is." Tonelli continued his inspection.

"Who was this one? You ain't got no name down for this call," he said.

"I think—but I'm not sure—that one was Dr. Kramer's call. I don't remember and it might have been Miss Pierce's. I couldn't get the name of the party they called."

"How did you get the names anyhow?"

"I called the number and then when I found out who it was I just says 'Excuse it plee-uz, wrong number.'"

Tonelli grinned.

"Sister," he said earnestly, "if you ever need a job you come and see me. I think I know a place you'd fit in."

"Honest!" she breathed. "At headquarters?"

Tonelli chortled.

"Nope. Not there, but a friend of mine needs a smart girl he can trust on his switchboard and I'd speak a good word for you."

"Don't forget!"

"I won't."

Moran, who had been standing guard outside for the twin purposes of intercepting Commander Betts and making assurance doubly sure they were not being followed, stuck his head in.

"On his way, Pete!" he reported.

"I gotta blow now," Tonelli explained hastily. He folded the telephone list carefully and placed it in an inside pocket. "I'll let you know how we come out."

"And don't forget my job," Miss Klein called after him.

The sergeant nodded and ducked out, leaving an admiring clan of Kleins behind him.

Commander Betts, examining door numbers, setting his foot on the lower step of the stoop, was accosted by the sergeant. The commander being in uniform was easy of identification and Tonelli presented himself and Moran succinctly.

"You were a pretty good friend of Dr. Holstead's, weren't you, Commander?" was the first question Tonelli shot his way, after the preliminary courtesies were over and the three men were proceeding westward on 47th Street.

"Where did you get that idea, Sergeant? I've only seen the man once in my life and that was when I went to see him day before yesterday—"

"When he called you yesterday was it to tell you Tom and Jerry had been to see him?" was the sergeant's counter question.

Betts laughed quietly, good-humouredly.

"Fine work, Sergeant! I'm sufficiently impressed now. You can let up on me. Do you want to hear what I've got to tell you or do you want to tell me?"

Tonelli grinned his answer.

"You tell me, Commander."

"Did you know Dr. Holstead had promised to co-operate with us, I mean the Coast Guard of course, in trying to trace this new gang of smugglers? They are a new gang we're convinced."

"Work with *you?* Then that's the reason why he didn't notify the police when Tom and Jerry came to see him, was it?"

"The exact reason, and I wish—"

The commander left his words hanging and hurried on to his next statement.

"Dr. Holstead called me yesterday before noon. I had not expected to hear from him for several

days—"

"Wait a minute, Commander. Why did you expect to hear from him at all? How come—"

"Excuse me. I'd forgotten you knew nothing of my call on Dr. Holstead about his nephew. I'm going to tell you all there is to know, Sergeant. It's a chance I'm taking. I don't know whether or not I should. Our orders from Washington were—"

"Murder comes ahead of orders," Tonelli said softly.

"Right as rain, Sergeant. That's what I think and I'm taking the chance even if it means my commission because you look to me like the kind of man I can play ball with. Anyway, Washington can't blame me under the conditions. Red tape has to be cut at times like this."

"Do you mind walking over this way, Commander?" Tonelli interrupted. "Over here to this drug store while I call my chief? There's something I just thought of I gotta do, but don't let me stop you. Go right on. I'm listening hard."

Betts made no protest. Here in his own province Tonelli naturally took the lead and as naturally the sailor fell into step. In as few words as possible he told the sergeant the whys and results of his visit to Dr. Holstead as they crossed over. Moran, trotting beside them, kept quiet although he was all ears.

"Could you get us a report from your boats on patrol tonight, Commander?" after a moment of thought Tonelli asked unexpectedly. "I mean by radio or something? Could you find out if the *Esmeralda* is lying outside now and if there has been any plane visiting her?"

"Do you think—"

"Commander, I'm past thinking on this case. There's too much to be done yet. We're doing all we can as fast as we can to cover every angle. When we get a break will be time enough for any thinking and I only hope the break won't come too fast. Excuse me a minute, will you?"

He stepped into a telephone booth without further explanation, swung shut the supposedly soundproof door and in order to insure its inviolability spoke behind cupped hand into the transmitter.

"Chief!" having got his number the sergeant exclaimed, "I've seen that telephone list. Yeah. I think you better send a coupla wise lads up to the Hotel Byington. I don't know just what to look for but tell them to lay low, watch everything and wait for orders unless something blows that looks like they'd oughta make a pinch. If they can get the chance they'd oughta bring in everybody. Guests, waiters, cooks, everybody they can lay hands on. That dump's lousy anyway.

"And another thing," he went on, having got assurance his tip on the Byington would be followed up, "I'm with this Coast Guard guy. He seems right. Can I go the limit with him?"

"Why not?" Henessy was irritated.

"O.K. I tell ya what I've got in mind." The sergeant rapidly outlined a plan of action that made his chief whistle doubtfully. "Well anyway if the Revenuers will stand the gaff why shouldn't I?" Tonelli demanded.

"Why ask me? I'm only Chief of the Bureau!" Henessy's sarcasm was implied permission.

Grudging as was this acceptance of his plans, it sent Tonelli beaming into the commander's company again.

"Now then," the sergeant said as they resumed their westward way, "tell me everything the doctor said to you when he called you yesterday morning, but in the meantime—" he dug into his pocket and consulted a slip of paper, "—Mike! You dig over to this address, 56th Street ain't it? Well, get over there and stay on the job. Watch everybody that goes into Miss Sheila Pierce's apartment. Talk to the janitor, see if you can dig up her cleaning woman. Talk to the cop on the beat and the elevator man and the telephone girl if there is one. Get me all there is. All the dirt and low-down on Miss Pierce. And Mike—use your head. If Miss Pierce is out, try to find out where. If she's in, keep her there until I get there."

"Where you gonna be?"

"I'm gonna be on my way over to Park Avenue with Commander Betts. We're gonna call on Mrs. Mallon. At least I am. If you want me get me there. Now on your way."

"So long." Mike turned north at as brisk a pace as the others continued westward.

Commander Betts smiled.

"Everything off your mind now, Sergeant? Do you want to hear what Dr. Holstead had to say to me?"

"Shoot," Tonelli invited. "All clear now."

"You're going to be disappointed, possibly. The doctor told me few facts that you don't know. Something he said, though, seems to me more significant than any bare fact."

"Yeah?"

"He called me," the commander took a fresh start, "and told me that he had just been left by the two men you thought were Tom and Jerry. They're without doubt Tom and Jerry, Sergeant. The doctor gave me a detailed description and it was that precious pair to a 'T.' Then, he went on to tell me how the men came into his office, bullied him, threatened him—"

"Did they say why or how they got the lowdown on the doc?"

"Dr. Holstead told me he asked them that very question. You see we must look at this from Dr. Holstead's angle. When these men arrived Dr. Holstead was wrought up and excited by the report I made to him day before yesterday regarding Jack. He refused to believe his nephew was guilty."

"'Refused to believe' is good."

"That is a justifiable comment, Sergeant, but unless I'm very much mistaken Dr. Holstead was completely sincere in that belief. Not all of the circumstantial evidence I was able to bring to him shook his belief in his nephew for a single second. He was still strong in that belief when he was confronted by these two men who insisted and kept on insisting that they were aware, were sure, narcotics were being smuggled by the firm of Holstead & Co., Inc."

"And I think they were right at that."

"The doctor also came to think they were right, but he wouldn't give way an inch with these two men—"

"I'll bet Tom and Jerry never ran into one like that before. If more business men had guts like that rackets would be wiped out."

"Probably they never did meet a man like Holstead before and never will again. The doctor made them admit they didn't know about the smuggling and the distribution of narcotics through Holstead's. They finally admitted to the old gentleman they had been 'tipped off' about it. Somebody called them up and told them it was a soft lay they could muscle in on."

"The hell you say!"

"No, Dr. Holstead said it. Then he added something that, coming from him (and mind you while I didn't know him I was very much impressed in that one interview I had with him), he said something that I've been giving a lot of thought to ever since and I've come to the conclusion it may be the crux of the whole matter."

"Yeah?" Tonelli was amiably impertinent. "Don't keep me waiting. I'm all in a dither ain't I?"

"The doctor told me," Betts became maddeningly concise, "that he had come to the conclusion during that interview that his nephew Jack was being made a scapegoat and a dupe. Also, the doctor was beginning to have strong doubts as to whether or not cocaine wasn't being distributed by his own company. He not only suspected it but he had some proof, he said."

"Proof? What proof?"

"He refused to tell me what proof he had—then. He said he'd get in touch with me again as soon as he could—"

"And in the morning he was dead."

"Yes, he was dead, but isn't there a lead there somewhere? Have you seen anything that would make you think that Dr. Holstead was murdered to cover up some proof he may have unearthed—"

Tonelli was very thoughtful.

"The more I see of this case," he said at last, "the more I begin to think it is sorta simple. If I could only get hold of the right people and could get them to tell me the right things— This is one of those cases, Commander, where all the experts ain't much good except to tell you what was done and how—after you know how it all happened. I'm on the right track if I can only stay on it."

"But that doesn't quite answer my question, Sergeant—"

"That's because I ain't quite got the answer, Commander. But I'll tell you one thing. I betcha I know where Jack Holstead is this very minute, or I betcha anyway he's on his way there."

"Where is that?"

"Out to Rum Row."

"Is that why you want a report on the *Esmeralda?*"

"That's the reason, no other one but."

"All right, Sergeant, I'll tell you what I'll do. I'll hustle down to my office while you're in here interviewing these ladies and I'll get busy with the radio. By the time you've finished here I'll have you a report on every square mile of water the Coast Guard patrols can cover. Is that a bet?"

"Great stuff, but if they get a line on the *Esmeralda* you tell 'em not to go screwy. Tell 'em to lay off. That I'm coming out there. Will you do that?"

"How can you do that, Sergeant? Your jurisdiction—"

"Commander, my jurisdiction is in my hat when I get outside of New York City. If I go outside the territorial limits I'll be on my own. There won't be any skin off anybody's nose if Tonelli gets in a jam as a private citizen. Not anybody's but mine, anyway."

"I see how you feel about it, Sergeant, and I'll stand by, help all I can, get you all I can to work with. See you later."

"In about an hour I guess."

The sergeant stood in that doorway through which Dr. Holstead had strolled a few hours before on his way to visit Mrs. Mallor and watched the coastguardsman drive off downtown.

"Is Mrs. Mallor in?" he enquired of the solicitous doorman. "Or Miss Mallor? Tell the ladies Sergeant Tonelli from police headquarters wants to see them. Say, wait—" he stopped the flunkey with a gesture. "There ain't anybody upstairs there with them now is there?"

"Why yes sir, I think— No sir, I remember now— Mr. Gates was in, sir, but he left a while ago."

"Has Mr. Jack Holstead been here this afternoon or this evening?"

"No sir."

"Have you got a switchboard here?"

"No sir, only a house telephone to apartments to announce visitors."

"You wouldn't know about outside calls then?"

"No sir. All the apartments have direct lines."

"O.K." The sergeant had lost his interest. "Tell the ladies I'm here, will you?"

Tonelli was very, very busy with his thoughts as he rode upward eleven stories toward his interview with Miss Mallon Mrs. Mallor, it seemed, was far too nervous and ill to see him or anyone else tonight. Tonelli made a face reminiscent of an early youth spent among none too polite children.

"I betcha she'll be a lot worse than nervous when I get through with her," he promised himself. For no sane reason he had taken a dislike to Mrs. Mallor even though he had never seen the woman or heard of her before he took over this case.

13

Only Frances Mallor knew how much time she had spent gazing from the living-room window down onto the traffic in the Avenue below. The restless ebb and flow of the motor tide seemed in some measure to harmonize with the recurrence of her own surging emotions. She had long since recognized the futility of striving for peace. She had tried to occupy her mind, to forget, but endlessly the same questions battered at her inability to answer. It was here at this window that Dr. Holstead had found her when he came to add to the perplexity of her vain queryings and here again Tonelli found her.

"Yes," she said as she came forward to speak with him, "I remember you perfectly. You were in Dr. Holstead's office this morning, weren't you? I'm so sorry mother can't see you. She has one of her sick headaches. She's subject to them and anything that upsets her—"

"You can't blame her for being upset over this business," Tonelli condoled. "I didn't know Dr. Holstead myself, but I'm beginning to feel as if I did. Everybody that speaks of him to me says he was such a swell— I mean a fine man."

"Don't be afraid of the slang word. I understand, Sergeant. It is Sergeant, isn't it?"

"Yes ma'am."

"'Swell' is none too vehement a word to apply to my Uncle John Holstead— He was all of that and then some. He was not only swell but a peach and a bully sport."

"Did you say 'Uncle', ma'am?"

Frances flushed.

"He's not really my uncle, but I've known him for so long he seems to be related to me. He was my father's best friend and I'm sure he's been the best friend my mother and I have ever had and—you see, I'm going to marry his nephew."

"You mean Jack Holstead?"

"Yes. Jack."

"Have you seen Jack today, Miss Mallor? I remember you was looking for him when I seen— I saw you this morning." Tonelli made it a habit to be extra meticulous with his grammar in the presence of ladies.

"No. I haven't seen him."

"You heard from him though, didn't you?"

"Yes— O, yes—" Frances hesitated, bit her lip, then her head tossed defiantly. "Yes! He telephoned to me."

"Where from, Miss Mallor?" Tonelli was politely insistent.

"Why—from his apartment at the University Club. Where else?"

"Miss Mallor," Tonelli made his solemnity accentuated, "I don't know why you're lying to me, but I wish you wouldn't. There's a lot of things we gotta say to each other, and there ain't no use starting out by lying. Is there?"

Frances met his gaze frankly, squarely. She pondered her reply, making no pretense of the fact that she was weighing the pros and cons of whether or not to place her confidence in the sergeant. Evidently she decided in the affirmative.

"No," she admitted, "there isn't any reason why we should lie to each other and there isn't any reason why you should not sit down and make yourself comfortable while we talk. I think we're going to be friends." The smile that accompanied her speech was the nearest approach to an easy spontaneous action on her part for days.

Tonelli met the offer halfway, although he showed no eagerness to turn the conversation as he wanted it to go. His horsemanship was scanty, yet Tonelli would have made a good handler for young and blooded colts. He was gentle and he was firm. He knew his own mind and knowing his direction could force his charge to do what he willed. There was a quality of inexorability in the sergeant which could become brutality if the occasion demanded.

"What are all these things we have to say to each other?" Frances, already under his sway, began the talk without urging. "I know millions of things I want to ask of *you*, but what can I *tell* you? I know nothing of what is going on. I am completely in the dark."

"But there *is* something going on, isn't there? Something was going on even before—" Tonelli refrained from mentioning the tragedy.

"Yes. Besides Uncle John's death—" (Her mouth quivered pitifully whenever she spoke of Dr. Holstead. There were no tears, no false sentiments, no spoken regrets. Her grief was too genuine and deeply sincere to talk about.) "—There has been something going on for days, for weeks and I'm worried. Don't ask me why. I've nothing to bear out my—feeling—but the most minute things—"

"Your feelings count a lot. Nothing is big and nothing's small, Miss Mallor. You take it from me, I know. I've seen men go to the chair because of a safety pin out of place. I was in a case once where a man was caught and convicted because he was careless about a button."

"How could a button convict a man? Buttons can't talk, can they?"

"Yes'm, sometimes. This fella was making a getaway in women's clothes and he had his coat buttoned from left to right like a man. Women button coats right to left. That was the only thing that tripped him up. His buttons."

"And so you're on the lookout for buttons?"

"No'm. I'm here looking for skirts." Secretly Tonelli thought that a pretty snappy comeback.

"*Cherchez la femme*, eh? Are mine the skirts you want to see?" She stretched them wide across her knees as she spoke.

"Yes'm. Yours and a lot of others. I think there's a whole lotta skirts tangled in this thing. What makes me think so more'n ever is when you lied to me just now about Jack Holstead calling you up. Holstead is the kind of fella women will lie for and about. He didn't call you today, Miss. You ain't seen him today, as bad as you wanted to see him. I know that. We've had the University Club and this house watched. Mr. Jack Holstead ain't been anywhere near you. What I wanna get from you is where you think he has been—or maybe you know where he is. Do you?"

"I don't know where he is." Her voice was sunk very low, as low as her head drooped to hide her

shamed eyes from the sergeant. "I wish I did. He is avoiding me."

"Now listen," Tonelli's voice took on the crackle of authority necessary to make it apparent to her that he meant business and that there was to be no nonsense about injured feelings or reluctance to speak of personal matters usually hidden under a socially conventional exterior. "I know something about you—and your mother—" Her head came erect at the suggestion of contempt in the tone in which he spoke of her mother. "—And your relationship with Dr. Holstead, but I've got to know a lot more. I like you and I'd like to be friends as well as you would. If you help me I can save you and Mrs. Mallor a lot of trouble and embarrassment. If you won't tell me all you can without holding anything back, there are ways of making you talk that I don't want to use. But I'll use them if I have to. That's a promise, not a threat."

"You speak as if mother and—I—were involved—suspected—in Dr. Holstead's death—as if we had something to do with it. You can't believe that! You mustn't!"

"I do believe it though! You have something to do with this murder. How much I don't know just yet but I'm gonna find out."

Tonal maintained his grimness with difficulty. The girl appealed to him strongly. Enlisted his sympathy. He was willing to stake his badge she had not been engaged in any nefarious game with Dr. Holstead. He hoped that no part of Dr. Holstead's misfortunes would be traced to Frances Mallor's door, but he had no such feeling about her mother. She was hard and selfish, he believed. Of course he had only the gossip of the Holstead office to go on, but that meant much. Mrs. Mallor's age was against her, too, in the sergeant's eyes. He had a weakness for young women and women who grew old gracefully. In their youth and full attractiveness normally girls are not cold and calculating, Tonelli had found. When he searched for the woman in a case he was inclined to view with suspicion the females past their first blush of youth. Such women felt they had to fight to maintain their place in the world, and their combativeness grew and extended itself all too frequently to the point where they felt themselves in arms against an unfeeling and disdainful world. All were enemies who were not definite allies.

"But we—we—" That implacable something behind Tonelli, the man-hunter, cut Frances Mallor's protest short. She took hold of herself with a visible effort. Time enough to defend her mother when there was a definite accusation. "Very well!" Frances faced Tonelli like the good soldier she was, but her lips were white. "You must have some reason for thinking my mother and I are involved. What is it you want with us? Go ahead with your questions."

"That's the spirit," the sergeant applauded. "Now we're gonna get somewhere." He hitched his chair a confidential inch nearer to her. 'What's the matter between you and Jack Holstead, Miss Mallor?"

Her eyes showed her agony.

"I don't know, Sergeant. I wish I did."

"Is it something recent?"

"Yes—no—I don't even know that. I can't tell. Sometimes I think it is something that has been coming for a long, long time, for months—and then again it seems so sudden, so without warning that Jack changed. Became a different man."

"How is he different?"

"That's hard to say. Possibly I mean he's become *in*different instead of different. Indifferent to me."

"You mean he wants to give you the gate? I mean stop being engaged to you?"

"He's never said so, but ever since—it's foolish, Sergeant, but it seems to me that all of our difficulties started when he began to fly."

"Yeah? It might not be so goofy. Why do you think so?"

"There again I'm probably not saying what I mean. It was when he began to take flying lessons that he first started to—not exactly neglect me, but he didn't seem to have as much time to devote to me as he had when we were first engaged—"

Tonelli's understanding nod encouraged her to speak on. She was getting a sense of relief as the result of this endeavor to put into words the trouble that had been a gnawing pain for so long. Merely by telling it she was putting a part of her heavy load on Tonelli.

"That was natural, if you want to be rational about it. Only silly girls expect the first romance and interest of an engagement to last forever. We had been engaged a month or more when he told me he had decided to learn to fly. He had always been dabbling in radio and studying about aeronautics. He had some ideas he wanted to try out and he had come to the place where he felt he should be a pilot, and know conditions in the air at first hand."

The sergeant nodded again. The floodgates were opened and she needed no further prodding.

"He learned to fly remarkably fast—at any rate Vee said he learned fast. Maybe he was just giving out his usual line. Vee flatters everybody."

"Who is Vee?"

"Walter Gates. He's an aviator out at Newark Airport who taught Jack to fly. They call him Vee—"

"Pretty good guy is he? Regular with his friends? You know what I mean?"

"Why yes. He's very nice. He's been exceptionally nice to me. He rather guesses that I'm not too happy about Jack, I think, and in his nice way he does all he can to make things easier for me."

"Hangs around here a good bit, does he?"

"He comes nearly every day, telephones or sends some little thing he thinks I might like. He really is a dear."

"Sorta crazy about you, huh?"

"In a way, possibly. Only in a way, though. There's nothing serious about it."

"You mean that you ain't serious about it, don't you?"

"How could I be? I'm still engaged to Jack and I'm funny that way. I think that obligates me to keep other men at their distance."

"Atta girl! I'm all for that. Put me straight, though—you met Vee Gates through Jack?"

"Yes. Jack introduced us one Sunday afternoon when he took me out to the flying field for my first ride."

"What does Jack think about this Gates coming here so often? Don't he think he's pretty attentive?"

Frances laughed as sardonically as a frank nature would permit.

"I don't believe he thinks about it at all. He seems to have ceased to be aware of me other than as a bit of a nuisance. He—he's so wrapped up in his own affairs."

"Flying?"

"Yes, flying."

"Not another lady in the picture? What do you know about Jack and other women?"

"What other women?" She was fencing.

"*You* tell *me.* Jack does sorta go big with the ladies, now, don't he?"

"Yes, but not any more so than any other attractive, healthy man. I wouldn't have him be any other way. Don't think this is all the imagination of a jealous woman, Sergeant."

"Why try to stall, Miss Mallor? There is another woman, isn't there? Do you know who she is? Can you guess if you don't know for sure? I tell you straight it's important to me to know who this other woman is."

"Jack is an honorable gentleman, Sergeant. I know that if there was anything that mattered, anything I should know, he would be the first to come and tell me about it. He's too much like Uncle John not to do that. He's too fine and honest."

"Good for you. That's the way a woman oughta talk about her man, but just the same—it might not be serious, he may be kidding around—there *is* somebody he's been paying a lot of attention to, ain't there?"

"He—" she started to equivocate again, recognized its futility in the long run and came out flatly. "Why shouldn't I say it. Yes. There *is* another woman, I *know* he sees that Miss Pierce a lot. I think he sees her a great deal more than he does me."

"Dr. Holstead's secretary?"

"Yes."

"Has he been seeing her outside of the office?"

"Yes."

"Do you know how he started seeing her outside of business hours?"

"It was through this flying. Miss Pierce introduced Jack to Walter Gates."

"Is that so? How did that happen?"

"Jack used to see her in Uncle John's office and Jack is so enthusiastic. He told her all about his ideas for radio and airplanes and how he hoped to be able to make it as easy to talk from airplane to airplane as it is on the ground and then—this is how I piece it together, Sergeant, Jack and I haven't talked about this—I've avoided saying anything to him. I don't want him to feel I'm whining or complaining. If Miss Pierce can get him away from me that's as much my fault as his or hers, I believe—"

"You're a pretty wise little lady, aren't you?"

"I don't know. I *do* know it does no good to plague Jack about things— Anyway, I've never said anything to him about Sheila Pierce."

"Then Jack talked about his new ideas and found out that Miss Pierce had a friend who was an aviator—is that it?"

"That seems to be the way of it. She arranged for the two men to meet. They took to each other right away and eventually Jack began taking flying lessons from Vee—"

"When did he buy the airplane from Gates?"

"Do you know about that too?"

"It's no secret. Anybody could know about it. I been out to the airport this morning and found out all I could."

"Then why ask me all these questions? You know a great deal more than I do probably."

"No, I don't know anything. Besides, if I did, I wanna get your angle. You can tell me things nobody else can. Who suggested buying the plane? Was it Jack's idea?"

"Yes, in a way. Walter is always hard up. He's rather irresponsible. Flyers are like that, from what I've seen of Walter's friends. They have a pretty hard time of it. They take big chances in their work but when they have an opportunity to enjoy themselves they cut loose and haven't much regard for what may happen tomorrow—money slips through their fingers like water and they spend like—like aviators!"

"So would I."

"I too. You can't make whoopee on your insurance money, as Walter says, and there aren't any pockets in a shroud."

"Ain't that the truth?"

"To get back to the plane. Walter was hard up as usual and said he'd have to sell the plane. He named a ridiculously low price, said that's all he'd be able to get. Sport planes are rather a drug on the market this year. So Jack bought it."

"Where did Jack get the money? Has he got plenty?"

"Not plenty. Nobody has who isn't rich, but Jack has an income. Enough to get along on and he's always been rather careful with his money. Not stingy, but Dr. Holstead taught him the value of money and having been educated abroad Jack has the feeling that to make a display of money in any form is rather vulgar. Nice people don't do it."

"Yeah?" Such a philosophy was a trifle over Tonelli's range. He changed the subject. "It musta been sorta hard on Gates not to have a plane of his own."

"Yes, I think Jack had that partly in mind when he bought it. He left word at the airport that Vee was to have the use of it any time he wanted it. When Jack wasn't using it, that is."

"Come again, sister? You say Gates could use the plane any time he wanted to?"

"Yes. But he seemed to have lost interest. He never used it."

"Never used it? Are you sure?"

"Yes, pretty sure. Jack told me something about Vee's being rather sensitive and proud about it. And then, it was about that time, Walter got a job—"

"He didn't have a job before?"

"No. That was why he was willing to teach Jack to fly. Walter is a transport pilot. Men out at the airport say he's one of the best. He had been working for the Tri-Continental people on a regular passenger liner until he had some sort of a silly run-in with the transportation superintendent. Walter is frightfully hot-headed and arbitrary. He told the superintendent where to go and was fired. While he was looking around for another job he took on Jack."

"What is this new job he's got? Flying?"

"It has something to do with flying, I gather. He's quite secretive about it. He hasn't told me what concern it is, I don't even know the name of the firm, but he has to do business with a man named Gomez."

"Where does Mr. Gomez hang out, do you know?"

"Yes, he lives in the Hotel Byington. If—"

The sergeant, unprepared, let slip a sharp exclamation at the name of the hotel.

"Excuse me," he covered up as well and as rapidly as he could. "I musta swallowed the wrong way or something. Go right on."

Wisely, Frances smiled into his eyes.

"What's the use of trying to fool me, Sergeant? I know what a bad reputation the Hotel Byington has, but you mustn't blame poor Mr. Gomez. He's a foreigner. He doesn't know. He's an awfully sweet little man. He has the most charming manners."

"Then you know Gomez?"

"Yes indeed. He comes here with Walter now and then. He and my mother are great buddies. They both like to do jig-saw puzzles and they both lost money in the market. They condole with each other and make plans to win a fortune as soon as things pick up."

"That must be nice. You say you don't know what sort of business Gates and Gomez are doing together?"

"They can't be induced to mention it. I'm dying to know all about it and I've teased Walter to tell me but all he's said is that it has something to do with flying. I think, but I don't know, that it is connected with the government of Mr. Gomez' country."

"What is his country?"

"I can't even tell you that. It's all so intensely secret. Even the tiny hints Vee has let drop to me he has made me swear I'd never tell a soul. I have my suspicions though. Between us, Sergeant Tonelli, I think the great mystery has something to do with a revolution or something like that. I don't know, that's just my impression."

"Pretty dangerous business, isn't it?"

"Vee wouldn't be in it if it weren't dangerous. He loves to do things that are dangerous. That's the reason he is flying. Everything else is too tame for him. It's an adventure to ride in a car with him, Sergeant. He cannot drive slowly. He can take Jack's car and make it go faster than the maker ever supposed it would."

Tonelli was thoughtful for a moment.

"Well," he remarked at length, "that disposes of Mr. Gates and Mr. Gomez, doesn't it? I didn't mean to get you off on a sidetrack. You were talking about Jack."

"Actually, I've told you all I really know about Jack. I may be very foolish and unjust. He may be so busy he's forgotten the little things he used to do for me—girls think so much more of those things than men do, only—I'm sure Uncle John was worried about him too."

"Why do you say that?"

"Uncle John said as much. He was here only the day before yesterday, the day before he—"

"—he died—" Tonelli said it for her. She nodded.

"On his way in to see mother Uncle John stopped to see me, and by the way, Walter was here too. Uncle John was in pretty good spirits even though he was busy and in a hurry. He joked about warning Jack that a handsome man like Walter was sticking around too much, but he needn't have bothered about that. Jack knew it and Jack isn't bothering."

"You say Dr. Holstead was in good spirits?"

"Very. Mother had sent for him to talk over some business matters; he advised her, you know. He was very happy because he told mother he had finished with his experiment—"

"Do you and your mother know what that experiment is?"

"No. I don't and I'm sure mother doesn't. She hasn't a head for that sort of thing. She wouldn't know a chemical if she stumbled across it. All we knew about it was that Uncle John was working on some grand thing that he expected to make his fortune."

"But he told your mother that he was finished. Did he tell you too?"

"No. All we talked about was Jack and we didn't say much about him. Uncle John was in a hurry to get back to his lab, and we made a tentative date to have lunch together to talk over the whole thing. You see, Uncle John knew I was worried. He—he liked me a lot, Uncle John did, and he knew I was as much interested in Jack's welfare as he was himself—"

"Did you keep that lunch date?"

"No. Uncle John called me up the next day and postponed it. He said something important had come up that might have a bearing on what he had to say to me and we had better wait—"

"Did he say what the important thing was?"

"No. He didn't drop a hint of what it could be."

"Miss Mallor, did you ever suspect Jack takes dope?"

"What?" The blunt question took her off her mental feet, but she rebounded vigorously, defending the man. "Of course not! Whatever made you think such a thing is possible?"

"Everything's possible. This great change that came over Jack— are you dead sure it wasn't caused by him taking some sort of a drug? People do, you know. It ain't their fault lots of times. They get sick, have a big pain somewhere and a doctor gives them a shot of hop and the first thing you know—"

Frances Mallor laughed him to scorn.

"Jack Holstead never had an ache or a pain in his life. He is disgustingly fit and healthy. He has never even had a toothache. I don't know where you got your information, Sergeant, but if anybody has told you Jack is a dope-fiend he's all wet. You've been talking to someone who has it in for Jack."

"I guess you're right at that," Tonelli admitted. He returned to the attack, began to count on his fingers as he recapitulated her information. "Now, let me see. First you notice Jack is acting queer. That is right after he has been introduced to Walter Gates by Miss Pierce." The index finger was turned down to mark the item. "Then Gates begins to give you a buzz." The second finger marked this. "You get an idea Jack is playing around with Miss Pierce." Noted on the third finger. "Next thing Gomez shows up and he and you and your mother get to be great buddies." Four fingers were down. "Last of all, Dr. Holstead comes here to see your mother and he tells you he is worried about Jack and he warns you Gates shouldn't oughta be playing around here so much. Right?"

"It's a little blunt, Sergeant Tonelli, but that's about what it amounts to. None of it is important in itself, but the whole thing—"

"Who is this person?"

Mrs. Mallor, in her favorite lavender negligee, stood in the doorway of the drawing room balancing precariously on the teetering heels of her golden mules. Her plump form was drawn to its full five feet two inches and she was glowering at Tonelli with an air of hauteur that was only slightly marred by the circumstance that her blondined mop of hair was gathered into a tall knot on the top of her head with a hastily placed hairpin or two and that the golden mound wobbled as she balanced on her insecure footing.

"Who *is* this person, Frances? I declare you're for all the world like your father. No consideration for me. No matter how badly I feel, with my head splitting, you fill the house with strangers—"

Tonelli rose awkwardly to his feet and Frances hastened to soothe the irate lady.

"Sergeant Tonelli *is* rather large, mother, but he doesn't quite fill the house. He is from the police, trying to find out all he can about Uncle John—"

"The police?"

Deathly white, Mrs. Mallor started back, clutching at her throat from which her breath was being expelled in panting gasps.

Frances moved quickly to her and, passing an arm around her waist, supported her as she sagged against the wall.

"Now mother, I knew you'd do this. You must not excite yourself. I tried to keep you out of it. There is no necessity for you to bother. I can tell all there is to tell. You see, Sergeant," the girl explained bravely, "my mother is so delicate. Her health is not good and she is very fragile. The least shock acts on her heart—"

"Sure. Anybody could see she was delicate," Tonelli agreed. "There ain't nothing to be afraid of, Mrs. Mallor. We gotta get a line on all the angles, that's all there is to it—"

"That's all, mother. I've finished telling the sergeant all there is to be told," Frances spoke soothingly to the woman whose color was gradually returning. "We've been having a friendly little chat. The sergeant and I have become good friends—"

"I'll say we have," Tonelli supplemented. "We been gabbing along about your friend Gomez—"

"Gomez!" There was no mistaking the terror in Mrs. Mallor's shriek. "You know! You know! But I didn't do it, I tell you. I didn't know anything about it. I didn't know it was important. I wouldn't have done it if I'd known. I wouldn't have hurt John for the world—he was my husband's best friend—Frances—Frances! Keep him away! Don't let that policeman come after me! I—I can't stand it! Don't let him touch me, Frances—"

Her voice trailed off in gasping sobs. Her body went limp in her daughter's arms and she slumped, a rotund, boneless heap against the baseboard.

Frances, speechless with an amazement that could not have been simulated, could only stand and stare from her mother's fainting figure to Tonelli. Back and forth her eyes darted, questioning. Back and forth from the huddle of lavender to the detective who never lifted his intent stare from her mother. The sergeant was nodding slightly as if acknowledging some inner advice. His lips were tightly compressed and there was stern resolve in the drawn down corners of his mouth.

"I think—" he began to say.

From another room came the insistent thin summons of a telephone bell. The maid, apparently unaware of the drama being enacted, passed by the drawing room on swift feet along the hall. In a moment she was back.

"There's a man who says his name is Moran on the telephone asking for Sergeant Nelly somebody," she announced, "and he says he's in a hurry."

"That's me!" Tonelli started for the door. "I gotta ask you, Miss Mallor, to get some clothes on your mother. She can't go down to headquarters in that rig. Can you hurry it up? I gotta lot to do."

"But—"

"Sorry, ma'am!" Tonelli clipped her protest short. "I can't argue about it. She's gotta come and you better come with her. Where's this here telephone, sister?" he asked the maid.

14

"He didn't get away this time!" Moran was exultant.

"Neither will you if the nut inspectors lay eyes on you!"

Tonelli glowered at the Mallor maid who stood inside the door listening with all her ears.

"Get out!" he commanded, and shut that door. "If I catch you listening on the other side I'll send you to the Tombs."

Wall-eyed with fear, the maid stumbled out and closed the door.

"Wassat?" Moran had caught the aside to the maid and thought Tonelli was speaking to him. "You'll do what to who?"

"Dry up, stupid. I wasn't talking to you. I was fanning a snoop. Now what's eating on you?"

"I got that guy. That guy that was tailin' me and that I lost when Henessy gimme the razz. He walks right in here—"

"Where are you?"

"Where do you think? At Miss Pierce's apartment like you told me."

"Are you right in her apartment?"

"Naw. I'm downstairs. There's a pay telephone here in the hall and I'm talking from that."

"Where's Miss Pierce?"

"She's upstairs in her flat."

"How do you know?"

"I seen her."

"What did you do? Walk in and tell her you was a big shot dick from headquarters?"

"Naw. I ain't made no nutty plays. Didn't you tell me to use my head?"

"Yeah? Well how did you see Miss Pierce?"

"When she come in. She come in from the delicatessen store. I seen her come in with a big armful of bundles. That's when I seen her."

"How'd you know it was her?"

"The janitor told me. I went down and buzzed the janitor like you told me to do and I stands in his front winder with him. He's got a flat on the basement floor front and we watched for her to come in. He said she'd just gone out a while ago to buy some eats. Pretty soon in she came."

"O.K. Mike. Now what about this guy you got?"

"That's what I'm tryin' to tell you, ain't I? I was just comin' up from the janitor's apartment, up the steps from the basement, when I sees a guy easin' through the front hall door. I takes a good look an' I sees it's this same bozo that's been tailin' me. Boy did I grab him! I landed on him so hard he's just turnin' over for a breath now. He ain't gonna be no trouble at all for a while."

"Have you talked to him?"

"He ain't in no condition to talk yet. But I frisked him and guess what I found?"

"Two lollypops and a bag of peanuts."

"Be nice, can't you? In his inside pocket I found a sweet little package of cocaine all wrapped up in one of them wax papers. It was put up neat in a little envelope and addressed on a typewriter to Miss Sheila Pierce—"

"The hell you whisper!" Tonelli's alarm was vociferous. "You ain't opened that package of coke yet, have you?"

"No, I ain't—"

"Don't touch it! Don't handle it no more'n you hafta. Get this and get it right! Act fast! Put the jewelry on this guy you got. Don't stop to question him, slam him into a taxi— Then get the harness bull off the beat if you need help to attend to your friend, and get along upstairs and get this Pierce moll. Get them both, the guy *and* the jane, down to headquarters as fast as you can travel. You got it? Don't make no slips!"

"I got it. I'm on my way. Anything else?"

"Watch yourself. Don't let the Pierce woman communicate with anybody. Don't let her touch anything in her flat if you can help it. If she has to have a coat or a dress get it for her yourself. I'm gonna get the expert squad up to that place on the run. Ready?"

"O.K. Pete, let's go."

Tonelli jiggled the receiver hook impatiently.

"Spring 7-3100 and make it snappy, sister. Hello! Sergeant Tonelli speaking. Let me have Captain Henessy. Hello! Chief? I gotta break I think. Yeah? I'll be in as soon as I can get there with Mrs. and Miss Mallor. Moran is on his way downtown with Sheila Pierce and the bozo he lost this afternoon just before they bumped Slim the Sailor. That's a break, ain't it? And I got the name of the party at the Byington Hotel. Yeah. Party by the name of Gomez. Yeah, I believe you! We got plenty to say to *him*. Now listen, Chief, what do you say to this? Why not let the boys up there at the Byington bring in Gomez on the q.t. and set a mousetrap in his room? You can't never tell what you'll get. Whatda you think? O.K.? Swell. I'll be on my way in three shakes— Hey! Wait a minute! I gotta 'nother idea! You heard anything from Commander Betts? Good! Where did he say the *Esmeralda* was? Yeah? Holy Saints! I'm on my way ahopping. And Chief. What about sending up the gang to frisk Sheila Pierce's apartment? Yeah? It won't hurt none and if we find anything we're all to the good. What's the latest on le Mai? He still ramping around? O, he is, is he? Yeah? Sure he ain't satisfied with what we done, them fellas always expect miracles! Are you still with me? O.K. If you're with me this far, I'll keep on going. I might not be able to finish up but I gotta damn' good start. How's the round-up? Why couldn't they find Tom and Jerry? Jeest! We gotta round up them guns. They're bad actors and how're we gonna find out how come they went to see Dr. Holstead if we can't grill them? O, all right! All right! I'm coming!"

Tonelli's three shakes were stretched to an hour and more. He had reckoned without an hysterical female who was used to pampering. Mrs. Mallor had a weeping fit which switched into a tirade on the brutality of the constabulary. That in turn became a sickening exhibition of wheedling during which Tonelli found himself apostrophized as a "great big strong man" and Mrs. Mallor classed as a "poor, little bitsy weak girl." Weeping followed again almost without transition and slid into a "brain storm" with hair brushes and mirrors hurled about with reckless abandon. The sergeant fumed and was helpless.

The delay, however, had one good result as far as the sergeant was concerned. In the midst of it Walter Gates presented himself. Under pretense of talking over the situation and enlisting his help, Tonelli arranged for him to accompany the party to Centre Street: "You know, as a friend of the family," Tonelli explained guilelessly. Gates grinned. The sergeant's diplomacy was transparent. Even had he not wanted to go along with the party there was no reason for Gates to refuse.

Fully two hours after his call to Henessy, Tonelli's safari began to move. Mrs. Mallor, supported on the dexter side by the sergeant, on the sinister by Gates, tottered out to the elevator with the maid following after. The servant carried steamer rugs and smelling salts, while Frances closed up the rear with a smallish overnight bag containing necessities for both herself and her mother.

Frances had stood the ordeal like a Trojan woman. There were deep shadows under her eyes, her cheeks were drawn and she was the color of old linen. Her mother, on the contrary, having vented all of her emotion in tantrums, was actually in splendid condition. Once, on the way to the elevator, she so far forgot herself as to stand erect and vigorously berate the maid for having neglected to replenish her (Mrs. Mallor's) make-up kit.

Of them all, perhaps Tonelli was the most anxious and perturbed in appearance and actuality. His mind was busy, far away in several places at once. He wondered whether or not Moran had reached headquarters safely with his prisoners. If the mouse-trap" was functioning in Gomez' quarters at the Hotel Byington and if the searchers were turning up any new evidence in Sheila Pierce's apartment. Last but not least, he had begun to worry about Jack Holstead.

"Hell!" he told himself. "I ain't but one man and I done the best I could." But that was scant comfort. It had been at the very least seven hours since Holstead had slipped away from the New Jersey officers. Seven hours was a long time for a desperate man dealing with a group of murderous accomplices or foes. To ease himself somewhat, Tonelli spoke over Mrs. Mallor's head to Gates.

"Besides the plane at the airport Jack Holstead has another one down at the flying field in Staten Island, ain't he?"

"Not that I ever heard of," Gates answered easily, "he uses a ship down there that belongs to the National Guard. They have an aero squadron there, you know."

"You're a good friend of young Holstead, ain't you?" Tonelli demanded pointblank.

"He's a friend of mine, certainly," Gates admitted frankly.

"Would you do him a favor to help him outa a jam?"

"Walter would give his right arm for anyone who was a friend of his," Frances spoke quietly from their rear. "Wouldn't you, Walter?"

"I'd do a lot for you and Jack."

"Then get this," Tonelli offered. "I've got some information on Holstead that leads me to believe that he's been flying out to Rum Row on dark nights and visiting a certain ship that lays out there. Did you know that?"

"You're telling me." Gates was noncommittal.

"All right. I'm telling you. That's the lowdown. Now you're a good friend of his. I think he's in a jam. It's my idea he's gone out there to that ship looking for the guns that bumped his uncle off, and if he has he's in a bad way."

There was a cry of terror from Frances.

"You've held this back! Why didn't you tell me before? Jack's in danger and you're standing here—talking—and you too, Walter! You're his friend—"

The ascending elevator stopped at their floor and the door slid open. Tonelli, guiding Mrs. Mallor into the cage, glanced back over his shoulder.

"What could I do?" he defended himself. "If Jack's on Rum Row he's way outside the jurisdiction of the United States, much less the city of New York. My badge ain't worth its weight in old metal out there. I'd be a fine sap sticking my nose in that hornets' nest—"

Frances, her eyes blazing, advanced into the elevator pouring her scorn impartially on Gates and the detective.

"Such a big brave officer of the law, and a dash-log aviator, too. So cautious about authority and official boundaries where there is danger. You haven't been so meticulous, Sergeant, about legalities and police niceties in coming up here and questioning my mother and me. You're big enough and willing enough to take a chance with a pair of women but you're not man enough to face men—even though Jack may be murdered—'

The elevator boy, open-mouthed, stood waiting. Toward him Tonelli jerked a curt thumb.

"Bear down on the lever, son. We've gotta get outa here sometime tonight." The car shot downward and the sergeant allowed his attention to be drawn back to Frances Mallor.

"Use your head, Miss Mallor," was his plea. "Would you have me take a police boat out beyond the territorial limit and tackle a foreign vessel without extradition papers? You want me to start a war between the Bronx and Belgium or something?"

"There must be some way—" Frances insisted stubbornly.

For the thousandth time Tonelli admired her iron control. Not for an instant during this long and trying evening had she really lost her head. He wondered when the break would come. Flesh and blood couldn't continue under the strain this girl was sustaining.

"Besides," Tonelli continued his argument smoothly, "a motor boat, a small boat, any kinda boat I could get, wouldn't stand a chance in the open ocean with a fast rum-runner. If we did close up on them they'd give us such a dose of lead poisoning there'd be an overdraft on the Police Relief Fund for a lotta brand new widows."

The elevator stopped at the ground floor; the gaping boy slid back the folding grilled gate.

"An airplane might do the trick." It was Gates who made the suggestion as the sergeant ushered Mrs. Mallor into the lobby.

Tonelli turned his face away to hide the gleam of satisfaction he knew he would be unable to keep from showing.

"Yeah," he said, "an airplane might do it, but where am I gonna get a plane?"

"Why not at Staten Island—I know the commander there. He's a good egg—if he let Jack have one ship he'll let me have another to go after him—"

"Walter! You will! You'll go after Jack!" Frances, sobbing, laughing, bubbling with joy, quivering with anxiety, grasped the aviator's arm.

"Easy does it, darling! Sure I'll go. We can't leave old Jack in the pirates' den, can we?" Gates scoffed. "Where *is* this rum-ship, Mr. Policeman?"

"I'll know as soon as we get down to Centre Street," Tonelli promised.

They had progressed to the awning on the sidewalk, the starter tootled on his whistle to summon a taxicab, there being none at the curb as would have been the case earlier in the evening. It was the hour when all of New York is beckoning to cabs to get them to theatre before the curtain rises. The hour for the exodus of late diners.

"I'll know a lotta other things when I get to Centre Street, too," Tonelli told himself. "I hope to God Mike didn't make a botch of it—"

A taxi slipped in toward the curb, the doorman stepped forward to meet it. Far down the Avenue there welled up the whirling, mounting cataclysm of sound, the insistent alarm of a police car's siren. There was another behind it and a third. The traffic scattered to the sides of the street like overgrown black beetles scuttling to cover. Two police cars swept past the apartment building like furies released from torment; the third skidded to a stop beside the frozen group at the curb.

His face mottled, purple, bursting with rage, Captain Henessy fell rather than sprang out of the car. Over his shoulder Tonelli could see the pale, calm, aristocratic features of Henri le Mai, a half smile, half sneer on his thin lips.

"Tonelli! You—!" Henessy delivered himself of a string of oaths as lurid and high pressure as his complexion. "Where the hell you been for the last two hours?"

"Why, Chief—"

"Don't Chief me! I ain't no chief of yours. Back to a precinct desk is where you're gonna go. That's all you're fit for. You never was any good. You gotta coupla lucky breaks and—"

"What's all the stew about?" Tonelli's choler, equal every whit in intensity to Henessy's, rose and choked discretion from him. "What the blue-bellied hell's eating you? Chief or no chief, no God-damned, brass-bound Mick's gonna get away with that kinda talk to me! Snap out of it and say your say or else dry up!"

"Gentlemen! Gentlemen!" Henri le Mai's face inserted itself between the fiery visages of the two policemen. "This is no place to indulge in personalities. It seems to me we're wasting time that might be more profitably devoted to looking for Moran and his prisoners!"

"Moran? Where's Mike?" Tonelli forgot his personal grievances in his alarm. "Holy Saints, I hadda hunch—"

"Yeah! Well hunch this for us if you can! Where *is* Mike? That's what we wanna know. Him and the gal and the fella he snatched is *all* gone. The janitor is lying on the floor in Pierce's apartment with his head caved in and"—Henessy was climbing back into the police car as he flung the words at his erstwhile pet—"the search squad just found the handle to Slim the Sailor's knife."

"Where?"

"Under Miss Sheila Pierce's mattress and with it was another knife just like Slim's. What kinda hunch does that give you?"

"And you say Mike's gone?"

"Gone! Disappeared! Vanished!"

"What's my orders? Shall I get going after Mike?" Tonelli's cry had in it a note of anguish. Henessy stuck his head through the window as the police car got under way.

"You take the ladies to headquarters and wait there with them. Them's your orders for now. That's all you can be trusted to do without a bungle!"

The rising wail of the siren drowned out the rest of the captain's valedictory which was at least as insulting as the first part, judging from the contortions of his face and his gesticulations. The car leaped up the Avenue howling its fiendish warning and was lost in the swarming traffic.

The sergeant took two steps out into the street, his body strained forward in the instinctive urge to shout and follow after. Discipline and habit won after a struggle. His face a stony mask, he turned back to his small unshepherded flock waiting for his bidding.

"All right." Courtesy, compromise, consideration—there was no shadow of these in his curt command. "Tumble into this cab! Step on it. I've got no more time for fooling!"

Mrs. Mallor made a brief, fluttery gesture and the sergeant thrust his face into hers.

"Listen, lady!" he snarled, "I got just about enough of your capers. If you'd snapped out of it an hour ago maybe my partner wouldn't be missing right now. You do as you're told! From now on I mean business—"

"It won't hurt you to be ordinarily courteous," Gates spoke up. "After all it wasn't Mrs. Mallor's fault that you got a dressing down from your profane friend in the police car."

"Yeah! I think different, see! And right now, right here I'm boss! If you wanna be sure, start something! There's been too damn' much courtesy around here if you ask me. This is murder, not a pink tea— and I'm a cop, not a waiter."

Gates shrugged and occupied himself with making Frances and her mother as comfortable as possible in the rear seat with the maid. He and Tonelli sat on the two folding seats. Whatever her opinion of the change in the sergeant's manners, his direct talk had a most salutary effect upon Mrs. Mallor. For the first time since she had entered the drawing room demanding to know who Tonelli was, she settled into the role of a sensible, co-operative human being. She made no fuss about the close quarters, she docilely lifted her feet over the luggage, she even shifted to allow the maid room enough to breathe. In her heart Mrs. Mallor adored a masterful man. If Tonelli had slapped her face he would have made a life-long slave.

The sergeant, staring straight ahead as they sped downtown, was busy with his thoughts. The blocks rolled by in silence until, as they bumped over the car tracks at Eighth Street, he flung a question at Mrs. Mallor.

"What did *you* have on Dr. Holstead?"

"Why—what do you mean—I don't understand—"

"You get me all right. Holstead's notebook, the one that was found in his pocket when he was picked up dead in the street at Newark—you remember that, don't you? Dr. Holstead was murdered and thrown out of an airplane—"

She cowered and Frances indignantly protested.

"It's not necessary to continue to be so brutally vile, is it?"

"You're witnessing the beginning of the third degree, Frances," Gates sneered. "Refuse to answer, Mrs. Mallor! You're within your rights. Demand your lawyer. If you haven't one I—"

"Buddy, I'm coming to you," Tonelli spoke quietly, ominously, "and when I get to you I'll comb your hair good. As for you, Mrs. Mallor, I ain't got either the time nor the inclination to be nice now. I want information, and if I don't get it something's gonna happen and happen sudden. Dr. Holstead paid you over thirty thousand dollars in a little over ten years. What did you do for the money? Why did he give you thirty thousand berries? Because he liked your smile?"

"That was money he owed me!" Directly attacked, Mrs. Mallor developed unexpected spirit.

"For what?"

"From my husband's estate. My husband owned a share of Dr. Holstead's business. He loaned the doctor money—"

"O.K. Now what about Gomez?"

"I introduced Gomez to Mrs. Mallon." Gates attempted to shift the questioning in his own direction. "If there are any questions about Gomez—"

"There are plenty. You better start thinking up the answers right now. In the meantime don't butt in! Keep your trap shut or I'll shut it for you!" There was no doubt Tonelli not only meant what he said but yearned to put the threat into execution. Gates subsided.

Frances unexpectedly spoke up as an ally. In the soothing tones she reserved for her mother, she said:

"Sergeant Tonelli is right, mother. You and Walter are acting like sulky children. Tell him all you know, won't you please, so he can do something about Jack and his friend Moran?"

"There isn't anything to tell—"

"Yes there is, Mrs. Mallor," Tonelli took her up. "What have *you* told Gomez—and when?"

There in a taxi, bumping over the cobbles of Lafayette Street, Mrs. Mallor grew up, became an adult woman. The tears flowed, but they were no longer pettish, childish, hysterical tears.

"I don't know what I've done," she sobbed. "I suppose I've made a terrible, terrible mistake, but how was I to know?"

"Tell us, mother, it can't be so dreadful," Frances urged.

"Mr. Gomez was so sweet, so polite, so nice. He—I don't remember how or when—we were talking about Dr. Holstead—Gomez said he understood Dr. Holstead was working on a great invention and why didn't I find out something about it—"

"And you did?" Tonelli was hanging eagerly over the back of his narrow seat. Gates seemed to have lost all interest. He was staring straight ahead. The pressure of Tonelli's shoulder against his must have warned him of the futility of trying to do anything but sit and wait. The sergeant dominated the interior of the cab as the Rock of Gibraltar looms over the Bay.

"There seemed to be no harm in it," Mrs. Mallor continued, "Mr. Gomez explained that if we knew what the doctor was doing and exactly when he would be finished, we, Gomez and I, would be in a position to make some money speculating on the market with our advance information. Everyone does it—"

"You bet they do," Tonelli encouraged her now that she was talking, "and so you told him that the doctor was finished—*how* did you tell him?"

"I—I called him on the telephone after the doctor left the house— he—Mr. Gomez told me the information was very valuable and he— he would give me five thousand dollars—"

"Mother!" the single word wrung from Frances was steeped in pain.

"Did you get the money?" It was Tonelli the practical who asked this.

"Yes, I got it. I needed it so, it didn't seem to be wrong! Mr. Gomez told me—"

"The double-crossing snake!" Gates was seething with rage. He burst his silence savagely, forcing the sergeant's attention to him. "What's the use of trying to pump Mrs. Mallor, she doesn't know anything that will do you any good!"

"Is *that* so? Do you?" Tonelli swung his batteries on Gates as the cab came to a stop before headquarters. Neither he nor the man to whom he spoke made a move to disembark.

"Suppose I do, what of it? Are you man enough to make me talk? Are you man enough to come with me to the *Esmeralda* and make the whole damned gang talk?" Gates' jibe was as barbed as a fish hook and he sank it in as remorselessly as an angler who has hooked a fat trout.

"How did you know the name of the boat was the *Esmeralda?*"

Gates laughed nastily.

"Come and see, copper!"

"O.K." Tonelli made his decision. He swung his bulk erect. "I like to go places and see things! You lead the way, I'll come with you. Let's go."

He sprang to the street with a brief "Wait here" to the driver. The first blue-coated man he saw inside the door of the building with the green sidelights he ordered:

"Take these ladies up to Captain Henessy's office and see that they are taken care of. Let them stay there until Captain Henessy comes in. Mrs. Mallor, you'll be doing all you can to make up for the harm you've done through this rat Gomez by either telling your story, all of it, to Captain Henessy as soon as he comes in, or, better still, write it all out so it'll be ready for him when he comes. Will you do that?"

Mrs. Mallor nodded. She was a much chastened woman.

"Where are you going, Sergeant?" Frances greatly dared in asking the question.

"Me?" Tonelli laughed. "You heard Henessy bust me, didn't you? I ain't a sergeant any more. Maybe I ain't even a cop. I guess by the time I get back I won't be, and I say to hell with it. Me, and Mr. Gates here, two private citizens, are gonna go out to the *Esmeralda* and see what we can see. I gotta hunch we'll find Jack out there, Miss Mallor, so don't you worry and when you see Captain Henessy hand him this with my compliments, will you please?"

Frances Mallor, in the entrance to police headquarters, stood looking in perplexity at a gold police shield, Tonelli's badge, which he had laid in her hand.

"Sergeant Tonelli!" she called, but as she started down the stairs the cab that had been waiting at the curb moved off at a reckless clip. Inside, ex-Sergeant Pietro Tonelli and Walter Gates, known to his friends as "Vee," were taking each other's measure.

15

Contrasting strongly to Tonelli's grim and set look, Walter Gates was merry, bright and blithe. He lolled back in his corner of the swaying car, his cigarette cocked at an aggressive angle, and now and again snatches of song issued along with the smoke.

"Take us about an hour and a half, with luck, to get down to the flying field. It's right down at the end of the Island," he reminded the sergeant. "If we catch a ferry—"

"The news I been broke ain't travelled all over the department yet," Tonelli stated. "Maybe we can improve on that ferry stuff."

"'He loved to hunt the bounding stag all through the Royal Wood,'" Gates caroled happily. "Any method of transportation is an improvement on a ferry boat as far as I'm concerned." He dropped into commonplace prose to make the last declaration.

"If you'll back me up in this I think I can get away with it," Tonelli plotted aloud. "You're a coastguardsman, see?"

"'His only outer garment was a threadbare woolen shirt,'" Gates sang, nodding his head vigorously to show he heard the sergeant, understood and agreed to everything suggested.

"We go to Pier 'A,'" Tonelli continued, thinking aloud, "and I'll pull the hurry-hurry stuff. Henessy has had a police plane standing by all afternoon—"

Gates clapped his hands violently in enthusiastic applause, his "Sweet Adeline" baritone rose and swelled, explaining to all and sundry who cared to listen: "'Every time we leave the ground the undertaker hangs around—'"

Tonelli had switched the course of the taxi which first off was headed for South Ferry. Now they aimed further west along Battery Park to the station of the harbor police, which is known as Pier "A."

They were moving south, past docks and piers along West Street. Gates, at Tonelli's insistence, had ceased shouting his ribald songs, but he continued to light one cigarette from another and hum excitedly under his breath. The cab slued around in front of the Whitehall Building; the Aquarium loomed like a gigantic bandbox in the starlight.

"Here we are," Tonelli warned. "Remember we're in a hell of a hurry and you're a coastguardsman. Come on!" He led the way into Pier "A" on a trot.

Gates followed at the pace the sergeant set, but, running as he was, the cigarette still wobbled from his lips and he hummed:

"'The general got the Croix de Guerre, parlay vous!'"

At the desk the lieutenant looked up and the sergeant called across from the door:

"Where's the plane?"

"What? How? O—"

"Captain Henessy gave orders that a plane was to stand by for me," Tonelli snapped.

The lieutenant came at once alert and understanding.

"It's moored off the end of the pier, Sergeant."

He spoke to the officer on reserve duty standing by the squad room. "Tell Roberts Sergeant Tonelli is here and wants the plane."

The message was not necessary. A young police officer wearing a Sam Browne belt over his tunic and pulling a flying helmet on as he came appeared in the doorway.

Tonelli switched his attention from the lieutenant to the police aviator.

"Can you carry three including yourself?"

"Yep. Easy."

"How long will it take you to run us over to the National Guard Flying Field on Staten Island?"

"Five minutes." The flying patrolman grinned.

"O.K. Let's go." Intent as he was on carrying through this commandeering of the plane with all that depended on the time element, Tonelli couldn't resist a question to the lieutenant.

"Is there a general alarm posted for Moran?"

"Yes, came through a long while ago. There's another bulletin too."

"Yeah?"

"They've found a man who saw Moran being forced into a car. The car was a roadster, sport model, with the curtains up. Blue body with light colored striping. Bulletin says it is probably the same car John R. Holstead, 2nd, was using this morning and for which the previous general alarm was posted."

"Shoot back a report from me, will you?" Tonelli directed over his shoulder. Outside he could hear the roar of the motor of the seaplane warming up. Gates had already followed the police flyer out to the end of the pier. "Advise Henessy that I recommend all roads leading to the water front, particularly Long Island and Jersey, be watched for the escaping car. The ferries and bridges are the points where you're most apt to pick it up. The men who got Moran are making a break for a boat somewhere. So long."

The sergeant had reached the amphibian plane and it had taken off on its long slant across New York harbor before the lieutenant had finished reporting in to headquarters, and in Captain Henessy's office there was no one on duty who felt it devolve upon himself to inform Pier "A" that Tonelli was in bad repute with his chief.

The boast of five minutes for the trip was a slight exaggeration, but it was under fifteen minutes from the moment Gates and Tonelli entered Pier "A" to their landing in Staten Island. Almost before the wheels had stopped rolling both men had tumbled out of the cockpit and Gates set off on a run across the tarmac to the flying field.

"Shall I wait?" the police aviator yelled above the purr of the idling motor. He had dropped to the ground beside the sergeant, his goggles were shoved back on his forehead and he absently wiped a smear of grease across his chin with the back of his gloved hand.

"Stick around for a minute—" Tonelli only half heeded him. He watched the door of the office. Even as he spoke it was wrenched open and the slim form of Gates catapulted from it. Tonelli sprang forward to meet him halfway.

"We can't have a ship!" Gates gasped. "The Squadron's out on a practice flight. Holstead got the last one and the officer in charge is having puppies because he hasn't got back with it."

The sergeant's jaw sagged. His mind raced with the problem.

"Can you drive that plane we crossed over here in?" he asked, lowering his voice.

"I can fly an egg crate if it's got a big enough motor," Gates bragged.

Tonelli in action was a man of few words. He was moving purposefully toward the police plane.

"Hey you! Richards, Roberts, whatever-your-name-is, come here!"

Unsuspectingly the sky-rider of New York's Finest, obeying his superior officer, walked toward Tonelli.

"Did you see anything of a motor boat on the bay as we crossed?" Tonelli asked. His eyes were fixed on the smear of grease on the other man's chin. His question was asked at random.

"I couldn't tell one from the other small boats in the dark," the patrolman explained. "I was too busy—"

Tonelli's ham-sized fist, swung without warning, clipped the officer neatly where the smear of grease marked the target and he went down like a log.

"Pretty baby!" Gates breathed from behind the sergeant.

"There's your bus," the sergeant spoke gruffly, "and," he leaned over to jerk the police aviator's goggles and helmet from his head, "here's your flying doodads."

For an instant Tonelli's hand rested on the fallen man's forehead and moved to his heart. "He'll wake up in a minute or two," he decided, and swung up over the side of the fuselage following Gates' example.

"Step on it, kid!" he advised. "Let's see what this *Esmeralda* looks like. At that," the sergeant's statement was not without grim humor, "we're safer three miles out than we will be in New York when that laddie buck comes to and gets to a telephone."

"What the hell did you hit him for?" Gates enquired, not with accusation, simply out of idle curiosity.

"He's a cop, starting out in the force," Tonelli explained, "but he's young and if I'd asked him to come along tonight he'd acome for the hell of it and like as not got broke and dismissed when we got home—if we did get home. It was easier to put him out than to argue with him."

"That fist's a damned near unanswerable argument," Gates grinned. He "gave it the gun" and the motor, ripping into life, made further comment hopeless.

Without direction from Tonelli Gates set his own course, while in the darkness and isolation of whirling sound from the motor and the song of the wind through guy-wires and struts, the sergeant smiled happily to himself. Far below, dotting the lower end of the bay, he could see flashing points of radiance, lighthouses which from above were insignificant in contrast to the great luminous blur of Manhattan with its spinal cord of fire formed by the Great White Way at the peak of its glory.

Prince's Bay Light passed almost directly beneath them, and Sandy Hook, with Navesink far to the right. Scotland Lightship ahead and to the right with Sandy Hook Lightship flashing behind it passed in review as the plane heeled slightly and turned east and north along Long Island. Jones' Beach, from Tonelli's viewpoint, was parallel lines of white—beach and surf. Fire Island light blinked under their bow; the guardians of Montauk Point were pin pricks far ahead. Where the beacons of Southeast Point and Sandy Point on Block Island lined up with Point Judith on the mainland to make an intangible barrier across their course, Tonelli became aware that the riding lights of the plane, controlled from the pilot's seat, were behaving in queer fashion. They went on and off, stuttering in rhythmic cadence, and, search the dark waters beneath as much as he might, Tonelli was incapable of seeing any answer. Somewhere, he surmised, along the shore line was a signal outpost of the off-shore rum fleet or one of the hidden radio stations which kept the hovering runners informed through short-wave length sending.

Tonelli had been in the air before but never at night. He had the impression of being encompassed by warm, viscous fluid which made progress smooth and easy. The sky above with its solidity embossed by stars was as likely a landing place as the smooth blackness below. Here and there the inky depths he gazed down into when he peered over the side were flicked with the lace of whitecaps.

The motor was the only fly in the ointment. It was an annoyance, it was a regularly intermittent yet constant battering on the eardrums that after a time became a pressure on the base of the throat.

Abruptly the plane heeled again to the left and the sergeant found himself gazing along the broad surface of a down-pointed wing, felt the solid gloom rising with tremendous pressure against his face as they side-slipped toward that real intangibility below. Only an effort of will could translate it into myriad tons of resistless salt water.

The circle they described in landing was centered, Tonelli saw, on two small, dark shapes. The one, smaller, long and thin, pointed and needle-like, left frothy divergent streaks behind it and grew as they dropped until it was recognizable as a speeding motor boat cleaving through the swell, its wake widening after it. The other shape was rapidly becoming a fairly large ship, black and sinister, apparently motionless while actually tossed and heaved on the long swell.

The motor of their plane died with a last protesting whir and became an occasionally even-spaced flutter which spun the propeller languidly. The flying craft straightened to even keel, its nose headed downward as the vibrations of wires and struts, the hiss of air along the supporting surface rose to a wail. There was a thud as the pontoons took the water and the ship bounded, a second and a third shock of impact, the motor burred into action and they taxied along on a sea which was far from smooth and imparted a jouncing effect to the passengers not unlike riding in a heavily-springed dray on a cobbled street.

Opening and closing the throttle in short bursts, Gates jockeyed the plane riding the waves in a wide circle, taxi-ing to within a few yards of the heaving deck of the dark and silent ship. They touched only just after the motor boat made fast to the ship's side.

His eyes whipped by the wind, his ears full and dull with the sound of the motor, strangely sleepy and listless from his enforced dose of oxygen and ozone, Tonelli willed himself alert and peered intently through the starlighted night. There was no moon, yet as he became accustomed to the surface glow of the sea, outlines, then solid surfaces became visible.

Two men were busied on the far side of the deck, which was unbroken in surface except for a low deck house and a stumpy slim rod which carried a radio antenna. The blunt bows of the ship headed into the rolling seas lifted and fell, slued and paid off with splashes and slaps of water against stout planking. A sound Tonelli was ever afterward to associate with this particular scene.

The motor boat which had come alongside had been secured and the two men were helping its passengers to the deck. One in particular had almost to be lifted bodily, and from the distance he was weird in his armless helplessness. One was a woman. Tonelli, watching, sensing that he was nearing the end of a double quest, sank back in his padded bucket seat relaxed and satisfied. No need to worry now. Time enough for anxiety and action when action would be effectively indicated.

From the roof of the deck house the figure of a man was gesticulating toward them and the hail came across the water.

"That you, Gates?"

Who the hell you expecting?"

Gates, his goggles pushed up, his hawk profile bent over the side of his high cockpit, was gleefully in his element.

The answer from the deck was the thud of a weighted line which dropped over the cowling within reach of the sergeant's hand. That hand pounced on the thin strong rope and hauled with a will until the heavier hawser attached to the heaving line snaked wet and dripping aboard the seaplane. Gates, standing now on his seat, lent his aid and the plane, its motor dead and silent, was warped so closely to the deck that the rise and fall of the waves caused the two ships to bump and scrape.

"Where are your fenders?" Gates called. "This isn't my crate. Me and my friend here borrowed it. We can't afford to have the paint work all scratched up. We'll catch hell when we take it back if we do."

As he spoke the two men who had helped the boarders from the speed boat had moved toward the rail and set two woven coir mats to cushion the impact of the larger seagoing vessel for the more fragile ship of the air.

The man atop the deck house scrambled down to them and Tonelli saw he was huge. Side by side with the sergeant he would have assayed an ounce of bone and muscle to every ounce of meat and sinew in the big policeman, and, like Tonelli, he was trig and trimly clothed.

A cap of naval design set at the seagoing angle on his close-cropped head. His blue coat was double-breasted with winking brass buttons, and wound around his neck and tied like a stock was a voluminous white muffler. He might have been a watch officer in a crack vessel of His Majesty's Navy superintending the landing of an admiral's cutter. With side-boys and a bos'n's pipe the illusion would have been complete.

"This is a little tricky!" Gates remarked conversationally to the sergeant. He was hanging over the side, one foot on the stirrup that gave a foothold for ascent and descent into and from the cockpit, the other foot dangling, seeking a firm hold on the pontoon over which the rolling waves washed. Gates found his footing, dropped to the pontoon, turned, balanced for an instant, leaped and caught the rail of the ship with his hands, one foot clinging to the beading which ran along the side below the level of the deck. Another heave of his arms and he slithered safely over onto the boards. "Can you make it?" he called back.

More clumsily the sergeant duplicated the feat. Beyond a wet trouser leg and a skinned knee he landed in good order, straightened and found himself looking into the cold eyes of the captain of the *Esmeralda*.

"Who," demanded that jaunty personage, "is this, Gates?"

His voice was cultured, his words clear, clipped, as English as his uniform.

"Excuse me." Gates was busy with helmet and goggles. He grasped his nose between thumb and finger and inflated his cheeks, blowing out his breath to exert pressure on his eardrums and clear them. "Allow me to present Detective Sergeant Tonelli of the Homicide Squad of the New York Police. Sergeant Tonelli, meet Captain McMurtrie of His Majesty's Merchant Ship, *Esmeralda*."

"Honored, I'm sure!" McMurtrie was suavely disagreeable.

"Pleased to meetcha," Tonelli was still sizing up his man. "Gates made a mistake though. Out here I'm just plain Pete Tonelli. This ain't exactly an official visit, Captain. I'm looking for a coupla friends, that's all."

Captain McMurtrie's glance swept across the bare deck of the ship, peered as far as the horizon on all sides searching a deserted sea. As plainly as if he had spoken the action stated it a singular business that a detective should be seeking friends in the midst of the reaches of the Atlantic Ocean.

"Ah—and what makes you suppose that you have any friends on the *Esmeralda?*"

"I don't suppose nothing—I know—"

"Pete! Here I am! It's Mike! Pete! Help! Hel—"

From somewhere under their feet, inside the deck house, the cry came. It was a hoarse and croaking scream, yet even the last gasp, smothered and quivering into a strangled yelp was recognizable as the far from melodious voice of Moran.

Involuntarily Tonelli tensed, sprang forward to find himself gripped from behind. At his right a grinning, black bullet head towered over his shoulder, an ape-like hand yanked his wrist backward and upward, pinning it in a hammerlock between his shoulder blades. At his left a squat and swarthy man gripped his forearm and elbow in such a manner that if Tonelli struggled he would only serve to increase the pressure that would ultimately snap the bone. Held in this painful position he felt the negro's free hand slide in expert fashion over his hip pockets and the service .32 caliber revolver was jerked from its holster at the back of Tonelli's belt. Butt forward, the grinning black man handed the weapon to his uniformed master.

"Sorry if we seem a bit inhospitable," McMurtrie grated, maintaining the semblance of an exaggerated courtesy as he took the gun, "these little formalities are necessary when we receive visitors who arrive without proper credentials."

Tonelli stared into his face. The sweat stood out on his forehead, for even the light pressure on his right arm was an agony. His body was bent forward to ease himself from the force being exerted from both sides. He was as helpless and as dangerous as a wolf in a steel trap.

"O.K." he said between his clenched teeth. "You win. I'll be good. You got my gun now, let me go."

The polite mask McMurtrie maintained left his face for a revealing instant.

"Good!" His laugh was a nasty bark. "We'll jolly well see to it that you're good, and stay good, you sneaking, spying hound!"

His hand slashed, open palmed, and his fingers left a row of stinging white welts on the sergeant's cheek.

"Take him below and keep him in the saloon until I get there!", McMurtrie ordered curtly, and turned on his heel, thrusting his jutting jaw into Gates' unperturbed countenance. "What do you mean by coming out here and bringing this offal with you?"

"Goodness me, aren't you pettish!" Gates, one-third of the captain's bulk and a good half head shorter, stood his ground nonchalantly. "Don't you remember the lovely little ditty? 'Every little movement has a meaning all its own,'" he sang.

"This is not the time for your bloody silly monkeyshines, Gates!" McMurtrie was working into a towering rage.

Tonelli, half dragged across the deck, was being bundled down the companionway into the saloon. As his head sank below the deck level his hearing strained for every word. In spite of the difficulty he was having with his footing on the sharply sloping ladder, Gates' drawled answer carried clearly to him.

"Don't be an ass, McMurtrie. You're better off with Tonelli here than on shore. He was getting uncomfortably close to the truth."

16

BEAUTY OF LINE OR APPOINTMENT was not one of the attributes of the *Esmeralda*. The cabin was smallish, square and dark, lighted during the day by a skylight let into the deck and, when needed, by an oil lamp swinging in a bracket from a deckbeam over the fixed table. A transom against the after bulkhead was provided with a cushion and formed a seat along one side of the table; heavy chairs were cleated to the deck on the remaining three sides. Two doors opened from the cabin, that on the port side leading into the captain's "room," the starboard to another cabin where the negro and the swarthy man who had captured Tonelli slept. These two men acted as McMurtrie's "officers." The negro who answered to the name of "Ha'penny" could neither read nor write, but the other, a half-caste who called himself "Da Sousa," held a Board of Trade ticket as chief officer in sail or steam.

These were things that Tonelli found out afterward. At the moment of his introduction to the cabin of the *Esmeralda* he had plenty to occupy his mind without bothering about the details of Captain McMurtrie's command.

Half mad with rage and pain he was booted down the companionway at the foot of which his captors loosened their hold and half-pushed, half-threw him into the room. He stumbled forward and fell sprawling across the table.

Unhurt, he lay there for a few precious seconds getting his breath and composing himself. The sergeant was capable of berserk rage once unleashed, but now he knew that the prime essential was to keep his temper, keep cool at all costs.

The tremendous paw of the black fell on his shoulder.

"Git up, mon!"

Taking account of every minute detail, Tonelli was almost constrained to laugh by the extraordinary circumstance of a negro with a Scotch dialect. The sergeant's acquaintance with the colored race was confined to Harlem and "Mammy" singers. He had known the exaggerated Anglicisms of "high brown" West Indians who lorded it over that dark section between the upper end of Central Park and the Harlem River, known as "San Juan Hill," but this was the first time he had heard broad Scots emanating from what he called a "dinge."

Nevertheless, far from laughing, the sergeant groaned and slowly pulled himself upright. He made of it a convincing bit of acting which might not have passed an expert but served to throw the two men off their guard.

"Sit down!" Ha'penny ordered, and the sergeant, to all appearances completely cowed, sat in the center chair with his back to the entrance.

There were voices on the companion steps as McMurtrie, followed by Gates, came down. McMurtrie jerked his head toward the ladder.

"On deck Da Sousa! You too, Ha'penny! All hands turn to. Set a southeast course at half-speed, Da Sousa. Keep the motor boat and the plane in tow. Look alive now! Smartly does it!"

"Ay, ay sir!" the two voices chimed as one as Ha'penny followed the half-caste on deck.

McMurtrie threw himself in the chair at the head of the table. Tonelli, his face in his hands, groaned as if involuntarily and shuddered. McMurtrie sneered.

"That'll be about enough of the theatricals. You aren't hurt. You can't make me think you are."

"O.K. I'm not hurt." Tonelli sat erect. "What happens now? You've got my gun, you've got me here on your ship with your gang to manhandle me if I speak out of turn. What's the next move?"

"'Where, O, where are the Generals, I wonder where they are? O, I wonder where they are? O, I wonder where they are?'" Gates, singing softly, passed behind the sergeant and took his seat at the third chair at the table. "'They're up in gay Paree! I saw them, I saw them, up in gay Paree, I saw them—'"

McMurtrie paid no attention to him.

"You know," he said to Tonelli, "I rather like your cheek. By gad I do. It's too rotten bad you're a policeman. I could use a fellow like you in my business."

"I draw the line at murder, McMurtrie," Tonelli stated quietly. "I wouldn't be the man for you. I don't like killers."

"Murder!" The captain's eyes narrowed into cruel slits. "Who said anything about murder?"

"I did, McMurtrie. I came out here to get a murderer."

"'*Apres la guerre fini, Les Americains parti*,'" Gates hummed. He had hung both legs over the arm of his chair and with bright and eager face was watching the by-play between the two big men glowering at each other over the opposite ends of the table.

McMurtrie had leaned back again, once more affably sneering.

"You change your mind a lot, my good man. I thought you came out here to fetch some of your friends ashore."

"Sure I did," Tonelli snapped. "I'm gonna take Mike Moran ashore with me and Sheila Pierce and Jack Holstead, McMurtrie. And with them I'm gonna take the men who stabbed Dr. Holstead. What do you know about that?"

From somewhere forward came the sound of Diesel motors turning over. The lumpish rocking of the ship changed to a smoother rise and fall, a more evenly spaced roll. McMurtrie took a cigarette case from the side pocket of his coat and selected a smoke with meticulous care.

"You hear those engines, don't you?" he challenged. "We're headed for the Bahamas, Mr. Detective. We're on a British vessel with British papers in order and we're headed for a British port. I doubt if you'll take anybody ashore with you. Certainly you won't take anybody back to New York. As a matter of fact," a flaring match illuminated his cruel features, "it may be that you won't *get* ashore. Only Gates knows where you are and *Gates* won't talk, *will* you, Gates?"

"Me?" The aviator showed all the surprise of a child awakened from sleep. "I never talk. I only sing—and fly."

Tonelli spread both hands flat on the table. In his mind was a picture. This McMurtrie was the man who had bound Chinese back to back and tossed them overboard when a revenue cutter got too close for comfort. Ha'penny was the murderous black who always followed him. The sergeant licked his dry lips.

"You mean you're gonna bump me off?"

In McMurtrie's hand was an automatic, its squarish end with the small deadly round hole that was the muzzle of the barrel trained steadily on the sergeant's chest.

"Don't get jumpy, Sergeant!" McMurtrie warned. "Take your hands off the table and settle down. It's a long way to the Bahamas and nothing has been decided yet. I don't like the way you talk. You speak too freely of murder and bumping people off to suit my quiet style. This is a peaceful merchant ship and I'm going to keep it so."

"'Yo, ho, ho and a bottle of rum!'" Gates trolled.

"Pete! They got me in here! Over here!"

Moran's voice came to them muffled by a heavy marine door built to be watertight in case of need. The sergeant, glad of a diversion that enabled him to look away from that menacing automatic in a natural fashion, jerked about in his seat facing toward the starboard as if he expected Moran to come tumbling out.

"That's your friend." McMurtrie's information was superfluous. "He's rather a sight, you know. Handcuffed with his own irons. Looks a bit like an overfed fowl trussed up for cooking."

"He ain't so funny, Mike ain't. He may look like a fool but if you buy him for that you'll get stung, I'm telling you."

"Exactly how he comes to be here I haven't heard yet." McMurtrie was blandly conversational. "It might be rather amusing to know why it was necessary for him to be knocked on the head—"

"He was in Sheila Pierce's apartment, that's why he's here. Like me, maybe he was finding out too much."

"Impossible, Sergeant. Our lives, mine and my associates', including the slightly disreputable Gates, are open to the public gaze. You seem obsessed with this idea that we are all scoundrels. I can assure you that—"

"Yeah? Bring Mike in here then and let's hear what he has to say and I'll lay my cards on the table. Maybe you *can* explain away knives and cyanide. Are you game?"

"Your taunts are rather childish, Sergeant. Is there any good reason why I should reunite you two old friends?"

Tonelli shrugged.

"I can't see's it'll make any difference to you. Like you just said, we ain't going nowhere and we ain't gonna land nowhere so there won't be no story to tell. It's up to you."

"Put like that it does seem cruel to keep you separated—"

From the captain's room a woman emerged, a woman who made Tonelli sit up and blink. She was tall, slim and her face was pallid with the clear pallor of a perfect olive complexion. Her hair was black, so black its waves caught and seemed to repeat the purple overtones cast by the light of the swaying lamp. There were great dark circles under her eyes; her hands were long and thin, sensitive hands that might caress a man or claw him. Her frock was of some rough woolen stuff that clung in draped simple lines and its deep red threw the sable of her eyes into stronger contrast with her creamy skin so that they seemed to be blazing under her curved brows.

"We're moving!" she said. Her voice was a husky contralto which held the same burning quality of her eyes. "Where are we going? When can I get ashore? I must get ashore at once."

"Hello, Sheila. Sit down and make yourself at home," McMurtrie invited.

She stared at him insolently, contemptuously, yet there was haggard fear behind her contempt.

"I have no desire to be at home anywhere that you are, McMurtrie. Where is Vincent?"

"Vincent?" McMurtrie, from his tone, had never heard the name before.

"Yes, Vincent! Where is he? He promised—"

"My dear Sheila—"

"Don't, McMurtrie! I've had enough! I can't stand any more of this horror. Vincent said this was the end. That you would land me in Connecticut. He said I could go—anywhere I wanted to go and I don't care where I go if I can only get away from this horrible boat, if I never have to see any of you again—"

"But you must be reasonable, Sheila. Who is this Vincent you're talking about?"

Tonelli chortled aloud. "Ain't that a shame, now, McMurtrie? Completely lost your memory, ain't you?"

"Sure, you know who she's talking about, Mac." Gates, who had not turned his head to look at Sheila Pierce on her entrance to the saloon, was flicking at an invisible grain of dust on his knee. He was deliberately insulting, deliberately passing the lie to McMurtrie. "She means the doc. Why not have him in? Why not have 'em all in? I'm bored with this show."

"You—" McMurtrie, snarling, half-rose, leaned over the table, menacing Gates.

"Hell, Mac. Be yourself. We're all here in the same boat. We're all in the same mess. What's the idea? You can't fool Tonelli any more. He and his partner in there have all the dope they need. They know all about us now. Why the hell does Kramer have to hide? I'm like Sheila. I'm damned fed up with all this mystery hoorah!"

"Yes?"

It was like one of the old marionette shows once so popular in the Italian section of the big city when he was a kid, Tonelli thought to himself. The puppets came in through the two side doors to the cabin as if pulled by the strings of the puppeteer. The latest addition was Dr. Vincent Kramer. Sleek, suave, affable Kramer who made a quietly effective entrance. Except that he had shed his white laboratory overall for a grey topcoat and wore a snap-brim soft felt hat, he was the same dapper, well-dressed person.

"We can't have you bored, Gates. Can we, McMurtrie? And it would never do for Sheila to begin having hysterics. If she were to scream someone might hear her." He chuckled silently, his lips stretched back in a joyless grimace.

Tonelli sat and waited, bided his time. He said nothing. There was nothing to say. He let the rest talk and listened and imbibed knowledge.

"I won't scream. There's no good screaming. I couldn't scream now if I wanted to." Sheila Pierce, taut, every nerve and muscle tensed, stood with her back to the door, braced against the motion of the ship. "I have wanted to scream all day. All day yesterday I wanted to cry out—to warn him. I wish to God I had made him leave with me—I would have made him leave if I'd known you were going to—"

"Shut up, damn you!" McMurtrie's command crackled like a rifle shot. "Keep your mouth shut or by heaven I'll close it for you and make it stay closed!"

"You're all on edge. Touchy. Let's calm down." Steadying himself with one hand on the back of Tonelli's chair, Dr. Kramer passed behind him and stood confronting the woman. "What you need, Sheila, is a little sedative. I'm sorry our man was delayed in delivering it. That clumsy interfering detective, this fellow Moran, got the package that was intended for you—"

"And plenty more, fella, plenty more!" There was Moran, his collar torn off and hanging in shreds, his necktie around on the back of his neck, his face a mass of purple bruises, his mouth puffed and bleeding, his lips cut—Moran, staggering, standing upright with difficulty, his wrists linked together at his back with his own handcuffs. A battle-scarred figure but indomitably still in the game, Moran swayed in the starboard doorway through which he had followed the chemist.

"You swine!" McMurtrie sprang to his feet. "Get back there!"

"Mac!" Once more it was Gates who intervened. "Lay off the poor devil. He's out on his feet."

"Who asked you about it?"

"Why nobody, now that you bring it up. But then nobody has asked me anything about this business. You didn't ask me if you were to hold Jack Holstead out here. You didn't ask me when you murdered his uncle. All you've asked me to do is the dirty work. To hold the bag. I think it was about time both you and Kramer asked me for advice or at least consulted my wishes. Or am I being as unreasonable as hell?"

"You got what you wanted. Quick money!" Kramer threw the words at the unperturbed aviator.

"But not enough, old bean. Not half enough. There isn't enough money in the world to pay me for flying that plane over—?"

"God Almighty, are you all mad?" McMurtrie howled. "Have you—?"

Suddenly Sheila Pierce began to scream. She crouched cowering with her back against the door, trembling all over, her body jerking spasmodically while shriek after shriek permeated the room. Shrill, rasping, jagged sounds that ripped through the eardrums like broken fragments of glass.

"Stop that!" Dr. Kramer strode forward grasping her by the shoulders, shaking her until her head wobbled limply on her neck. "Stop those damned hysterics! Here!" He fumbled in his side pocket and produced a small folded wax paper. Carefully he unwrapped it, spread the powder it contained on the back of his hand and approached it to her nostrils for her to sniff.

How he did it neither he himself could explain and certainly it seemed almost a miracle to those others in that crowded small space, but Moran propelled himself forward, around or over the table and, smashing into the doctor, spilled the powder.

"Took out for that stuff, lady!" Moran croaked. "That's the same stuff they slipped to Slim the Sailor. It's poison, it ain't coke!"

The doctor had gone down, his head against the bulkhead, half doubled beneath the table, and Moran had sprawled onto the floor. Handicapped by his chained hands, Moran could not move with speed and Kramer was the first of them to recover. One foot in its elegant shoe struck out, the heel catching Moran full in the face and squashing his nose into a pulp. It was then that Tonelli, at first as much taken by surprise as the rest, went into action. With one sweep of his arm he smashed into the swinging lantern, tearing it from its bracket and shattering it against the bulkhead behind McMurtrie. One bull-like roar Tonelli gave as the cabin plunged into a fury of black darkness except for the licking flames along the corner of the deck where the oil from the lamp ignited.

With that one roar he was silent, deadly silent, driving forward with the battering irresistibility of a python in attack.

"Ha'penny! Da Sous—!" McMurtrie's outcry stopped short there. Tonelli's hands had found his throat. The automatic cracked and cracked again. There was an answering roar from the floor where Kramer was struggling to his feet. In their corner, McMurtrie and Tonelli, equally matched bulk for bulk and strength for strength, thrashed and pounded in titanic throes.

"Cheerio! Coming up!" Dimly through the pounding blood in his eardrums Tonelli heard Gates chirp, and then all minor sounds were submerged again in Sheila Pierce's marrow-freezing screams.

Through the haze of his terrific efforts, the muscle-tearing strain he was under in his endeavor to grasp and hold the twisting, heaving man he was entwined with, Tonelli was aware that there were clattering steps on the companionway and then in rapid succession the hammer blows of four revolver shots. It was a dim memory, however, because for once in his life the sergeant had found his equal in a rough and tumble. He was fighting for his life and all decencies of combat had been cast to the four winds.

McMurtrie had the heel of the palm of one hand under Tonelli's chin, his other arm locked tight around the sergeant's waist and slowly, slowly he forced the sergeant's head back and back. Somewhere in the darkness lay the automatic which Tonelli had succeeded in wrenching from the captain's grasp, but both men had forgotten it.

The fingers of the sergeant's right hand dug into the hair at the back of McMurtrie's head; short hair but curly, affording an excellent grip. The groping left hand closed around the biceps of the arm which held the sergeant in a vise. Throwing himself backward Tonelli managed to loosen that grip a trifle and instantly his knee yanked upward in the terrible blow to the groin.

Involuntarily, in his agony, McMurtrie loosed his holds and the sergeant was free to take a quick step backward, as he moved driving his left fist into the solar plexus and his right to the face in a savage one-two. McMurtrie went down, pitching forward as he struck. His lashing arms encountered Tonelli's ankles and he jerked them out from under him, bringing the sergeant crashing to the floor.

Both men were winded, panting for breath. The sergeant was still fighting in grim silence, but the other, his jaunty pose of stoicism completely shattered, gasped obscenities and curses in an endless filthy stream.

By the weird, uncertain dim light of the flames burning themselves out along the bulkhead, Tonelli, as he rebounded from his crash to the floor, could make out the form of his opponent straddled almost across his feet. Half blindly the sergeant flung himself forward bringing up against the stanchion of the table with a force that almost shattered his shoulder. Completely mad with rage and pain, he stabbed forward with both arms, his groping fingers closed on McMurtrie and he drew the writhing, snarling figure toward him.

Striking out with clenched fists, kicking, butting, biting, Mc-Murtrie, half under the table, strove in vain to free himself from the inexorable pressure of Tonelli's resistless enveloping movement. In an insane convulsion the captain turned completely over and lay on his side, his bowed back to the sergeant, his feet and head the extremes of an arc at the greatest distance from the detective. Tonelli's right hand was wound in the slack collar of McMurtrie's jacket so twisted it was impossible for him to release it, his left arm, extended around the leg of the table, had a firm purchase on the captain's thigh.

Like an archer straightening a huge bow across his knee, Tonelli drew in with both arms. He had hooked his feet around the legs of the chair in which he had been seated a few seconds before and the stout oak secured to the deck was equal to the strain. McMurtrie, thrashing, floundering, tearing at Tonelli's hands with both of his own, could not fight off the slow, pitiless drag of the sergeant's mighty arms. Under the inexorable pressure the captain's body straightened, his back, just above the hips, jammed against the leg of the table, was coming into line. His hands flailed the air uselessly and still Tonelli pulled as the man's curses rose in a weird bubbling outcry.

His pulses pounding, his brain whirling in a disordered vortex of primeval passion and strife, the sergeant felt rather than heard the crackle as McMurtrie's spine snapped. The captain's shrieks died in a gurgling, rattling groan and the great body went limp.

Fainting, sick, his senses reeling, the sergeant let go his hold slowly. In the darkness he had great difficulty in freeing the hand wound in the seaman's jacket and in those few instants he was aware that a peopled silence lay over the cabin, broken only by his own labored breathing and the groans of the dying man from whom he struggled to free himself. Clinging to chair and table, he staggered to his feet. His bloodshot eyes searched in the gloom.

"Mike!" he called. "Mike!"

His mouth was dry, he licked his lips with his swollen tongue. "Mike, are you there? Are you hurt?"

At his right there was a soft sighing sound. The ghost of a laugh.

"Nice little party, Sergeant! Looks like we're the only survivors."

It was Gates. Tonelli could make out his form, slumped shapelessly over the corner of the table.

"Are you all right, Gates? Where are the others! Moran? The woman? Kramer?"

There was no answer, only the groaning of the man at his feet, his own rattling breath and the sound as of water dripping slowly drop by drop, spattering to the deck. Those few slight sounds, and gradually, growing more sharply defined until it was the one real thing in the world, the one thing that mattered, the sickening odor of fresh blood clogged Tonelli's nostrils.

He lurched in Gates' direction, his groping hand encountered the huddled figure and with the slight touch the aviator crumpled and thudded to the deck, the revolver in his hand slithering across the slippery boards.

With some dim idea of getting lights and aid, Tonelli staggered toward the companionway. It was blocked; his awkward feet stumbled over inert heaps lying at its foot. Painfully, his throbbing head a torture as he bent forward, he investigated in the faint luminous light from the midnight sky and the stars that filtered through the hatch.

Two bodies lay there and as the sergeant bent closer to identify them a brilliant glow swept across the square opening above him. Clawing and scrambling his way up the ladder, Tonelli was caught and held in the beam of a searchlight as he emerged on deck. To the port the sharp bows of a destroyer headed for them and distinct across the water came the hail:

"*Esmeralda* ahoy! Stand by to receive a boat!"

17

His teeth champing on the dead butt of a cigar, Captain Henessy paced his office growling defiance at his distinguished visitor. The dirty dawn was creeping in at the windows, the place stank of stale cigars and Henessy was tousled and unkempt.

"I don't give a damn if all the millionaires in New York are peeved," he orated heatedly. "By God, Commissioner, Pete Tonelli's little finger was worth a thousand of them."

"But we must be reasonable, Henessy. Henri le Mai is a very powerful man. If he should get the impression that the New York police are letting him down—"

"Letting him down hell! If he hadn't come barging in here ranting and raving—"

"Ranting and raving, Henessy? That doesn't sound like le Mai to me—"

"Well he was polite and snarling then and that's worse."

"Besides, you can't blame le Mai—"

"I blame him for me bawling out Pete. I'll never forget the look in the big fellow's eyes when I drove up the Avenue leaving him there on the curb. I ought to have had more sense. Just because a lousy millionaire is crying about some papers I go and bawl out the best flatfoot that ever put cuffs on a crook. Now Pete's gone off there to Rum Row and I'll bet a good hat he's been killed— If he is I'll haunt le Mai in his sleep!"

"The odds are always even as far as Tonelli is concerned. *You* know that, Henessy. He can take care of himself—"

"How'd you like to be out there with him?"

"I've been in some pretty tight places in my day, Henessy." The commissioner remarked it as a matter of fact and not a boast, but Henessy calmed down somewhat.

"What the hell's happened to them damn Coast Guards!" The detective chief had to vent his spleen against somebody. "You'd think they could at least report once in a while."

"They'll report as soon as there is anything to report," the commissioner soothed him. "Let's run over this thing again, will you?"

"All right, but what good'll that do?"

"Let's see. The way we stand now is this, isn't it? You've got Gomez—"

"The sneaking skunk—"

"—and he claims to be the agent for a syndicate from abroad. Is that right?"

"He says he don't know anything about Holstead's murder. He says he was directed to get in touch with McMurtrie and that McMurtrie told him he would deliver the papers Gomez wanted—and this here notebook of Dr. Holstead's. He claims he don't know how or why or where McMurtrie planned to get it—"

"Where does Mrs. Mallor come in?"

"That poor old jane! Honest, Commissioner, I feel sorry for her. She's just an old fool. She met Gomez through this aviator Gates—"

"Gates was a friend of McMurtrie's?"

"That's what Gomez says. He says that McMurtrie brought Gates to him and this Dr. Kramer—and that's the hell of a note when you think it over. Henri le Mai was so dead sure that Kramer was on the up and up— You know I got an idea that's why le Mai's so nervous. I'll bet Kramer was an undercover man for le Mai and double-crossed him and now le Mai's scared stiff he'll be involved in this murder—"

"Le Mai isn't involved, Henessy! Why should he want Holstead out of the way?"

"Why does anybody want anything in this mess? Tom and Jerry for instance. What I can't quite figure out, Commissioner, is where they come in on the deal. They swear that they were tipped off that the Holstead company was dealing in coke. Then they say that they got a telephone call from the Holstead office itself—"

"That was Kramer, most likely—"

"Or the Pierce woman. One of the two. Anyway, Tom and Jerry say that they had this telephone call telling them that if they wanted to horn in on the racket they'd better get down and see the old man. That was Dr. Holstead. They went to the office and the doctor stalled them, according to them. They say they never had any dealings with Kramer and they never heard of the Pierce woman—"

"It's pretty complicated, isn't it? Do you think they had anything to do with the murder?"

"If they did they've both got air-tight alibis we can't ever shake. They've got every minute of their time accounted for. They was at a fight at the Garden. There was dozens of people there that could identify them, and after the fight they went to a party that lasted until six in the morning and there were twenty or thirty people at the party. Between you and me I've got a sneaking suspicion they're telling the truth for once in their lives. I don't believe they were in on the play and I don't believe they had anything to do with the dope racket as far as Holstead's was concerned."

"So that leaves us Gomez—we've got him, and the Pierce girl, but we don't know where she and Moran have gone. And Dr. Kramer and Gates—"

"And McMurtrie and the two Mallor women," Henessy finished the list for him. "And all we've got of the lot is the Mallors and they're no good to anybody as far as I can see except to sit out there with the matron and look sad."

"Where does young Holstead fit in?"

"He don't fit in. He's just an odd piece floating around. It don't none of it make sense and Tonelli told me that much early this morning."

"Yesterday morning now," the commissioner corrected quietly.

"Now what do you make of these two cars for instance? The one down at the Staten Island Flying Field, that's young Holstead's. But that one we found abandoned out at Montauk, whose is that?"

"What does the license bureau say?"

"It's registered in the name of Baker. That's a phony name and a phony address was given, so where does that leave us?"

"Could it belong to Tom and Jerry? After all, Henessy, this murder was committed by two men and that airplane stuff in Newark certainly looks like the kind of play a coupla of coked-up gangsters would make."

"Tonelli had an idea it was done to throw us off the track by making us think gangsters did the job, and Pete's right a whole lot of the time. No, I tell you Commissioner the only thing that makes me feel sort of funny about Tom and Jerry is Slim the Sailor," Henessy continued his own thoughts aloud. "Slim was working with them once I know, only—that pair aren't the kind to kill a man by sending him a package of cyanide put up like coke. That's too slick for them to think out all by themselves. If they bumped off Slim there's a new man in their gang, a fellow with a lot different kind of brains than Tom and Jerry's got."

"Is Gomez a killer?"

"That rat? He wouldn't swat a fly if it was caught in flypaper. He's one of the boys that gets somebody else to do his dirty work while he hides around the corner."

"Where was he on the night of the murder?"

"He's got a non-skid alibi too, Commissioner. Don't worry about that. On the night of the murder he had a headache, so he says, and he kept damn near every bell-hop in the Byington on the run getting him ice water and seidlitz powders. There are a half dozen of them ready to swear he was in his room all night and not only in his room but in bed."

"Sounds conclusive." The commissioner rose and stretched. "Henri le Mai has asked to be notified if anything of importance turns up, and I wish you'd let me know as soon as you hear from the Coast Guard or have any other news—"

Henessy's telephone jangled and he grabbed the instrument while the commissioner stood eagerly waiting.

"Hello! Yes, Henessy speaking. The hell you say! He did? You don't mean it! They are? All of them? Can you give me a list?" Henessy caught at a scratch pad and a pencil and began writing, repeating names as he wrote. "Sheila Pierce—Kramer—Holstead—Moran—Tonelli—what? All right, give that list too. Gates—McMurtrie—what kind of penny? O, Ha'penny, going English on me, huh? And Da Sousa. That all? What's the message? What's the name? Hooker? Five feet nine, weight one hundred and forty-five, about thirty to thirty-five years of age but looks younger. Has a record of imprisonment for peddling narcotics? All right. I'll get the boys out after him. In two hours you say they'll be in? O.K. We'll have a brass band at the dock to meet them. Thanks, so long."

Henessy turned to the commissioner, beaming.

"See, I told you so. Tonelli's on his way home. The Coast Guard destroyer picked up the *Esmeralda* but Pete didn't need it. He'd finished. Cleaned up before the revenuers got to him. That's a great lad, Commissioner."

"He is, Henessy, but what about the murderers?"

"Pete's got them. He'll bring them in when he comes."

"Fine! And the notebook?"

Henessy's face fell.

"Say Commissioner, they didn't say a word about the notebook. If that damn flatfoot has gone and lost that notebook I swear I'll break him back to a harness bull as sure as my name's Henessy. The big palooka. You send him out to get a notebook and he goes and gets into a big scrap and has him a time—" Hennessy's eyes grew dreamy. "Say Commissioner, that must have been a whale of a fight. Wouldn't you give your right eye to have been there?"

Commissioner O'Rooney laughed.

"Both of us, Henessy. If Tonelli can walk bring him up to my office as soon as you can. I'll notify le Mai and Tonelli can tell us all about it."

"O.K. Commissioner, it's five o'clock now, the destroyer will dock in a couple of hours. What do you say to making it nine o'clock, that'll give Pete a chance to wash his face and hands?"

"Nine o'clock it is, Henessy."

The captain, his face wreathed in smiles, snatched up his telephone as the commissioner took his leave.

"General alarm!" he snapped. "Put every available detective and plainclothes man as well as the uniformed force on a search for a man going by the name of Hooker. Thirty to thirty-five years old but looks younger. Five feet, nine inches tall—"

COMMISSIONER O'ROONEY, officially at his desk flanked by Henri le Mai and Captain Henessy, listened eagerly while Tonelli told his story.

In a corner of the room, surreptitiously holding hands, Frances Mallor and Jack Holstead seemed happy in spite of Jack's battered appearance. A big man with a shapeless lump of bandages where his head should have been was Moran, considerably subdued. Beside him sat Commander Betts of the Coast Guard. Tonelli himself sported an unusual assortment of lint and absorbent cotton. A tight wrapping held one ear in place, which otherwise had an inclination to sag on its hinges, and his right hand was enormous in a plaster cast and supported in a sling. Two or three tastefully decorative crosses of adhesive tape showed minor abrasions of his face. Altogether he had the general appearance of a Tom cat who has been wooing unwisely in a strange neighborhood.

He held in his comparatively undamaged hand (only the thumb was swaddled) a sheaf of closely typewritten notes to which he referred from time to time.

"They're pretty swell, these Coast Guard boys," he said by way of introduction. "They had a kid on board, one of the slickest stenographers I ever saw. He took down every word, wrote it out and here it is all signed and witnessed and it was done before we touched shore."

"They seem to have had a pretty able surgeon on board as well," smiled the commissioner.

"Nope, they didn't. A fellow that called himself a pharmacist's mate did all this. Pretty fancy, ain't it?" He grinned in Moran's direction. "Anyway, there they was when I came up on deck, a whole boatload of them with a machine gun and everything and they took over the ship. The cabin was a mess. There was still a little fire burning. McMurtrie was dying. Mike was out cold, Dr. Kramer was unconscious with a broken shoulder and a bump on the head where Gates tried to bend the barrel of the doctor's own gun over his bean. The girl was sorta delirious.

"Ha'penny and the other one, Da Sousa, were both out of commission but they weren't dead. They'll both live. Gates got them with the doctor's gun as they came down the steps. That kid is a fighting fool. He's the gamest bantam I ever saw and if it hadn't been for him I wouldn't be here, nor Mike nor Jack Holstead."

In the corner Frances squeezed Jack's hand tighter and snuggled closer.

"Is there any hope for Gates?" Henri le Mai asked the question. Tonelli shook his head.

"He took it through the lungs. It must have been one of the shots that McMurtrie fired when I jumped him. How that kid held on as long as he did—" Tonelli gulped. "He—he laughed just before he toppled over. He's not afraid to die, he's glad to go I think, and he told me he had the time of his life. 'Sergeant,' he says to me, 'if I'd known they had planes I'd have joined the cops long ago.' What do you know about that for being game?"

"But he was a criminal," le Mai coldly reminded Tonelli.

"I don't suppose you ever broke a law, did you, Mr. le Mai?"

"Possibly, but why did Gates go with you and why did he fight on your side? Wasn't he one of the gang?"

"Sure he was one of the gang, but, you probably couldn't understand this Mr. le Mai, Gates had his limits. He was a real friend of Jack Holstead's. When the rest of them kept on their dirty work, Gates changed sides. He figured he'd got Jack in the jam and it was up to him to get Jack out. And then Gates was sorta sweet on Miss Mallor—" The sergeant stopped. "—Anyway that ain't our business now. Gates came through and I don't mean maybe. He did a bad job at first, but he's paying up now. He's dying. Where was I at anyway—" He shuffled over his notes, blinded perhaps by a watering of his eyes he'd have died rather than admit.

"Get on with your story, Tonelli," the commissioner relieved the situation.

"All right. This is sorta hash I'm giving you—"

"First," it was Henessy who spoke, "where did you find Holstead here?"

"He was in the engine room, damned near choked to death by an oily rag they'd stuffed in his mouth but otherwise in pretty good shape, weren't you, Jack?"

"Bully, Sergeant! But I was awfully glad to see you and those Coast Guard boys."

"I betcha. We didn't make a clean round-up at that. There were three more men in the crew but when they heard all the rumpus they took their feet in their hands and beat it. Anyway the *Esmeralda's* small boat was gone and so were the men. The Coast Guard is on the lookout for them and may pick them up today sometime."

"Do we need them as witnesses?" asked Henessy.

"Not that I can see."

"Then to hell with them. Excuse me, Miss Mallor. Go on with your yarn, Pete."

"Like I say, this is hash I'm giving you. I have a lotta statements here and with what I know, this is the story. It began about four years ago when Sheila Pierce first came to work for Dr. Holstead. Dr. Kramer took a good long look at her it seems and fell for her—"

In their corner only Jack Holstead and Frances knew that Jack winced. She patted his hand and whispered:

"Never mind. It's all over now."

"—then," Tonelli went on, "Kramer found out that Sheila was a hop-head."

"I beg your pardon?" This was le Mai's polite interruption.

Tonelli was disgusted with his ignorance.

"She took dope! Cocaine! Now I didn't quite get this straight and it doesn't make much difference. I don't know if Kramer began to get cocaine for her to keep in solid with her or if she came to him first, anyway, Kramer began to handle cocaine. That went on for a while and then Kramer began to get ambitious."

"Has Kramer made any of these statements?" the commissioner asked.

"Kramer has made a complete confession and signed it," Tonelli stated calmly.

"How did you get him to do that?" Again it was le Mai who was the target of Tonelli's carefully veiled contempt.

"I asked him to," the sergeant answered briefly, and continued to give his statement while the commissioner and Henessy exchanged amused glances.

"Kramer saw a chance to make some easy money by bringing in cocaine. This wasn't more than a coupla years ago, so you see this affair between him and Sheila was going on for some time. It was when he began to branch out that Gates came into the picture. Gates was a friend of Sheila's. Kramer saw the advantage of having an aviator in with them and he got Sheila to play up to Gates. That's Sheila's story, but between us I don't believe that it took much urging to make Sheila play up to any man.

"Through Kramer, Gates met McMurtrie, who brought the cocaine up from the Islands. Kramer and McMurtrie had been working together for quite a while. Gates would fly out and bring in the stuff, Kramer, through Slim the Sailor, Hooker—say, by the way, did you pick up Hooker, Captain Henessy?"

"Yep, we got him, Pete."

"Good! Well, this new combination of Mac, Gates and Kramer worked fine for a long while because Gates would bórrow planes from friends of his and make the trips in between the times he was flying the passenger route for the Inter-Continental people where he worked."

"Gates didn't use cocaine himself, did he?" asked the commissioner.

"Neither Gates nor Kramer used it. Kramer handled it for money and Gates did it for the hell of it and because he was always hard up. It was a game with Gates, a risky game and he couldn't live without taking risks. All this while Kramer was using his connection with the Holstead Company to mask his game of smuggling and distributing dope. He started small and built up. He got so big that Tom and Jerry heard about this new source of snow and Kramer began to worry about them. Then in steps Jack Holstead. Jack was young and it looked like he was going to come into the company. That would gum Kramer's game on that end so he sicked Sheila on to Jack. I guess maybe Jack fell for her—"

Jack in his corner nodded in corroboration.

"—and between Kramer and Sheila they persuaded Jack that he was better off out of the drug business doing independent research on radio for himself—"

"That's only partly right, Sergeant," Jack spoke up for himself. "I didn't need persuading about that. What they did do was to convince me that the business didn't offer sufficient scope for independent work of my own."

"You see," Tonelli thanked Jack with a crooked smile that peered around his bandages, "they didn't want Jack actively in the business. Dr. Holstead kept conveniently away."

"But what has this to do with the murder and Dr. Holstead's notes?" Henri le Mai interrupted impatiently. "I'm not at all interested in Kramer's peccadillos."

"Mr. le Mai," Tonelli sounded bored but patient, "one of the first things I savvied in this case was that Kramer was your hired man. I told Captain Henessy so. Now officially I've kept that part of Kramer's dealings out of the record because it would confuse a jury. I know that Kramer double-crossed you. He got so busy with his sidelines he forgot you were paying him to keep tabs on Dr. Holstead, but take it from me no jury would be able to swallow these fine points. If you want your connection with Kramer to go on record, just say so and—"

"Are you threatening me?"

"No, only telling you, like I'm telling this story. It's a long story and it's pretty involved if you don't take it from the beginning. I began to get on the track when the telephone girl told me that Jack was sweet on Sheila. I figured that some way Kramer and Sheila and Jack were mixed up and I thought Dr. Holstead knew something about it. The doctor was nobody's fool—"

"Actually," Jack Holstead spoke again, "my uncle warned me against Sheila. He knew that she had the drug habit. He noticed it. Anyone familiar with addicts can tell, and when he told me I saw it too. Then," he hesitated, "I thought I might be able to do something to help her and when my uncle suggested that I let her alone I refused to stop seeing her. That's the cause of our quarrel. That's what he sent for me to talk about the night he was murdered. That's why I was in such a state of mind. I knew then that I loved Frances but it didn't seem quite sporting to walk out on Sheila even though both she and I regarded it as a passing affair."

"Sheila introduced you to Gates, didn't she?" the commissioner put the question to Jack.

"Yes sir. She—"

"Better let me tell that part as I got it from Gates," Tonelli, seeing Jack's embarrassment, intervened. "When Gates had the fight with his superintendent (he'd gone off on a bat and missed a trip) he lost his job and found himself cut off from using a number of planes. He knew his own plane had been seen by the Coast Guard and it was getting too dangerous for him to use that. Along about that time, through McMurtrie, Kramer met Gomez—"

"So that's where *he* comes in. I was wondering," Henessy said softly.

"Yeah, that's where he comes in. Gomez wanted somebody who was on the inside of the Holstead Company to get him Dr. Holstead's notes. How he met McMurtrie I don't know, but he did. McMurtrie brought Kramer and Gomez together and from then on the three worked together. Kramer was the brains behind what came after. He had too much brains. If he'd done a little less fixing he might have got away with it."

"Then Kramer did the murder?" Henri le Mai was leaning forward anxiously.

"Hold your horses, will you," Tonelli was losing his temper, "this is my case and I'll tell it the way I want to tell it. Kramer figured that if he could get Jack to flying in Gates' plane he could kill two birds with one stone. They took Gates in on the plot, but Gates didn't know that Dr. Holstead was to be murdered. Neither did Sheila Pierce, so she says, but the evidence shows the murder was deliberately planned well in advance. They were prepared to go to any lengths, though, because Gomez was showing a lot of dough and with both the doctor and Jack Holstead out of the way the dope racket could go merrily on on a bigger scale than ever.

"They planted the airplane on Jack. I found that out at Newark Airport. Then they tipped off Tom and Jerry. I knew that from the telephone calls that Kramer and Sheila made. The idea was that they would frame Slim the Sailor and through him the murder would be traced back to Tom and Jerry. Getting Tom and Jerry to come to the office was just another dodge to hang it on them.

"When Tom and Jerry came in to see Dr. Holstead, Kramer didn't know that the doctor already knew about Jack's airplane and the dope smuggling from Commander Betts. Kramer thought that the old man would go off the handle and accuse Jack and they might quarrel and that would be another out. Another motive for the murder. That didn't quite work. The old gentleman pretty nearly upset the game by having Jack come to his house the night of the murder.

"Then everything happened at once. Mrs. Mallor called Gomez and told him the formula was finished. They made all their plans.

Kramer killed a guinea pig in his laboratory and smeared Slim's knife with the blood. They used another knife like it for the murder. At the last minute Sheila lost her nerve and went to warn Dr. Holstead. She told him Kramer and McMurtrie were coming to get the formula but he laughed at her. She tried to get him to give *her* the formula and he showed it to her and then while she was looking he went and hid it. That's why she came back in the morning. She came to see if she couldn't get it. I think she had some idea of crossing them all by bringing the notes to Mr. le Mai. All the time she swears she didn't know there was to be murder, that she thought Kramer and McMurtrie would scare the doctor into giving up the notes. It was McMurtrie who killed the doctor, but Kramer planned it and is equally guilty of the murder.

"Gates was told to meet Kramer and McMurtrie outside of the house and he did, not knowing anything about it. McMurtrie and Gates went in, Kramer stayed outside. Before Gates could do anything about it McMurtrie stabbed the doctor and then Gates had to go through with it. The airplane stunt was another of Kramer's ideas to pile up more evidence against Tom and Jerry and Jack Holstead. Gates pretended to be Jack Holstead and the dumb attendant at the airport thought he was. And there you have it, all sworn to and signed and sealed. McMurtrie's dead, Gates is dying, Sheila will turn State's evidence and Kramer is an accessory before and after the fact along with Gomez. Is that O.K.?"

"Fine work, Sergeant," the commissioner commended. "How did Jack Holstead get out to the *Esmeralda?*"

Tonelli smiled. "He made Sheila talk after he saw me at the doctor's apartment. Sheila told him how to find the boat, gave him the signals and he went out to avenge his uncle."

"Yes," Jack spoke up, "and I'd have been dead now if you hadn't come and got me out of the mess. McMurtrie was utterly ruthless. He let me come on board, tied me up and then knocked holes in my plane's pontoons, and let the plane sink."

"But the notes, where are the notes?" le Mai insisted.

"I thought you was more anxious to get the murderers than the notes," said Tonelli pointedly.

"Well, of course I am, but then—"

"There's always a but with you fellows. Go look behind the portrait of Dr. Holstead's father in his. living room. That's where the notes were hid. I hope you don't get blood all over your fingers when you try to use them."

"Hell!" Henessy swore. "We're gonna have a time burning Kramer and Gomez. They're the real murderers all right, McMurtrie and Gates were only the instruments, but we'll have a time pinning it on the brains."

"Not so hard," Tonelli reassured him. "You forget Slim's murder. That's why I had you gather in Hooker. He delivered the cyanide that Dr. Kramer handed to him in Gomez' room in the Byington while Gomez was present!"

"You win, Pete!" Henessy gave up.

"Then we got a coupla minor charges like attempted murder and assault. I gotta tell you a funny one about Mike, though. It's too good to keep. Mike started the rumpus in the *Esmeralda* thinking Kramer was gonna poison Sheila. Mike sorta liked Sheila's looks and you can't blame him at that. The funny thing is that the powder Mike spilled in the *Esmeralda's* cabin was real cocaine." Tonelli paused to chuckle.

"Now Mike took a package of powder away from Hooker up at Sheila's flat. He had that in his pocket all the time. He's got it now and that powder is cyanide."

"Who kidnapped *you*, Mike?" the commissioner questioned.

Mike mumbled through his bandages and the sergeant answered for him.

"Kramer did. Kramer got scared that Sheila would talk so he sent her the same dose he'd sent Slim. Then he got scared Hooker would get caught so he followed him. He knocked the janitor and Mike over the head, he and Hooker and Sheila loaded Mike into a taxi and drove to where Kramer had his roadster parked. That roadster, by the way, was the one they used to take Dr. Holstead's body out to Newark in. It was almost a duplicate of Jack's. They drove out to Montauk, took a fast motor boat out to the *Esmeralda* leaving Hooker when they changed cars. Simple when you know how it was done. The point is, we got enough on Kramer and Gomez to burn them!"

Henri le Mai rose and started to say something to the commissioner.

"You getting worried about them notes, Mr. le Mai?" Tonelli asked. "Don't! They're O.K., locked in Captain Henessy's safe. I put them there yesterday. I found them behind the picture when I made my visit to Dr. Holstead's apartment. I noticed that picture was crooked and I knew Dr. Holstead never would have stood for that. He liked everything four-square. So I looked to see why the picture had been moved."

"Why wasn't I informed of this before!" Henri le Mai demanded angrily.

"Well you see, Mr. le Mai," Tonelli was very bland, "nobody knew about it but me. I didn't tell Captain Henessy what was in the package and I'm about as dumb as the average juryman. I wanted to be dead sure that your arrangement with Kramer stopped short of murder. That's why I held the papers. I hope you'll make a lotta money on the formula, Mr. le Mai."

COACHWHIP PUBLICATIONS
COACHWHIPBOOKS.COM

THE HEX MURDER

Alexander Williams

COACHWHIP PUBLICATIONS
COACHWHIPBOOKS.COM

THE JINX
THEATRE
MURDER

ALEXANDER WILLIAMS

COACHWHIP PUBLICATIONS
COACHWHIPBOOKS.COM

COACHWHIP PUBLICATIONS
COACHWHIPBOOKS.COM

THE
RUMBLE
MURDERS

Henry Ware Eliot, Jr.

COACHWHIP PUBLICATIONS
COACHWHIPBOOKS.COM

COACHWHIP PUBLICATIONS
COACHWHIPBOOKS.COM

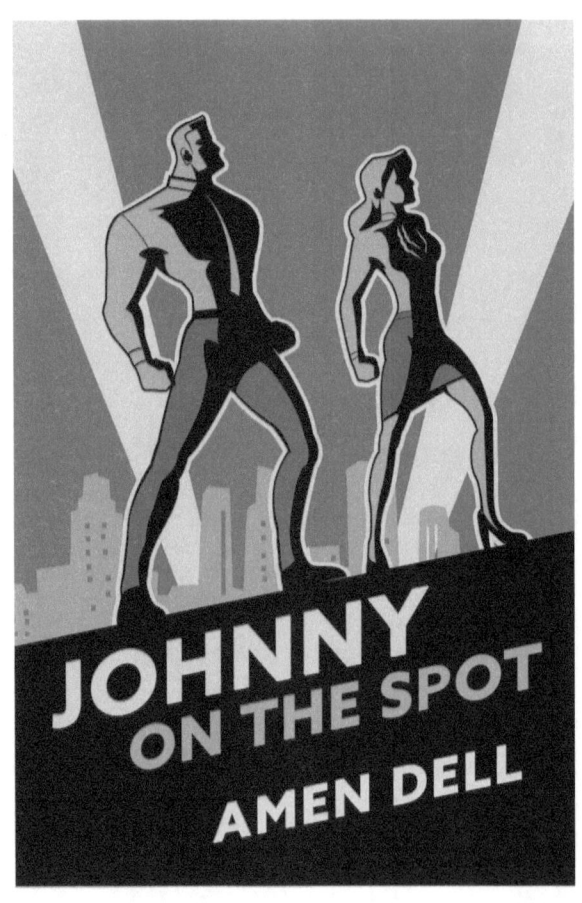

JOHNNY
ON THE SPOT

AMEN DELL

COACHWHIP PUBLICATIONS
COACHWHIPBOOKS.COM

ANONYMOUS FOOTSTEPS | JOHN. M. O'CONNOR